FIND ME A VILLAIN

For the first time in her life, Nina was alone in unfamiliar surroundings. She had lived in only three homes: her childhood one, the small house she and Martin had bought when they were first married, and Silverlea. She had not expected to feel so strange. How long would it take her to settle down?

She turned up the televison and tried not to think of the weeks ahead. The news on ITN had just ended when the telephone rang.

It would be Jenny or Sarah, wanting to know how she was getting on. Both had said they would ring her often, and both had promised not to tell their father where she was. Nina hurried to answer.

When she lifted the receiver and gave the number of the Hall, no one spoke. All she heard was a shuddering sigh.

Also in Arrow by Margaret Yorke

Find Me a Villain

MARGARET YORKE

ARROW BOOKS

Arrow Books Limited
17-21 Conway Street, London W1P 6JD

An imprint of the Hutchinson Publishing Group

London Melbourne Sydney Auckland
Johannesburg and agencies throughout
the world

First published by Hutchinson 1983
Arrow edition 1984

Printed and bound in Great Britain by
Anchor Brendon Limited, Tiptree, Essex

ISBN 0 09 934800 4

In tragic life . . .
No villain need be! Passions spin the plot:
We are betrayed by what is false within.

George Meredith

1

Rain fell from the leaden sky. It dripped from the few dead leaves which remained on the trees, and from the spiky hedgerow brambles. Water collected in pools on the paths through the copse, and the tall withered grasses drooped under their burden.

There was no wind.

A mile from the copse, lorries sped past on the new by-pass. No one stopped here now, but once, not so long ago, lovers had carved their names on the trees and ramblers had kept open an unofficial footpath through the undergrowth. In the meadows beyond the copse, cattle grazed peacefully.

It was a heifer who disturbed the covering of earth and leaves over the body. More venturesome than her sisters, she leaned against a post that had worked loose in the fence round the field and pushed it over, catching a leg in the wire as she crossed into the copse. She gave a bellow of pain, but moved on, and soon three others from the herd followed. They trampled the leaf-strewn ground and nibbled at shoots as they passed. It was some hours before their escape was discovered and they were driven back into the field. By then they had moved past the shallow dip where the body lay, but their passage had shifted the soil and leaves, exposing a foot to which still clung shreds of the dead woman's pale, patterned tights. There was no shoe.

Rain went on falling, pattering on the rotting leaves and woodland soil, dripping from the trees, trickling into the shallow grave.

2

When she smiled, she reminded Nina of a cat. Her eyes
seemed slanted, and they glinted green. There were lines
etched round them. At any moment, Nina thought hysteri-
cally, she would lick a paw and begin to wash her whiskers.
She was gazing into the eyes of Nina's husband with an
intensity which was, to the woman watching her, obscene.
Her claw – no, her hand – rested on his jacket sleeve as they sat
at a small table in the restaurant.

Nina had expected her to be young, but she wasn't, though
her hair hung straight to her shoulders in youthful style and
the dress she wore was pleated and ruched like those sold in
boutiques catering for teenagers. Martin was smiling into
those green, slitty eyes; his was, Nina thought, an inane,
fatuous grin. She peered at them both from the shelter of the
round felt hat she wore, holding the menu before her face as a
screen.

Nina felt like a character in a gangster film as she sat there,
in semi-disguise, watching her husband and his mistress
lunching together. She had waited in a telephone box near
Martin's office and had followed him when he emerged. In
dark glasses and an old raincoat, with her hat pulled well
down, she had walked along the road behind him as he strode
away from her, Nina knew, for ever. The woman, whose name
was Caroline, had appeared from the other direction and the
two had embraced, for all to see, on the public pavement.
Passers-by had to alter course to avoid them. Then, arms
linked, heads turned to talk to each other, faces almost
touching, they had walked on and entered the restaurant.

Nina felt physically sick as she stood on the pavement
outside. She walked past, then turned back and entered the
restaurant. She sat at a table separated from theirs by a screen
which was festooned with climbing plants. She had been there
before, with Martin, and knew that concealment would be

possible behind this barrier. Watching them, Nina saw that she need not fear recognition. Martin had eyes only for Miss Kitty-Cat. Even if he were to glance round, he would never expect to see Nina; he would imagine her, if he thought about her at all, at home at Silverlea, still in tears as he had left her last night.

No doubt he'd already described the scene to Miss Kitty-Cat. He would have told her how Nina had wept and stormed and refused to believe that he meant to leave her and marry this other woman who was, it seemed, pregnant by him. At last he'd walked out of the house and driven off in his red BMW, saying that he was sorry to hurt her but there was no point in prolonging their interview.

He and Caroline had met at a party, Martin had said. It was something to do with his work – he was in advertising – and she'd handled the promotion material for a firm whose account he looked after. The affair had been in progress for over four years. Four years! Nina found it hard to take in what he was saying. How many others had there been, before this one, she had demanded, and Martin had not replied. That meant that Caroline was not the first. Nina's instant reaction was sheer, physical jealousy as she imagined Martin in bed with another woman; she felt ill, thinking of it. Then came awareness that what she had thought was good, had believed in and had worked for throughout her adult life, had been a myth. That knowledge was almost more painful. She had loved Martin and trusted him, and had thought that he was as content as she was with their life. How long ago was the first betrayal, she wondered. Now he had met someone who did not intend to let him go.

Martin did not like cats: it was strange that he had fallen for this one, Nina thought. Her throat felt choked; she could not eat or drink anything now, and she rose and left the restaurant. She had seen enough.

A bus stopped just as she stepped on to the pavement, and without looking to see where it went, she boarded it, moving right to the front where there was an empty seat. She sat there, unaware of the route the bus took, heedless of anything except her own misery. Tears flowed down her face. The conductor came to take her fare and she thrust several coins at him, forgetful, even, of what the minimum fare was. After several stops a woman with a large shopping bag came to sit beside her, and Nina, turning her head away, peered out of the window at last. They were in Oxford Street. At the next stop she got to her feet, blundered past her neighbour and left the bus. She walked on, still not heeding where she went, chivvied and jostled by shoppers on the crowded pavement.

It began to rain.

Nina went into John Lewis's and wandered around among the handbags and into the fabric department. Here, in an islanded space, she stood still and endeavoured to regain her self-control. She blew her nose on a crumpled tissue found in the pocket of her daughter Jenny's old school raincoat which she wore, and which she had borrowed as part of her disguise. Then she walked on through the store and out into Oxford Street again. It was raining harder now. She crossed the road, and when she reached Woolworth's, went in. The only tissue she had was sodden, and she could not find her handkerchief, so she bought a small packet of tissues and wandered on. In a display of pottery objects arranged on a counter, Nina saw a row of painted cats. She halted, staring at them. They were moulded in various postures, and, to Nina's prejudiced eye, they all wore smug, self-satisfied smirks on their glazed faces. Nina's gaze focused on one of them. It seemed to have exactly the same expression as she had seen on Caroline's face earlier.

She bought the cat and carried it out of the store in a paper bag.

Nina walked on in the rain. Drops pattered off the brim of her hat past her nose. Her feet, in her smart black boots, were warm, but her hands, one holding her handbag and the other the Woolworth parcel, were cold. She had left her gloves on the bus. The Woolworth's bag was getting wet and it began to disintegrate. Nina put it in her handbag and walked on. In her mind she was following Martin and Caroline away from the restaurant. Maybe they would go back to her flat now, before he returned to the office. He had spent many nights in her flat, Nina knew, nights when he had said he was at a conference or attending a business dinner. He had left Surrey for good. Last night he had said he had already consulted a solicitor and would be putting the house up for sale. She should have part–

he did not say how much – of the proceeds. He would be in touch with their daughters. He would see that she was looked after in a financial sense. He had not explained his feelings at all, although, amid stormy tears, she had wanted to know what she had done wrong, where she had failed. They had been married for twenty-four years. Nina had had no other romance in her life.

On she walked, shivering. She felt dizzy and sick, and at last her own physical distress began to impinge on her mental anguish. She looked vaguely about to see where she was and found that she was almost at the bottom of Bond Street. Piccadilly lay ahead. Nina had no memory of how she had got there, what had made her go in that direction.

Swan and Edgar's, she thought: the snack bar there would have tea, coffee, a sandwich. But Swan and Edgar's was no more. Nina paused on the pavement outside Burlington House. Across the road the clock outside Fortnum and Mason's began to strike, and some tourists stopped to watch. Inside, there would be warmth and shelter. Nina crossed the road and passed through the portals into the fragrant, muted bustle of the grocery department and went on, up the stairs, to the Mezzanine Restaurant, where she looked vaguely round. She felt rather dizzy. All the tables seemed to be occupied, but ahead, at the counter, she saw a vacant seat. She climbed on to it, stowing her packages, and ordered tea and a Danish pastry. When they came, however, she could barely swallow the tea, much less eat the pastry. Her throat seemed to have closed up. She forced some tea down, and the warmth did help a little. I really need a brandy, she thought wryly, and wondered if they would serve her with one at four o'clock in the afternoon. Her recollection of the past hours while she walked the streets was a blur; she was quite shocked to see how late it was.

The spaces on either side of Nina at the counter were occupied, but now one neighbour descended from her tall chair to leave and someone else took her place. Nina barely noticed the movement; her horizon had shrunk to the limits of the counter before her, the cup and saucer, and the plate bearing the glistening pastry, now battered and in disarray after her prods at it with the fork supplied.

Nina's new neighbour settled her handbag in the shelf

space under the counter and took off her coat, hanging it over the back of her chair. She knocked Nina's arm as she did so, and apologized.

'So sorry – do forgive me,' she said.

'What – oh –' Nina was barely aware of the contact. 'It's quite all right,' she mumbled.

'These seats are awkward if you're rather short,' said Priscilla Blunt.

'Oh – er – yes,' Nina answered, and prodded her pastry again.

'What a terrible day,' Priscilla Blunt went on. 'Fortnum's is always so reassuring, isn't it?' Now she was taking off a plastic rain hood. She looked round for somewhere to put it, and, finding no handy spot, pushed it under the counter with her handbag.

Nina slowly turned to look at her.

'I suppose so,' she agreed.

She saw blonde-rinsed, freshly coiffured hair from which came a faint scent of expensive hair-spray, and a well-made up face that was not in the least feline. Priscilla, whose husband said she was inclined to be too friendly and outgoing, was aware only of a drooping figure in a navy gaberdine raincoat and a round waterproof hat, an entirely respectable person to address. Priscilla often talked to strangers in trains and cafés because she liked to speak her thoughts aloud; she never looked for much response but she was seldom snubbed and would scarcely notice if she were.

Nina needed to blow her nose. She rootled in her handbag for the tissues she had just bought, and to find them took out the packaged cat, which she set on the counter. Because, in her distress, she was not coordinating properly, she had to rummage in the depths of her bag and drew forth other possessions – a zipped make-up bag, her purse, a diary – before she found the tissues. Priscilla could not fail to notice all this burrowing. Nina blew her nose and began putting everything back in her bag.

'Have you got a cold?' Priscilla asked, and frowned. She did not want to catch one, and she drew away from Nina, though germs, of course, abounded in every public place, even Fortnum's.

14

'No – no, it's not a cold,' said Nina.

Priscilla opened her own bag and extracted her spectacles, which she put on and through which she then inspected Nina. In spite of the lowered brim of the hat, it was obvious that she had been crying; her face was blotched and mascara had run round her eyes.

'Are you feeling all right?' Priscilla enquired.

'I'd got a bit chilled, walking about in the rain,' said Nina and turned a face of misery towards her.

Priscilla did not like having to notice other people's problems in case she felt obliged to help them, but if confronted with them she would not evade them. She had a lot of energy herself and thought positive action was the remedy for most difficulties; tackling them head-on and going straight through them enabled, in her view, normality to be swiftly restored behind the upset.

As can be the way with strangers, Nina found herself relating what had happened.

Priscilla wanted to drink her tea and enjoy the slice of coffee cake which she had ordered. She sipped and munched, saying 'Oh dear,' and 'Really?' at intervals, while the tale was told. Nina spoke in a low voice, and disjointedly, but her story was coherent; it was an old one.

'Perhaps he'll come back?' Priscilla suggested, pouring out more tea.

'I don't want him, now,' said Nina. 'Not after this. How could I ever trust him again?'

'Lots of men stray,' Priscilla said. 'It needn't mean a great deal.'

'But it does,' said Nina. 'I hadn't realised – all those years – our married life – I thought that we were happy, but he had other women then. I was a fool.'

'You know about them? These other women?' asked Priscilla.

'He didn't deny it,' Nina said. 'It makes all our life together a – a sham.'

'Awful for you,' said Priscilla vaguely. Then, more collectedly, for soon she must be on her way and she could not abandon this wretched creature altogether, she asked, 'What will you do?'

'I don't know.'

'Have you a good solicitor?'

Nina hadn't thought so far.

'There's the one we used when we bought the house – twelve years ago, that was. We moved from a small cottage into such a lovely house, Silverlea. It's not far from Oxted,' she said.

'Perhaps he's acting for your husband,' said Priscilla. 'But there must be others. I should consult one quickly, if I were you.'

'Yes. You're right,' said Nina.

'And what about a job? Find something to occupy yourself,' said Priscilla. She already knew that Nina had two daughters, both grown up, one married and one in her second year at university.

'What can I do?' asked Nina. 'I'm not trained for anything.'

'Didn't you work before you were married?'

But Nina had married Martin fresh from secretarial college, and Sarah had been born within a year. She had never used her office skills.

A dim warning thought came into Priscilla's mind as she recalled her own son's matrimonial difficulties.

'If you earn, it may prejudice the settlement you get,' she said. 'Your husband must provide for you.' Her only son, now married for the second time, was having to provide for his first wife, though there were no children.

'He said he'd see I was looked after,' Nina said.

Priscilla had asked for her bill and had taken her purse from her handbag. Now she drew a card from it and gave it to Nina.

'I've had an idea,' she said. 'My husband and I are going away at the end of next month, to South Africa. It's partly business, partly pleasure. We'll be away two months. We had a Spanish couple who looked after our house in the country, but they have had to go back to Spain because of some family trouble; and there won't be time to get and train a new couple, and make sure they're trustworthy, before we go. We don't want to leave the house empty for so long, and I was going to engage a house-minder. There are agencies where you can find such people – they're often retired policemen, I believe.' She laughed. 'You could mind our house,' she said. 'We wouldn't want you until just before we go, so you'd have time to sort out your own affairs. And we would say that what we paid you was expenses, so that there would be no question of it affecting your entitlements.'

'But you don't know me! You know nothing about me,' Nina said.

'On the contrary, I know a lot,' said Priscilla. 'And I'm sure you can provide a character reference – the vicar – a JP from where you live – someone like that who has known you for some time.' She gave the card to Nina. 'If I haven't heard from you by Thursday, I'll go to the agency,' she said. 'Tell me your name.'

Nina supplied it.

'Good,' said Priscilla. She laid notes and some coins on the plate bearing her bill. 'Do finish your tea,' she said. 'And think over my idea. It would give you a chance to recover and make a long-term plan.' And help me too, she thought, for there was no doubt about Nina's utter reliability; anyone who looked like that, dressed so dowdily, just had to be respectable and honest.

Nina helped her into her coat and handed her her umbrella.

'Thank you very much,' she said. 'I'll think about it.'

When the stranger had gone, Nina poured herself out another cup of tea and ate several mouthfuls of her pastry. She was feeling better.

She looked at the card the other woman had given her.

Mrs Leonard Blunt, she read, and an address in Berkshire: The Hall, Netherton St Mary, near Murford. Nina hadn't heard of it. She put the card away in her own notecase.

When she asked for her bill, she found that Mrs Blunt had paid for her.

Now she would have to get in touch with her, if only to thank her for that.

3

There were lights on when Nina reached home that night.

Rain was still falling as she drove her Metro from the station, swishing through puddles that had formed in the lane. Each house in this neighbourhood was set in an acre or more of land, with trees around to ensure seclusion. You seldom saw another person, except by design; there was no village near, no community feeling, and the nearest shop was two miles away.

The house should be empty, dark; who was there? Was it Martin? Had he come back? Could he have changed his mind after all? Her stomach began churning as she stopped the car on the concrete path outside the garage, but then the front door opened and Jenny came running towards her.

'Mum – where on earth have you been?' she asked. She looked pale and harassed.

'In London,' said Nina. 'What are you doing here, Jenny?'

Nina had not gone straight home after she left Fortnum and Mason. She had walked round the corner into the Haymarket, and had sat in the darkness of a cinema for several hours. She had not wanted to go home at all, but in the end it seemed the only thing left to do.

'But you haven't seen Daddy. He told me he hadn't seen you,' said Jenny.

Nina had got out of the car and the two began to hurry towards the house through the rain.

'Did you ring him?' Nina gasped. How had Jenny known where to find him after he'd left the office?

'No. I've been to see him,' said Jenny. 'I had this mad letter from him, so I went to find out what it was all about.'

'Come inside,' said Nina, shushing Jenny ahead of her into the warm house, as she had done throughout the girl's life. Martin had said he was telling the girls his plans; had he already written to them before speaking to her?

It seemed so. It did not occur to Nina that Martin might

have acted thus in order to force himself into tackling her, something he had kept putting off.

'Mum, it's awful. I'm so sorry,' Jenny said. She turned to her mother and for a moment they clung togther in the hall, Jenny dressed in blue jeans and a loose sweater, her mother still in the old school gaberdine. Jenny suddenly realized what she was wearing. 'Good heavens, you've got my old school mac on, she said. 'Why on earth –?'

'It would take too long to explain,' said Nina, undoing it. She had taken her hat off in the car; at least Jenny hadn't seen the full disguise. 'Have you had any supper?' she asked.

'No. I wasn't hungry, somehow,' said Jenny. 'Have you?'

'No, but I had tea at Fortnum and Mason's,' said Nina.

'Did you? You were going it a bit, weren't you?' said Jenny. 'That's great.' She stood back to examine her mother, whose face seemed to have suddenly developed new lines and sags.

'Then I went to the cinema,' Nina said.

'Really?' Jenny began to smile. 'I wish Dad had known,' she said. 'He thought you'd be moping about the place drenched in tears.'

'I was,' Nina admitted. 'It was a terrible shock, Jenny. I simply had no idea. Had you?' she asked.

'No,' said Jenny. 'I thought he might have gone temporarily off his head – had a brainstorm – something like that, but he seems to mean it.'

She'd caught an afternoon train to London after reading her father's letter, and had gone to the address which he'd put at the top of the page. She'd found him there with this woman, Caroline, who was plain and bony, and quite old. Caroline had kept touching him. As she moved across the room to fetch a drink for him – Jenny had refused even tea – drawing the curtains – switching on the electric fire – it had seemed to Jenny that she sought excuses for passing close to him, resting her hand on his arm, brushing against him. The flat was Caroline's but her father was clearly very much at home there.

Jenny had clenched her fists and spoken harshly.

'What about Mummy?' she'd asked. 'What are you going to do about her?'

'She'll be looked after,' he'd said evasively. 'The house will fetch a lot of money and she'll be entitled to part of it.' There was no need to mention the mortgage repayment which would eat into whatever sum was obtained.

'But she's got to live somewhere,' Jenny had said. 'It's so cruel of you, Daddy.'

'These things happen,' her father had said. 'I'm sorry to hurt her, of course, but it can't be helped.'

'Couldn't you just – couldn't you – well – '

'Carry on as we've done?' her father had finished the difficult sentence for her.

'Mm.'

He'd told her, then, about the baby, which hadn't been mentioned in his letter. Jenny had felt rather sick. She'd left at once and come straight home, expecting to find her mother in need of consolation. Instead, the house was empty and her mother's car was not in the garage. There was nothing on the kitchen diary to indicate where she might be, and when an hour passed and she still did not return, Jenny had telephoned her sister, Sarah, to see if their mother was with her.

But Sarah did not know where she was. She had received a letter from their father, too, almost a replica of the one he had written to Jenny, and had at once telephoned their mother, but there had been no reply. She had been worried, Sarah confessed, and they had decided that Jenny should telephone various friends in the district to see if anyone knew where she had gone. Jenny had done so, but with no success.

Now, the telephone rang as Nina was taking off the gaberdine raincoat.

'Answer it, Jenny, would you?' she asked. She hung the raincoat up in the downstairs cloakroom and there, in the mirror above the basin, saw how distraught she looked, her face grubby from where the mascara she had put on from habit had run, her lipstick not restored. She washed her face and was patting it dry on the big, mushroom-coloured towel when Jenny called to her.

'It's Sarah. Will you talk to her?'

'Oh,' said Nina. 'Of course.' She tried to hide her dismay; at the moment she didn't feel strong enough to talk to her elder daughter, whose personality was rather overpowering. She always knew what was best for everyone else, including her son and her husband as well as her mother.

Jenny was pleased to see, as Nina took the telephone receiver from her, that she looked more like herself now, with her hair combed, though her face shone after its wash; normally her mother was always well made up and her complexion matt; it had frightened Jenny to see her in disarray.

That Caroline had rotten skin, Jenny thought: she'd got acne scars all over her face. How could Daddy fancy her, after Mum?

'Yes, Sarah?' Nina was saying into the telephone. 'How are you, darling?'

'Never mind that,' said Sarah. 'What about you, mother? Where have you been? We've been so worried. You shouldn't have gone off without letting someone know where you were.'

'I've simply been to the cinema,' Nina said. Why should she, she thought rebelliously, have to account for her movements to Sarah? Why should Sarah be trying, now, to put her in the wrong? Martin had done it, too, telling her she was dull; that she bored him.

'The cinema?' Sarah was saying. 'At a time like this?'

'Why not?' Nina asked. 'I'd no dinner to cook for your father. What else was there to do?'

'Well – see a solicitor, for one thing,' said Sarah. 'Jeremy's found the name of a good one, who goes in for this sort of thing.'

What sort of thing, wondered Nina. Adultery? Betrayal?

'Very kind of him,' she said, managing not to point out that most solicitors closed their offices at five o'clock or so.

'You're not to worry, mother,' Sarah instructed. 'We'll organize you. You'll always have a home with us.'

'That's kind of you, darling,' said Nina. 'But I've made no plans so far.'

'Well, of course not. It's all so sudden,' said Sarah. 'I want you to know that Jeremy and I are thoroughly shocked. We're right behind you, one hundred per cent.'

'I'm glad,' murmured Nina. She saw that the conversation would not be swiftly concluded and gestured to Jenny, who was standing at the foot of the stairs watching her, to bring her a chair. Jenny did so, and made winding-up signals indicating that Sarah was getting into gear for a peroration. Nina winked at her and Jenny grinned.

21

'Yes, darling,' she heard Nina meekly agree, as she went into the dining room, and thereafter heard more such short utterances as she took glasses and bottles from the sideboard. She reappeared by her mother's side and handed her a full tumbler.

'Brandy and soda,' she said.

Gratefully, Nina took the glass and drank half of its contents at a gulp. It gave her dutch courage.

'Sarah, dear, you're both so kind. Please thank Jeremy,' she said, cutting into her elder daughter's flow of speech. 'I'll ring you tomorrow. It's too late now to go on talking. Jenny and I haven't had supper yet. We all need time to think about what's happened. He's your father still, after all, and he still feels the same about you and Jenny, remember.'

But what did that feeling amount to? He'd admired the girls for their prettiness when they were small, and had been quite indulgent, but he'd taken small part in their various activities. 'That's girls' stuff,' he'd often said, and 'You girls deal with that,' bundling them all together, dismissing them, going off to play golf or to business commitments, or so he had said.

'He's ashamed,' Jenny said, when Nina had hung up. 'Perhaps he does love us – but then, what is love?' She gave a huge sigh.

Nina knew that the concern both her daughters, in their different ways, were showing for her at this moment was love, in one of its forms.

'It's like soup – comes in a good many varieties,' she said, lightly. 'Now, Jenny, you must be starving. Shall we have scrambled eggs?'

In the kitchen, over scrambled eggs – six between them – Nina said that Sarah intended to organize her.

'Don't let her,' said Jenny. 'She's already got her eye on some cottage in the village for you to buy – she thinks Daddy will give you the money. She means you to take up full-time grannying. She said it will make you feel wanted.'

'It's kind of her,' said Nina. 'And I'm sure she could do with some help.'

'Very likely,' said Jenny. 'But she loves telling people what to do, Mummy. You know that – I've seen you crumple when she gets into her stride. She saps you. If you once get under her

22

thumb you'll never escape. Just like Jeremy – but he needs it. She's pregnant again, did you know? Her and Caroline. Isn't it awful? They'll be sort of twins, yet an uncle, or aunt. Or something. I think it's disgusting.'

Nina knew that Jenny's warning was apt. If she once let Sarah start arranging her life, she would be committed and unable to withdraw.

'You're too young to give up, Mum,' Jenny went on. 'Look at Daddy, starting all over again, and he's older than you.'

'It's different for men,' Nina said.

'I don't see why it should be,' said Jenny. 'You just show him.'

'Well, I've got a job,' Nina said, suddenly making up her mind. 'It's only temporary, but it's a start.'

'Have you really? Why, that's great,' Jenny said. 'What is it? How did you find it?'

Nina did not describe the circumstances of her meeting with Mrs Blunt.

'I went to see about it today,' she said primly. 'Before the cinema. The details aren't arranged yet. I don't start for several weeks.'

'That'll give you time, then,' said Jenny.

'Time for what?' asked Nina.

'To pack up the house and all that. Daddy's got a buyer for it. Someone he knows through work. I suppose he can sell it over your head?'

'I don't know,' Nina said. 'I'll have to find out. It's his house – it's in his name.'

'Mum, you're not a bit liberated are you?' said Jenny gently. 'You've got your rights, you know.'

Nina had never thought about that before; she had been content with her role, a background one, supporting Martin, running his home smoothly.

'There's you, Jenny,' she said. 'You need a home – I'll only go where there's room for you too, in your vacations.' She'd only accept Mrs Blunt's offer if that was agreed between them, Nina resolved. She rose and went to fetch her handbag. From her notecase she took the card Mrs Blunt had given her and gave it to Jenny. 'That's where my job is,' she said.

'How grand,' Jenny said.

Nina had taken a tattered parcel out of her bag and set it on the drainer.

'She's nice, this Mrs Blunt,' she said. 'I'm to be a house-minder.'

'Whatever's that?' Jenny asked.

Nina was pleased to be able to tell one of her daughters something she did not already know. She explained.

'You don't need any special training,' she ended.

'How much will you be paid?' Jenny asked.

'That's to be decided,' Nina said.

'Well, don't worry if you can't have me there,' Jenny said. 'I can always go to Sarah – or to Alec's,' she added, lightly.

Nina had not yet met Alec, who was a year ahead of Jenny at university.

'I'm not quite sure if the job goes on until Christmas,' Nina said. 'Exact dates are to be arranged.'

'Well, don't let me be a problem,' Jenny said. 'I'm sure it will all work out. It's funny,' she went on.

'What is?'

'Well – you and Sarah. You both did the same thing – married so young, I mean – yet you're very different.'

It was true that both Nina and her elder daughter had married at nineteen and had their first baby at once. Both had immersed themselves in domestic, maternal life.

'I don't think Jeremy's very like Daddy,' said Nina.

Jenny, however, thought that he was: he was a rather selfish young man who intended to be well looked after.

'Sarah doesn't let herself be pushed around,' she said. 'She's much tougher than you are, Mum. She knows what she's doing.'

'And I didn't, at her age?' Nina asked.

'Well, girls didn't then, did they?' Jenny said, kindly. 'Things were different. Marriage was all the rage, wasn't it?'

It was true. When Nina left school, girls expected to work for just a few years, until reprieved by marriage and children. She had considered no other future and when Martin had singled her out, was elated.

'Yes,' she said.

She began collecting up their plates.

'See – there you are, automatically clearing up. You're

conditioned to the domestic scene,' Jenny said, but she was laughing. 'Leave that, Mum. You look shattered. I'll see to it.'

'Put them in the dishwasher,' said Nina. 'They can wait till tomorrow.'

'I will. I'm not two years old, you know,' said Jenny.

'No,' said Nina. 'Thank you, Jenny.'

'Go on up and have your bath,' Jenny said, waving her out of the room.

'I'm so glad you're here, Jenny,' Nina said, at the door. 'Thank you for coming. But you must go back tomorrow. You mustn't miss your lectures.'

'I'll go if I'm satisfied that you're all right,' Jenny said. 'Now, off with you!'

Nina went. Jenny heard her going slowly upstairs. Usually her mother, who was small and compact if a little overweight, moved briskly, with small, rapid steps. Jenny began clattering the dishes so that she could not hear the slow, dragging tread on the polished stairs. Then she noticed the parcel on the drainer and picked it up. The half-rotted paper fell away from it, revealing the cheap pottery cat.

What an odd thing for her to buy, Jenny thought, and put it on the dresser where it wouldn't get knocked over.

4

Nina would take from the house everything that was hers – her clothes, her books – mainly cookery books and works on home management or needlework. She made a neat list of the contents of the linen cupboard and packed up half for herself. She set out the crockery and kitchen utensils and catalogued all of them, then packed up what she wanted in large cardboard cartons from the supermarket. She needed no garden implements and those would offset any balance in her favour so far. The furniture was to be split by agreement and attention to value, as arranged by Mr Drew, the solicitor whom she had consulted, and Martin's lawyer.

Nina had found Mr Drew by means of the yellow pages in the telephone directory. She had seen him the day after her trip to London. A stranger, she had decided, would be a better choice than a solicitor recommended by some friend, or by Sarah's husband. Mr Drew was an elderly young man of thirty-two who advised her that she had rights and, when she explained about her house-minding job, said she should not move out of Silverlea just yet. Nina insisted that Martin had said she would be looked after. She trusted him, even without a written promise, and would not agree to Mr Drew registering the house to protect her interest.

Mr Drew's desk was stacked with neat piles of paper and several folders. He looked at her sagely across the top of them. He had pale-blue eyes and a small, fair moustache.

'You trust him,' he repeated. 'Well, I hope you won't be disillusioned.' Trusting Martin, he implied, had brought her to this office.

'He isn't mean,' said Nina.

'Wasn't,' corrected Mr Drew. 'You say this woman is pregnant. He'll be needing money, Mrs Crowther. Certain sums are your due, of course, but errant spouses are often reluctant to pay.' Much of Mr Drew's income came from this sort of tangle and the pursuit of entitlements.

'He's already got a buyer for the house, it seems,' Nina said. 'I'd like everything settled as soon as possible. Divorce can be quite quick these days, can't it?'

All things being equal, yes, Mr Drew agreed, but her future must be safeguarded. Years when she might have been building up her own lucrative career had been spent caring for husband and family, he pointed out; why should she lose now? His job was to see that she didn't, he added, not telling her that in his experience, and despite his skill, in the end she would. He saw that she was determined to take this temporary job. At least she was not due to begin it just yet, which would give him time to start striking bargains with the opposition. She must make a new will at once, he told her meanwhile. He would have it prepared straightaway, and she could sign it the very next day.

'But I've never made a will,' Nina said. 'I've nothing to leave.'

'Your jewellery – your clothes. You have a car?' Mr Drew

suggested. 'And eventually, what money we win from the sale of the house. If anything happened to you, it would all revert to your husband, and I'm sure you would prefer your daughters, for instance, to have it.'

He was right. Nina meekly agreed and went home to telephone Mrs Blunt.

That Sunday, Sarah, her husband Jeremy, and their son Sebastian arrived for lunch. Each evening, till then, Sarah had telephoned urging Nina not to give up. Her father would come to his senses, she said, and return. Nina refused to discuss his conduct or her plans on the telephone, and refused, too, to accept Sarah's repeated invitations to stay.

'My solicitor has advised me not to go away,' Nina said slyly, enjoying using Mr Drew in this way.

Hence the visit.

Sarah had told Jeremy, who was a computer systems analyst, that they must go and talk sense to her mother.

Jeremy, a balding young man with an incisive brain, narrow horizons and a strong sense of self-preservation, knew when to submit. A good lunch, at least, was a certainty at Silverlea. They strapped Sebastian into his seat in the rear of their Peugeot and arrived in Surrey with good appetites for the roast lamb and blackberry and apple pie which Nina had prepared.

Jeremy had brought a bottle of sherry as an expression of sympathy and a bottle of wine for lunch. He loomed gravely over Nina in the kitchen as she dished up the vegetables while Sarah potted Sebastian. Nina's plight was, in his opinion, worse than if she had been widowed, for then she would have been cushioned by Martin's insurances, and there would have been grief, but not humiliation.

'I'm awfully sorry about all this, Nina,' he said. 'And we do want you to move near us. If it's really final, I mean.'

Sarah, entering the kitchen, overheard, with approval, these words.

'There's plenty you could do, mother,' she said. 'Sebastian would love to see more of you. And this one, of course.' She patted her not-yet-bumpy stomach.

'I'm sure there are lots of ways in which I could be useful,' Nina said. 'But I might decide to go round the world before settling down. I've never had a chance to, before.'

Jeremy stared at her. He had no great perception of mood and could not interpret hers. Perhaps she had already been at the sherry?

'This job you mentioned,' he said. 'What is it?'

'I'm to work for Leonard Blunt,' Nina said, with perfect truth. 'You know who I mean? He's the chairman of Blunt's – the grocery chain.' Mrs Blunt had explained this when Nina had telephoned to accept the post. Leonard's father had founded the business with a chain of bakeries which had expanded first into tea shops and later into a network of supermarkets which now extended nationwide and whose turnover was vast.

'Good gracious,' said Jeremy, impressed, and added hastily, 'I mean, well done.'

Sebastian, who had come into the room with his mother, now noticed, on the dresser, the pottery cat Nina had bought in Woolworth's.

'Nice pussy,' he said, trying to reach it.

Sarah moved it out of range.

'I haven't seen that before,' she said. 'Where did you get it? It's rather crude, isn't it?'

'It caught my eye,' Nina said. 'Does it remind you of anyone?'

They'd met Caroline, she knew; they had gone to London the day before though they hadn't had time, yet, to describe their encounter. Nina, in any case, did not want to hear about it.

'It's just a cat, isn't it?' Sarah said, frowning. 'A pottery cat in rather poor taste.'

'Yes,' agreed Nina. 'That's all it is, my dear.'

Driving home in the evening after an excellent lunch, a short walk on the common and a large tea, Sarah felt baffled.

'She seemed very strange, didn't she?' she asked Jeremy.

'She looked very tired,' Jeremy said.

'She was making jokes,' Sarah said. 'She's never done that. Or not much.'

Jeremy had to agree that wit was not Nina's predominant characteristic.

28

'Well, she seems to have found a suitable job, at any rate,' Sarah said. 'Though I can't think what she'll really be doing. She's got no business experience at all. Perhaps she's to be some sort of receptionist. She always looks nice, after all. She dresses well, and she knows how things should be done.' She sighed. 'I can't understand Daddy.'

But Jeremy could. Just occasionally – not very often – he wondered what it would be like to be married not to Sarah, who was pretty, capable, even-tempered and affectionate, though, unlike her mother, rather untidy, but instead to come home to a tiger in disguise. It might not be very comfortable, he thought; it would only be a delight during a fit of fever in the blood: but it would be exciting. Perhaps Caroline was a tiger.

A fling would be possible, Jeremy thought, looking ahead: a minor fling, on a trip abroad, maybe, when Sarah could never find out, just to prove one's blood was red, but not this sort of thing, which was very sordid. Oh, no! He took his left hand from the steering-wheel and laid it on Sarah's thigh. She was always willing, as long as Sebastian was safely asleep, and sometimes, still, even eager. He loved her.

With such a name, Nina had expected Netherton St Mary to be a typical English village, with thatched cottages, a duck-pond and friendly inhabitants.

She had lived all her life in suburban Surrey, where her father had been a doctor in general practice. He had volunteered for the RAMC during the war but was rejected on health grounds; as a civilian doctor he worked, in those years, for very long hours and dealt with bomb casualties as well as day-to-day ailments. Her mother was involved with the Red Cross and ran First Aid courses. An elderly maid looked after the house, and as Nina grew older she learned, automatically, to cook and to clean as she helped Gertrude. Her older brother was sent to boarding school, but Nina, after some years at a kindergarten, went to a private day school where she shone at nothing but was content. Her mother continued, after the war, with her voluntary work, which she had enjoyed, and Nina, who was fifteen when Gertrude retired, took over many of the responsibilities of running the household. Her happiest hour of the day was when her father came home to the evening meal she had prepared. She enjoyed protecting him from importunate patients and hated it when he had to go out to calls at night. He died suddenly, of a heart attack, when she was seventeen.

Nina and her mother settled down uneasily together. Her brother was now at medical school and seldom came home. Nina left school and began a secretarial course. When she met Martin at a party, and he singled her out, she found him different from the boys she had known all her life – her brother's friends. He was older, more self-assured. Martin was drawn by her freshness and lack of sophistication.

After their marriage, her mother moved into a flat in Eastbourne where she lived in contentment for fifteen years. Then, to the amazement of her son and daughter and of her friends, she married a widower whom she had met when she went on holiday to the Algarve, where he had a villa. They lived there still, in perfect harmony.

Nina had written to tell her mother that she and Martin had parted, and her mother had replied kindly, hoping that the rift was only a temporary one and inviting her to stay. Time and distance might be helpful, she suggested. Nina replied calmly, saying that there was no hope of a reconciliation and perhaps she might come for a visit later on. She and Martin had been out there once, for a week, and her mother and her husband had come over for Sarah's wedding, but not since. Her husband was now rather frail, and the journey was very tiring for him.

Driving to Netherton St Mary on a cold day at the end of October, Nina reflected on her mother's reckless act in marrying, in her sixties, a man she scarcely knew. Hearing about it, Nina's friends all told worrying tales of other such matches hastily contracted between lonely survivors with nothing but their bereaved states in common, and which had not turned out well. But this one had; her mother was happy.

She must have been lonely in those Eastbourne years, Nina thought, but she had never complained and she had worked tirelessly for various good causes in the manner Sarah now thought appropriate for Nina herself. How much courage had it required to make that fresh start, Nina wondered now: as much as she needed herself at this moment?

She had had a second meeting with Mrs Blunt, in London, in the Blunts' Knightsbridge flat. Here, Nina was told about her duties, which included looking after a well-behaved, docile black Labrador dog. There was no cat. Mrs Blunt said her son, as a child, had an asthma-provoking allergy to cats so they had never kept one. The dog was present during the interview. He wagged his tail and gazed benignly at Nina.

'He'll be company for you,' said Mrs Blunt. 'I must warn you that the house is rather isolated.'

Mrs Blunt had been surprised to find Nina, at this encounter, no longer dowdy; but the impression she had of her reliability was unchanged.

Nina's neighbour and friend, Felicity Wainwright, listened to an account of the interview when Nina returned and said that it sounded fantastic. It would do Nina good to have a touch of high life.

'Bully for the Blunts,' she said. 'I expect he rose from behind the counter cutting up cheese to his present eminence.'

'It must have been the bakery counter, not cheese, since it began with buns,' said Nina.

'Did you meet him?'

'No.'

'Oh well, she seems nice. That's the main thing,' said Felicity.

Felicity had been wrathful on Nina's behalf when she heard about Martin's defection. She had undertaken to tell the rest of their circle, couples living in similarly secluded, expensive houses in the area, the bare facts. She'd made her husband check the credentials of Mr Drew, Nina's solicitor, and he had confirmed that the yellow pages had led her to a dependable representative of an impeccable firm.

Felicity offered practical help. Nina's summer clothes and her personal possessions were stored in her attic, although by the time Nina left for Netherton St Mary no final arrangements had been made about the house or its contents. Martin, through his solicitor, had indicated that the sale was going ahead, but, as contracts had not yet been exchanged, Nina expected to return, however briefly, after her job ended.

Mrs Blunt proposed that Nina should receive a cheque at the start of her time at the Hall.

'To cover expenses,' she said. 'Then, at the end, we'll give you a present – quite a substantial one,' and she named a figure. 'In that way you won't be obliged to declare a wage, which might prejudice your alimony.'

She was to draw on the contents of the Blunts' three deep freezes, where bread and other food supplies were stored along with fruit and vegetables from the garden, and was to charge anything else to the Blunts' accounts with local shops. All bills were to be sent to Mr Blunt's secretary who would telephone once a week to make sure that there were no problems. If any arose, Nina was to consult the secretary, or Mrs Jowett who lived at the Manor House. She and Mrs Blunt had been at school together, Nina was told.

Surveying her new surroundings on that cold, grey day, Nina thought it was rather like moving into a Hollywood film. The house, however, was neither as large nor as old as she had expected. It was a late Victorian gothic building, solidly built and expensively modernized so that it lacked no aid to comfort and convenience. The sense of unreality which Nina had felt ever since the course of her life had so suddenly altered grew stronger as she walked round with Mrs Blunt. She had found the way without difficulty, following instructions sent by Mr Blunt's secretary to take the slip road from the motorway and go through Murford. Nina was not a confident driver; she had passed her test years before, it was true, but she never drove on long journeys or on motorways; Martin did that. Hers were the school and shopping trips along local, familiar roads. She had felt quite a sense of achievement, entering the village at last without taking any wrong turning.

'We'll leave you lists and things,' Mrs Blunt had said, arranging that Nina should arrive a few hours before the Blunts themselves departed for London, where they would spend the night before catching their plane. 'And Dan Fenton will be up to do the garden. He's got real green fingers. I found him when our old boy retired. His own garden's a dream, but doesn't give him enough scope so he loves ours. It's saved him, I think, poor man. His life has been tragic.'

'Oh?' Nina thought interest was expected.

'His only daughter was killed – shot in a bank raid not long before he and his wife came to this village. His wife never got over it and she died soon after they moved.'

'Oh dear,' said Nina. 'How very sad.'

Her friend Felicity had looked the Blunts up in *Who's Who*. Leonard, she had told Nina, was sixty-eight, and Charles, the only son, had been born in 1942.

'Mrs Blunt must be about sixty-eight too,' Felicity said, but Nina disagreed. She looked much less: nearer fifty, she said.

'Well, she must be older than that, to have a son of that age,' Felicity pointed out. 'We're not much older than him.'

'I feel antique,' Nina had sighed.

'Poor old thing. You'll buck up,' Felicity said. 'Rot Martin.'

'We never quarrelled,' said Nina. 'Odd, isn't it? All that was going on, and I never knew.'

'A quarrel can clear the air,' Felicity said.

But the hardest thing for Nina to bear was the knowledge that for years she had trusted in something that didn't exist – had, possibly, never been there at all.

And now she was at The Hall, Netherton St Mary, its custodian for the next two months, alone in the house while the rain still fell outside, the keys in her care. The Blunts had been driven away in a large limousine.

Mrs Blunt had shown Nina all over the house while her husband, a short, cheerful man with sparse sandy hair, made some final telephone calls. He explained the complex locking system to her, making sure she understood. The various lists were handed over, and Rory, the dog, was patted and told to look after Nina. He looked very melancholy when the Blunts had gone.

There were fourteen bedrooms in the house. Nina went round once more and counted them. Some were in the attic, including the flat where the Spanish couple had lived. Nina was glad she had not been instructed to sleep up there, under the eaves. She had been allotted the yellow spare room, one of the nicest, with its own bathroom and a view across the fields.

'You can try out every room,' Felicity had said. 'Who's to know, when they've gone? I expect you'll meet everyone in the village.'

Like Nina, she had never lived in a rural village, and her impressions of life in one had been gleaned mainly from the novels of Agatha Christie. She thought Nina would have quite a social time.

33

Driving through Netherton St Mary, on that first day, Nina had felt doubtful of this. The place was larger than she anticipated. Several streets radiated from the main Murford road, and though there were some old buildings, she saw modern houses too. Her instructions were to bear right by the Black Swan, go past the Baptist Chapel and turn right again, then continue for half a mile until she came to the decontrolled sign. Now she would find herself driving along beside a high stone wall which marked the Hall grounds.

Tall iron gates were set between high stone pillars on which crouched carved lions. Nina had driven slowly up the well-kept drive which ended in a gravel circle around a rosebed in front of the house.

Mrs Blunt had said it was isolated, she reminded herself. That was why she was needed; otherwise, they would have locked the place up, she thought, and put the dog into kennels. But now she felt as lonely as if she were marooned in a desert. There was no other dwelling for at least three-quarters of a mile.

Nina put a great many lights on all over the house and went into her room to unpack. She hung her clothes in the fitted cupboard and put photographs of the girls and of Sebastian on the walnut chest. She unwrapped the pottery cat from several layers of tissue paper and looked at it consideringly. Then she put it in the bathroom, on the window-sill. Leaving the landing light on, she went downstairs and into the study, which Mrs Blunt thought she might find cosier to sit in than the drawing-room. In any case, the television set was kept there.

Rory, the dog, lay uneasily beside her as she tried to watch television. He kept lifting his head and gazing mournfully round, seeking his master and mistress, Nina supposed, but she could not help wondering if he was hearing unusual sounds and several times she got up to check all the doors and windows. The wind had risen and the earlier soft rain became heavy, lashing the latticed panes audibly in spite of the double-glazing.

For the first time in her life, Nina was alone in unfamiliar surroundings. She had lived in only three homes: her childhood one, the small house she and Martin had bought when they were first married, and Silverlea. She had not expected to feel so strange. Was it the size of the house, with its lofty rooms, that made her uneasy? Was it the responsibility of being in charge of so many valuable pieces of antique furniture and a collection of Meissen arranged in a Chippendale cabinet in the drawing room? How long would it take her to settle down?

She turned up the television and tried not to think of the weeks ahead. The news on ITN had just ended when the telephone rang.

It would be Jenny or Sarah, wanting to know how she was getting on. Both had said they would ring her often, and both had promised not to tell their father where she was. Nina hurried to answer.

When she lifted the receiver and gave the number of the Hall, no one spoke. All she heard was a shuddering sigh.

5

Nina slept badly that night, her first at the Hall.

She had said, 'Hullo? Hullo?' into the telephone several times, and stated her own number, all the while aware of a listening presence at the other end of the line although the sigh was not repeated.

'Who do you want to speak to?' she asked, deciding not to say that the Blunts were away. At last, when there was still no answer, she hung up.

A few minutes later the telephone had rung again, and once more no one spoke. There was no sigh this time, but Nina hung up instantly.

There had been no obscene remarks. Anyone's breathing could be audible on a telephone. It was a mistake, a wrong number, Nina told herself as she let Rory out for a final run. She was glad he was with her in the house, sleeping in his basket in the lobby beyond the kitchen.

Didn't burglars sometimes telephone to discover if a house was occupied before robbing it? Well, if her caller was a burglar, he'd know the Hall was not empty. But would a burglar dial the number twice? And if it was a straightforward wrong number, wouldn't the caller apologize?

She lay in bed, trying to sleep but starting awake at every sound, real or imagined. Her bedside clock seemed to tick very loudly. The heating system made a few ticking sounds. Outside, the wind still blew and the rain beat down.

Nina's single bed was soft and comfortable. She drew the primrose-coloured blankets and printed sheet around her shoulders. She was not accustomed, yet, to sleeping alone, although Martin had often spent nights away or come home late. Lying there, tense, she imagined him now, beside Caroline, and felt bitter hatred for them both. Would she ever stop feeling like this?

At last she turned on the light and looked at the time. Though she felt as if she had lain there for hours, it was only half-past twelve. Nina turned off the light and lay down again, trying to calm her racing brain, but at half-past one she gave up and went to the bathroom. Reflected in the huge mirror that filled one wall, she saw herself, in her pale green nightdress, moving about, getting a drink, swallowing two of the sleeping pills the doctor had reluctantly given her when she told him that she could not sleep. The pottery cat on the window sill seemed to watch her movements, smirking at her.

Nina got back into bed. Her mind was haunted by images of Martin and Miss Kitty-Cat, intimately linked. How about his snores? What did Caroline think about them, Nina wondered, with some malice.

She tried to turn her mind away from its obsession with her own distress and think about the village, Netherton St Mary, into which she had come, trying to recall what she had noticed as she drove through that afternoon. There was the pub, she remembered, and a shop or two; the long stretch before the decontrolled sign and the gateway to the Hall. She'd explore it all tomorrow.

At last the pills worked, and in the morning, when she woke, it was nearly half-past eight. Nina was still drowsy from the drug. The room was unfamiliar and her heart began to pound as she struggled to remember where she was.

The dog, she thought, remembering. He'd be bursting, poor thing. She swung her legs out of bed, pulled on her dressing gown and slid her feet into her slippers, then drew the curtains back. The rain had stopped, and a thin, wintry sunlight filtered downwards between clouds.

Rory rose to greet her as she came into the back lobby. He stretched and wagged his tail, not seeming desperate at all. His muzzle was grey; he wasn't a wild young dog, eager to be off hunting or courting, she thought gratefully. Though she had never liked dogs much, for they shed hairs and had messy wet feet and often sniffed at you quite rudely, she was glad to see him. They'd settle down together, she decided, patting him before opening the back door to let him out into the garden.

The air smelled damp. A bottle of milk stood on the step, and later, by the front door, she found a heap of letters on the mat. That seemed civilized enough, considering the distance from the village, Nina thought. At Silverlea the milk never arrived before noon, and the post not until ten o'clock. Her spirits rose. Would a paper also come?

She hadn't asked about them, and they weren't mentioned on Mrs Blunt's list. No doubt they took *The Times*. Martin always read it on the train. Nina thought it dull. She rather liked the gossip in the *Mail*.

She was sitting at the kitchen table eating bran flakes, the only cereal she could find, when the telephone rang. Immediately her fears of the night returned, but this time the caller was Sarah. Nina's heart warmed with gratitude as she gave a falsely reassuring report. In the background, as they talked, Nina could hear shrieks from Sebastian, due at playgroup later that morning. Sarah said she couldn't linger; she had to go to the ante-natal clinic after dropping Sebastian.

Nina felt guilty as she replaced the receiver. Poor Sarah had a lot to do; she might, in her pregnancy, feel tired and ill and in need of help, yet here was her own mother over seventy miles away from her, employed by a stranger.

But I had no help when the girls were small, Nina thought defensively. She'd washed and ironed and cooked and sewed, practising thrift, grateful as time went on for various aids Sarah had had from the beginning, such as an efficient washing machine and an electric mixer. But she'd been content. She'd wanted nothing more.

Yes, and look where it's got you, she told herself, returning to her cereal. She'd thought herself secure, but there was no safety anywhere. A wave of terror filled her. She might be only halfway through her life; certainly, in the ordinary run of things, there were many years ahead of her. What further blows lay waiting?

As if he sensed her sudden panic, Rory padded towards her, paws clattering on the tiled floor. He laid his head on her lap and stared at her mournfully.

'All right, boy,' she said. 'We'll go for a walk as soon as I've tidied up.'

Though there was no witness, she felt she must keep the house so spick that if Mrs Blunt suddenly walked in unannounced there could be no criticism of her custodianship. She'd do specific tasks each day, make a routine.

Scouring the sink after she had washed the breakfast dishes, Nina thought of the hours she had willingly spent in the same way at Silverlea. She'd seen Martin off each morning with a smile and a wave from the door; when he returned in the evening, dinner was already organized and the girls, when small, were almost ready for bed. Later, they were settled with their homework, pleased to see him but not expecting much communication. There had been anxieties – childish ailments, Jenny's adenoids and Sarah's appendicitis, and, at first, money had been short, but they had supported one another, or so Nina had thought. Martin had shown interest in the girls' guinea-pigs and later paid for riding lessons; then there had been worries about exams. They'd been, she'd thought, united as a family. At what point had the betrayal begun? Years ago, when Martin had started coming home late from the office, pleading extra work?

She shook herself. There was no point in going over it all again. If Miss Kitty-Cat had not got pregnant Nina might be still unaware of her existence. Perhaps Caroline had planned the baby to force Martin to act. Nina had asked him that, savagely, during their dreadful scene, but he'd ignored the question.

She went upstairs to make her bed. The room was so pretty. Just think where you might be, she told herself. You're lucky, living here in luxury. You might have had to live in digs and be a cleaning woman, with your lack of skills. Martin could have cut off all support. Men often did, Mr Drew had said, frowning over the fact that she had given Martin written consent to sell the house. Meanwhile, he was making her a small allowance.

Mr Drew warned that because Nina had made no contribution towards the purchase of the house, nor had a job after her marriage and thus no salary to put towards the mortgage, she might, in the end, get much less than she was expecting.

Nina's mind went on squirrelling round unhappily while she got ready to take Rory out. She had put her coat on and was tying a scarf round her head when a bell pealed piercingly through the house.

It was not the telephone. The front door? Nina went there and opened it, but no one stood on the step. The bell rang again, and Rory gave a loud bark from the rear of the house. Nina hurriedly locked the front door again and secured the various bolts, then went to the lobby by the kitchen and opened the back door.

A woman in an olive-green padded anorak stood on the step. She had tousled grey hair and a weatherbeaten face with the threads of broken veins giving her a florid look. There were women who looked like that in Surrey; you saw them about with dachshunds or corgis on leads.

'Mrs Crowther?' the woman said, and stepped into the house. Nina saw she wore green wellington boots. The visitor looked at Nina's beige suede coat and her printed headscarf. 'Going out?' she asked. 'I'm just in time, then. My name's Heather Jowett. I came to collect you for a good walk. I'll show you some of the best ways to go with Rory. Get your boots on – it will be muddy after the rain. I'll wait here – I don't want to dirty your floor on your first day here.'

This was the woman whom Mrs Blunt had mentioned, the one with whom she had been at school, Nina remembered. But surely they weren't contemporaries? Mrs Jowett looked at least fifteen years older than Mrs Blunt. She glanced down at her own legs. She was already wearing boots, but they were fashionable black leather ones, zipped and with small heels. She hadn't worn wellington boots for years.

'Oh – er,' she said doubtfully, as Rory made snuffling

sounds and licked Mrs Jowett's hand in a welcoming manner, clearly her friend. Perhaps she had been head girl when Mrs Blunt was the lowliest junior.

'I'll show you a splendid field walk,' Heather said, and smiled. Her face changed, its harsh lines dissolving. She had vivid blue eyes.

'I won't be a minute,' said Nina, and hurried off to the cloakroom where she had seen a row of boots neatly arranged. The smallest pair was still too large for her, but she stuffed the toes with Andrex from the roll in the lavatory and soon rejoined Mrs Jowett, who had moved outside and was surveying the garden with Rory beside her, leaving the back door open.

Nina carefully checked the various processes as she locked the back door and put the keys in her pocket. If she neglected any part of the ritual, a bogus meter reader might call and force an entry.

'I'm glad Priscilla took my advice,' said Heather as they strode off down the drive at a brisk pace. Nina's heels rubbed up and down in the too-large wellingtons as she stepped out.

'Oh?' she said, wondering if she should put Rory on the lead. He seemed to be walking meekly enough beside them at the moment, but if she were alone she would not have left him free.

'I said she should find someone to live in the house when Jose and Maria left,' said Heather. 'It's better than leaving an isolated place like this unoccupied, and better for Rory than kennels. I couldn't have him you see, much as I'd have liked to.' Why not, wondered Nina silently. 'After all, anyone could break in and no one would notice,' Heather went on. 'Except possibly Dan, that's the gardener. You know about him, don't you?'

The man whose daughter had been shot, Nina remembered. She said that Mrs Blunt had mentioned him, and commented on the size of the village.

'It's grown a lot lately,' said Heather. 'In the building boom a few years ago people sold spare land – fields and tennis courts and things – to developers, and there are several new estates where young people live. I rather like seeing babies about, but there was a time when one knew everyone in the place. It's not like that now.'

'Where do they all work?' asked Nina. 'Do they go to London?'

'Some do, but there's a big industrial area in Droxton – that's about twenty miles away. It used to be a quiet market town, like Murford.'

They were walking along the lane now, away from the village. Nina plodded on in her boots. Her new friend, who was quite tall, took long strides. Heather soon turned off the lane down a track where, after all the rain, deep puddles filled the ruts made by tractor wheels. Now, Rory ran on ahead.

'He'll get covered in mud,' said Nina.

'It won't hurt him. A big dog needs plenty of exercise and he doesn't get enough with Priscilla,' said Heather. 'Have you done much house-minding, Nina?'

'Not a lot,' Nina answered.

'It must be rather fun,' said Heather. 'No heating bills to pay – no rates. Everything found.'

'Yes,' Nina cautiously agreed.

'We never go away,' said Heather. 'Not now. We spent a lot of time abroad when we were younger. My husband was in the army, you see.'

'Oh.'

They were walking, now, along the headland of a ploughed field. Damp, heavy clay clung to Nina's feet so that every step involved lifting a weighty clump of earth. Her companion seemed unaware of any difficulty. Country life, thought Nina: she'd liked the idea of a friendly village, she reminded herself, and here, certainly, was a friendly neighbour.

Suddenly Heather stopped, rummaged in her pocket, and bent down by the hedge. To Nina's amazement she had drawn forth some small bulbs and a pocket knife. She carefully cut some holes in the turf near the hedge and planted the bulbs, shabby tweed skirt stretched over her lean hips, legs in thick wool tights set wide apart.

'Snowdrops,' she said, replacing the turf and treading it down. She cut another piece and planted more. 'I must put some scillas in here too.'

When she stood up again, she noticed Nina's astonished expression and explained, 'I always have something to plant in my pocket – bulbs or seeds, sometimes seedlings or a sapling, or a rooted cutting, depending on the season. Man is destroying his environment. This field was once divided into four, but now the hedges have been grubbed out to make it simpler to harvest. Windbreaks have gone. Wild flowers have been lost. I replace them whenever I can.'

Nina's surprise had become approval.

'What a good idea,' she said. 'But isn't it expensive?'

'Money's relative,' said Heather. 'One person's necessity is someone else's luxury. I collect nuts and acorns from the woods, so they cost nothing, and I save seeds from my own garden. Even the bulbs are some I've thinned from clusters of my own. To plant just one fine tree – one that reaches maturity – is worth doing, I consider.'

'I'm sure you're right,' said Nina.

She warmed to her companion as she trudged on, her mud-laden feet growing heavier by the minute. How far were they going? She tried to remember their route as they turned right and left, skirted a copse, clambered over stiles. Several times they stopped for further planting sessions. Nina's tight skirt hampered her when they climbed a gate which was securely locked, but Heather, in her pleated tweed, stepped nimbly over. They walked through a herd of steers who blew and snorted as they passed among them, something Nina would never have dared on her own. Rory's free running was controlled; he never moved far from them, and although he paused to gaze into the face of a steer which bent to inspect him, he soon moved on.

'He's a good dog,' Heather said. 'He's too old, now, to run away, and he's well disciplined. You won't have any trouble with him.' It was she who had undertaken the role of his controller during the walk, issuing the few commands required. Nina would never have allowed him all this freedom.

They did not talk much, but the silence was not uncomfortable. Now and then Heather indicated spots where trees – sometimes diseased elms – had been felled, or varieties of wildlife had once flourished. They paused on a humpbacked bridge over a fast-flowing stream which, said Heather, joined the river which ran through Murford further on; sometimes these low-lying fields were flooded after rain.

42

'It's like a lake,' she said. 'We often skated here, in icy spells.'

Who were 'we'? She'd mentioned a husband. She must have children too, Nina decided.

'The Manor's over there,' said Heather at last, and pointed across ploughland to a hollow where a large brick house with a grey roof was visible, among trees. She glanced at her watch. 'I'll go straight on home now – I must get back. You'll be able to find your way to the Hall again, won't you, Nina? Just follow this hedge the way we've come, go over the stiles and past the wood, and you'll be back within sight of the path where we started.'

Nina was far from sure she could manage this, and it seemed as if she must still walk several miles, but it wouldn't do to protest.

'I'm sure I'll find the way,' she said. 'Thank you.'

'Goodbye,' said Heather, and again the expression of great sweetness came over her face as she smiled. 'We'll walk again,' she said.

Nina watched her stride away, hands thrust into her jacket pockets. What a weird woman, but she was nice. She fitted into Nina's expectations about the inhabitants of Netherton St Mary by being eccentric with her flower-planting.

Rory displayed a wish to follow Heather. Nina called him sternly, and was relieved when he turned back towards her and trotted on beside her. She began to rehearse in her head how she would write to the girls about Mrs Jowett – whom perhaps she must think of, even address, as Heather, since the older woman had called her by her first name. 'A kind woman who has lived here in the Manor House for many years,' she would tell Sarah. Jeremy would like the touch about the Manor. 'A funny old thing in green wellies who's into nature,' she would say to Jenny, 'and not at all stuck-up.' She'd hurried off rather suddenly, after she'd looked at her watch, rather as if she'd remembered leaving the iron on, or a saucepan on the stove.

Nina would have to get some wellingtons of her own. These were most uncomfortable and she was sure they would have rubbed holes in her tights.

At last she and Rory reached the Hall again, and Nina

wiped her boots on the grass by the side of the drive in an attempt to rid them of some of their mud. On she trudged, and when she reached the house she saw a bicycle parked by the back door and a distant figure on the lawn, sweeping leaves. Rory left her, running towards the man who, with a besom brush like a witch's broom, had swept drifts of beech leaves into neat piles.

This must be Dan Fenton.

Nina walked slowly over the grass to meet him. She wondered how often he came. He was a big man, dressed in a stone-coloured anorak, with dark corduroy trousers tucked into ordinary black wellingtons. His feet were large. He paused in his sweeping to talk to the dog, bending to pat him. He did not realize, at first, that Nina was there, seeming totally absorbed in talking to Rory and fondling his ears, but then he sensed her presence and, straightening up, touched his cap.

'Good morning,' Nina said, shying from using his first name straight away, yet feeling 'Mr Fenton' would be too formal.

'Ah – good morning, Mrs Crowther,' Dan said.

'Rory and I have been for a walk,' said Nina. 'He's got rather muddy, so I suppose I'd better rub him down.' She'd only just thought of this, and had a sudden memory of her mother's Jack Russell; he'd had to be bathed in the kitchen sink, a task she had deplored, hating the woolly smell of wet dog.

'Mrs Blunt keeps a towel for him in the boiler room,' said Dan. 'I take him out for her sometimes, when she's busy.'

'Oh – do you? Thank you,' Nina said. 'We went over the fields. Mrs Jowett kindly called for me.'

'Oh yes – she likes a good walk,' Dan said. 'That's when she's not busy in the garden. She gets out of the house, one way and another, when the colonel's painting.'

'Painting?'

'He's an artist. Has a room there fixed up as a studio,' said Dan. 'Mrs Jowett takes the paintings off and sells them.' He smiled faintly. 'A neighbour of mine used to help in the house, but not any more.'

Nina longed to know why not, but knew she must not encourage gossip.

'Yes – well, I'd better see to Rory,' she said, repressively. 'Come along, boy.'

The dog looked enquiringly at Dan, who nodded to him and told him to go along.

'He's an obedient dog,' said Nina.

'Yes. Mrs Blunt isn't one to stand nonsense,' said Dan, returning to his sweeping.

Nina could believe it, not from dog, man or woman.

In the boiler room she found a large, brightly patterned towel with which she dried Rory's wet paws and coat. She cleaned Mrs Blunt's boots before putting them away, and sure enough there were holes in the heels of her tights. She went upstairs and changed them. By now she was longing for a cup of coffee, and she put the kettle on when she came downstairs.

What about Dan? He'd expect one, wouldn't he? The jobbing gardener they'd had at Silverlea had always been given coffee and a slice of cake, mid-morning. He'd expected to come into the kitchen for this refreshment, and Nina had quite enjoyed chatting to him as she worked there. Did the same apply in a mansion?

Cautiously, Nina decided to take a mug of coffee out to Dan in the garden today. She could be more friendly later, when she had settled in; after all, it wasn't her house.

Dan was grateful. He took his cap off and scratched his head when he had taken the mug from her.

'I put sugar in,' said Nina. Workmen, in her experience, always took two, if not three spoonfuls.

'Thank you,' said Dan.

He was very bald, she saw, though there was strong grey hair that curled above his ears, and he had thick, bushy eyebrows.

'I'll bring the mug in before I go,' he said.

'Oh – yes,' said Nina, and turned to walk back to the house. There couldn't be a lot to do in the garden at this time of year, she thought. At Silverlea, they'd had no help in the winter. The jobbing gardener had put in bedding plants in spring, and mowed. Nina had snipped dead heads from roses and cut blooms for the house. Martin, when he was young, had seemed to enjoy gardening but he'd done less and less latterly.

Nina had never done much outside although she liked arranging flowers and had even been to classes to learn how to do it more skilfully. She'd been to occasional cookery demonstrations, too, but she had never wanted to learn German, as Felicity had done, or take any sort of job, even a voluntary one, apart from rare fund-raising ventures for charities. She'd always been busy. After all, Jenny had been at home until last year.

How swiftly things could change! Only weeks ago she had been at Silverlea, taking the continuing pattern of her life for granted. Where would she be a year from now?

Again the large, strange house felt alien. She wished that, after all, she had invited Dan to have his coffee in the kitchen.

6

Death sometimes comes too suddenly for any goodbye. So it had been on a day, seven years ago now, when a young bank clerk had gone to work as usual. A few hours later she was dead, shot as she waited to be admitted past the inner security door on her return from lunch. Two masked robbers had held up the small branch and had got away with money being drawn for wages by men from a local firm, one of whom had been wounded. The girl had tried to run for it, to raise the alarm outside. The police caught the villains within days; they were still in prison but, with remission of their sentences, would not serve much longer. Dan Fenton thought that this was not punishment enough for murder.

Ellen, his wife, had never recovered from her daughter's violent death. Afterwards, she had become sad and silent and had sought refuge in religion, going to chapel twice on Sundays and praying a great deal in between, but none of it had brought her comfort. Dan had taken early retirement, hoping that would help, for they had long planned to move to the country and keep bees, but Ellen had died soon after they came to Netherton St Mary, simply fading away after a minor illness.

'She turned her face to the wall,' the doctor said. 'She had no stamina left.'

So now Dan lived alone in the pebble-dashed villa in Chestnut Crescent. It was one of a group that were built in a period of expansion between the wars, soundly constructed and with a large garden. Neither Dan nor Ellen had had the heart, when they bought it, to pursue the search for something more picturesque. Dan had done the house up inside, following, after Ellen's death, the scheme that she had limply approved, applying white vinyl paint over the purples and oranges of the previous, rather younger, owners. The couple who, a year ago, had moved next door found him reserved. They felt sorry for him, and often the young wife, when she had been baking, would bring him some scones warm from the oven, or a slice of moist fruit cake.

He didn't, in the end, go in for bees. The neighbours might not have liked them, and now there seemed no point. Instead, he set up a tank for some tropical fish and tried to get absorbed with them; they were company of a sort, and undemanding, not moping when he went out for the day, as he regularly did.

He had tamed the neglected garden, and grew vegetables which won prizes at the Netherton St Mary horticultural show. His neighbours, to whom he gave lettuces, tomatoes, beans and cauliflowers in return for their cakes, were proud of his success. Priscilla Blunt, presenting the awards, had noted how annually he won most of them, and made enquiries. Thus it was that she had arrived on his doorstep one day to ask if he would be interested in taking on the garden at the Hall.

Now Dan spent a great deal of his time there, keeping only the vaguest record of the hours he worked, for to him, they were the best ones of the day. His life revolved around the two gardens, his tank of fish, and his weekly trips to London.

Dan had made one of his journeys to London a few days before Nina arrived at the Hall. This was an extra visit, a pilgrimage to his daughter's grave on the anniversary of her death. To reach the vast cemetery where she was buried involved two changes on the underground and he had to wait some time for the second train. As, at last, he walked the last quarter of a mile up the hill, he stopped at a florist's. His choice of flowers for her had become part of the ritual: virginal white chrysanthemums now, spring flowers on her April birthday. If she had not been killed, by this time she might have been married, with children. Dan sighed, thinking this, as he stepped past headstones in the graveyard.

It was very quiet on this rainy day. He saw no other visitors, although a burial was in progress near the boundary wall. Dan stood by the simple tombstone which had weathered from its first early purity. His were the only flowers that rested there. Who else remembered her, he wondered sadly.

He stayed there some time, deliberately trying to call back her memory, finding it difficult, now, to picture her face. He remembered various birthdays: her first little bicycle: the day she cut off her long, fair plaits against her mother's wishes.

At last he felt that it was time to go. The rain still fell, spattering the path. His flowers would soon be faded, Dan knew, walking slowly back to the gate and into the road. He went on down the hill to the tube station.

Sometimes, on his days in London, he went to Euston or St Pancras; sometimes to King's Cross; sometimes Liverpool Street. Though the stations varied, there was almost always someone to be found.

He always picked the youngest girl he saw.

Today, in the buffet at Euston, Dan ate a ham sandwich and drank a cup of railway tea. There were several girls in the busy place; he noticed two at one table; at another table, a girl was on her own. She had shoulder-length dark hair, and smooth, plump cheeks. While she ate a pie, she kept her gaze fixed on her plate.

Dan watched her covertly. Soon, she rose, picked up a small case, and went off through the glass doors on to the station concourse.

Dan followed.

Twenty miles from Netherton St Mary, Police Constable Peter Downes was driving along on patrol, a happy man. He was enjoying his freedom, alone in the car after completing his probationary period in the force, and other spells of patrol duty with a more experienced officer.

His duty today was to cover a large area of the division

watching for crime and criminals, noting any suspicious activity, guarding the Queen's Peace and ensuring the preservation of law and order. In his career thus far, he had met a variety of incidents – a good deal of drunk and disorderly conduct, domestic disputes, vandalizing juveniles. He had been present at several road accidents, controlling the traffic at the scene, comforting the injured, measuring skid marks and reporting the facts. A patient civilian clerk at Murford Police Station had taught him how to write his reports clearly. Now he was fully trained to protect the populace. His awesome appearance, pink-cheeked and with a wispy fair moustache adorning his youthful upper lip, would be enough, it was hoped, to deter potential villains who might see him passing from their felonious intent.

It was Saturday morning, and Downes kept his eyes open for wandering schoolchildren with time on their hands who might be tempted to broach open windows and unlock doors in their quest for diversion. Downes knew that 77 per cent of all crime was preventable, being the result of opportunist activity.

He drove over Droxton common and past a warehouse, its gates secure. A car ahead of him dropped its speed as the driver noticed him in the rear-view mirror and Downes smiled to himself at this proof of the effect of his presence.

His was the nearest car when headquarters received a 999 call from two ten year-old boys who had been to the spinney on the by-pass looking for conkers. He was the officer sent to investigate what they had found, half-buried among leaves.

The boys were waiting for him by the telephone box from which they had made their call. One was white-faced and shaky; the other was already on the mend and would soon be enjoying his brief notoriety, but it was his friend who had actually discovered the body. Downes sent them off to wait at a distance while he approached the spot they had indicated, and verified for himself that it was, indeed, the remains of a human leg and foot which protruded from the leaves.

He felt a sour taste in his mouth as he noted the time and called in to report, stepping back from the spot where the body lay, anxious to disturb nothing that might be remotely a piece of evidence. He was too old, he reminded himself, to throw up at the sight of a corpse. He took the boys back to his car where all three waited until reinforcements arrived.

Nina had gone up the village with Rory that Saturday morning. She'd half expected Heather Jowett to come round again and had loitered a little before setting off, but the old woman did not appear.

Old woman: if she was the same age as Mrs Blunt, she wasn't really old, Nina reminded herself, and before she tied a scarf over her own fair hair she searched for grey strands and fresh wrinkles on her face. She had lost weight lately, and there were new lines on her forehead. Below her eyes were pouchy bags that had not been there three months ago.

Today, she wore her own neat boots for she did not intend to walk over fields. She buttoned up her suede coat and set forth with Rory on his lead, carrying the letters she had written to both the girls the night before, and the mail that had arrived that morning for the Blunts, redirected, as she had been instructed, to the London office for forwarding. Her notes to the girls were short. In addition to describing her walk with Heather, she had told Sarah how well equipped the Hall was and mentioned the size of the grounds. Jenny, she thought, would be more interested in the description of the study with the rows of neatly shelved books -- the complete works of Dickens, among others, so that Nina would have no excuse not to repair notable gaps in her reading. She kept the tone of her letters light and she did not refer to the telephone calls.

There had been another call the evening before, at much the same time as the first one. Again, no one was there when she replied. She'd spoken quite sharply.

'What do you want?' she'd snapped, and when no one answered had slammed down the receiver, trembling with a mixture of fear and anger. Now, walking up the road in daylight, with the dog, her idea that the caller was a burglar wanting to know if the house was occupied seemed silly. A child, perhaps, had picked up the telephone and dialled at random. But no child would do that at twenty minutes to eleven at night, surely? And no child would dial, by chance, the same number twice.

She had lain awake in bed wondering what to do. Perhaps she should tell the police. After all, she was responsible for the house and they might have ways of tracing such calls. She had got out of bed and gone round checking all the doors and windows and had left several lights burning to deter thieves. Once again, she needed a pill before she could sleep.

She might ask Heather's advice about what she should do, Nina thought: if she met her, that was: she didn't think she could call on her so soon, if at all, unless there was a real emergency; she really should wait to be invited. Nina passed a lane leading off the main road and decided that it must be the way to the Manor. Cars passed as she walked along, and a bus stopped further down the road. The activity was reassuring. She met, separately, two old men with dogs on leads – one had a spaniel, one a shaggy black mongrel. The men kept their gaze on the path before them, and Rory ignored the dogs. Nina went past a block of former almshouses, now privately owned, built of brick with slate roofs, then the Baptist Chapel which she had noticed when she arrived, a roughcast building with texts printed on posters pinned in a frame on each side of the open iron gates: *Mark ye the Way*, said one, and *God Sees You*, warned the other. The next houses were small detached ones of individual design, about fifty years old and not, to Nina's eye, attractive. She was looking for thatched roofs, leaded windows, beams, but she saw little that was picturesque on her way to the post office, which was part of a terraced block in the main street. She needed stamps for her letters and had to wait while earlier customers were served with sweets and toys, which the shop also sold. She had missed the outgoing mail, she saw, when at last she was able to put her letters in the box that was set into the post office wall. On Saturdays the only collection was at ten-fifteen.

There had been no near letter-box at Silverlea, but the postman would always take ready-stamped letters when he delivered, if you left them for him. Nina, then, had written few letters apart from those to her mother. The post had not seemed important and most of what came was for Martin, often bills or circulars. The thought that her letters to the girls would not start on their way until Monday was frustrating.

She could telephone Sarah, but it wouldn't be easy to get in touch direct with Jenny.

Don't be silly, she said to herself. You don't need to speak to the girls.

She crossed the road to look at the few shops on the other side. There was a grocer, a butcher and a greengrocer. They were all busy. Further on was a garage with petrol pumps and a workshop. That was lucky, thought Nina. Her Metro was fairly new and was in good order, but she was glad to know that there would be help at hand if it went wrong. Martin had been quite good at simple mechanics and had usually been able to cure the non-starting of the car she had had before. She didn't mean to use the Metro much; she'd walk a lot with Rory.

She walked on past a pub, the Black Swan, where the road forked, the main road going on to Murford through which she had come after leaving the motorway when she arrived. Now she took the other spur, a lesser road which led past, at last, some pretty cottages with tiled roofs and a few larger houses, old ones, set back behind hedges or low walls. Further on was a telephone box on the corner of a curving road, Chestnut Crescent, which seemed to be a collection of plain, squarish pebble-dashed semi-detached houses. Nina walked past the turning and came to a field in which several ponies were grazing. A drive led to a farmhouse some fifty yards from the road. Beyond the farm, at what must be the end of the village, stood the church, an old stone building with a Saxon tower. Nina hesitated, but now Rory drew her on, tugging gently at his lead. He led her towards the wooden gate, green with lichen.

Nina opened it and went up the path to the door of the church.

It was locked.

How odd, she thought. Weren't churches meant to be always open as places of sanctuary? She turned away and wandered into the churchyard. There were old tombstones set in the grass, the names often worn and hard to decipher. Flowers were laid on some graves, and in a corner there was a new one, the ground humped and covered with a heap of withering wreaths. Worms, thought Nina, and shuddered. She glanced at the names on some of the tombstones and saw that families were buried together in groups. She noticed several Jowetts, and stopped at one. Rory slumped down on the ground beside her as she read the inscription: *Robin Jowett 1942–1963 R.I.P.*

Could that be Heather Jowett's son? Nina felt shocked. What had caused his early death? She turned away, suddenly cold, and left the churchyard with its overhanging evergreens, its yew hedges and it silent memorials, walking briskly back towards the village.

Passing the newsagent's, on impulse she went in and bought a paper.

'You'll be from the Hall, then,' said the newsagent, who was a plump man in a green overall.

Nina was pleased at this recognition, which went with her theory that everyone knew one another in a village.

'Rory and I are old friends,' the man explained, bending to pat the dog. 'He used to come in with Jose. I'm afraid we can't deliver up there. It's too far – the boys don't have time before catching the school bus. There's only the Hall along that way.'

'Well,' said Nina, rallying. 'I have to take Rory out every day. I can fetch my paper then, if you'll keep it for me.' It would give shape to her day to have this task.

It was agreed. The newsagent asked how she was settling in, and Nina said, 'Quite nicely, thank you.' She felt reluctant to leave the warm shop and the friendly newsagent, but she could think of no way of prolonging the conversation. She and Rory left the shop and walked home. The wind was getting up, and leaves from the gutters scurried past them as they walked on. Nina tied her headscarf more tightly and Rory slunk along, tail down, his back to the wind.

She spent most of the evening watching television, even dropping to sleep for half an hour during one dull programme. On the evening news, the local programme reported the discovery of a woman's body in a copse near the Droxton by-pass. The body had not been identified, but it had lain there some time and the police were treating the enquiry as a case of murder.

How dreadful, thought Nina, switching channels. She had seen Droxton on a signpost in the village earlier; Mrs Jowett had said it was twenty miles away.

There was no mystery telephone call that night. She listened for it, expectantly, but there was no ring, and, although the wind grew stronger in the night, blowing a gale by two in the morning, she slept soundly, without a pill.

There seemed to be no good reason for getting up the next morning. There was no one to send off to school, no one hurrying to the office, no breakfast to cook. But there was Rory, always Rory. Nina, who had drowsed off after waking early, forced herself to get up and go downstairs.

The wind almost tore the door from her grasp when she opened it to let Rory out. A cluster of leaves blew in round her feet, and across the lawn she could see twigs and small branches from the trees. She turned on the radio and learned that there had been much damage during the night, with trees blown on to power and telephone lines, and across roads.

Nina already knew the lights were working. She lifted the telephone and heard the dialling tone.

Rory soon returned to the house, scrabbling at the door to be admitted. Nina was getting quite fond of him and she patted him warmly when he came in. She had breakfast in her dressing gown, almost succumbing to the temptation to get back into bed. She'd seldom had breakfast in bed at home; she knew Sarah did, quite often, at her own insistence, not Jeremy's. Sarah had said that her own father was the original male chauvinist pig and she had no intention of letting Jeremy go the same way. When Nina defended him, saying her own role had been responsibility for domestic chores as her share of the partnership, Sarah had laughed shortly.

'That lets you off the hook, mother,' she'd said. 'That way you don't have to try.'

Nina hadn't understood.

Now, she wondered if Martin would help Miss Kitty-Cat, who perhaps was suffering from morning sickness? Nina hoped it was very bad, and would last through the whole nine months. Swilling the water round the basin, she looked at the pottery cat on the bathroom windowsill. It seemed to watch her as she moved, its simper ever wider. Now, at that instant, Martin might be making love to that woman.

54

Disgust and jealousy nearly overwhelmed Nina then. She felt almost giddy, and picked up the cat in her two hands, holding it above her head, about to dash it down on the bathroom floor. But it wouldn't break on the soft carpet, she thought, laying it down again. How foolish she was being! Anyone watching her would think she was mad. Perhaps she was, a bit, she thought. Her heart thudded uncomfortably as she went back to her room and brushed her hair.

How was she going to manage, here on her own all day, and for nearly two more months? How could she pass the hours?

I must take it a day at a time, she thought, sitting down at the kitchen table, her head in her hands. Today is Sunday. I'll deal with that first – not look ahead. Then, gradually, the weeks will pass. She could go to church this morning. But church, except at Christmas and Easter, had never been part of her life.

If she were back at Silverlea, if nothing had happened, she'd be preparing lunch for Martin, who might have gone to the golf club. Even in bad weather, like today, he often went there for a drink with his cronies.

She'd have to eat something for lunch herself, she supposed. There was sure to be a chop in the freezer.

During the night Dan had heard the wind rising, gusting round the eaves. Ellen had hated the wind; she had feared the banshee wail it made when it blew from the north-east and came howling down Chestnut Crescent. She'd lived long enough to hear it there more than once. Dan remembered that now, lying in his bare room at the front of the house. He no longer used the bedroom at the back, where she had died; it was pervaded too much by memories and he had equipped the other more appropriately for his bachelor existence. It was starkly furnished, austere, but had all that a man required for an ordered life: a narrow bed, a plain wardrobe, and a chest of drawers on which were placed neatly his hairbrush and comb; he took pains with what hair remained to him, and went to the barber regularly.

When he got up, he could see signs of storm damage even in his own garden; twigs lay on the lawn and a bough had blown down from a plum tree. He wondered about Mrs Crowther up at the Hall, in a big house that was strange to her. No doubt she was used to such places, earning her living by caretaking in them, as he imagined she did. Nevertheless, when he had cleared his own garden of debris, he decided to make sure that she was all right.

It was too windy to go on his bicycle, and he seldom took his small car on such a short trip. He set off on foot, a big, broad man in boots and anorak, a tweed hat on his head and a scarf round his neck. The wind caught at him as he went past the telephone box at the end of the road. A single car passed him, but he met no one walking. He stopped at the newsagent's to get his own paper and to consult the newsagent about taking one up to the Hall. Mrs Crowther had asked for the *Sunday Express* to be kept for her, he was told.

Papers tucked under his arm, he went on up the road. He kept his mind busy with thoughts of the present, not of the past. When he was occupied in the garden – his own, or the challenging one at the Hall – he forgot everything but the job in hand, and he enjoyed using his strength to dig the beds and clip the hedges. He had enough mechanical skill to keep the large mower at the Hall in good order, and he liked cutting logs, laying turves, and the harder tasks, as well as growing plants from seed. He enjoyed climbing a ladder to pick apples and putting them into racks in the stables. He'd nailed fine wire mesh round the apple racks to frustrate the mice who had always made merry in there before he worked at the Hall.

A large branch, blown from a tree by the gate, lay across the drive entrance. Dan dragged it to one side. It would cut up nicely into logs for the study fire. He glanced at the telephone lines and the electric cable that led to the house from a pole outside, although most of the village now received its power from lines under the ground. Everything looked all right.

The closed windows of the house glinted dully as he approached. It was a gloomy sort of place viewed from outside, Dan always thought, though the interior had been done up in such style that it was quite light and airy. He knocked on the back door and heard Rory give a low bark. Soon the door was opened an inch or two, and Nina peered out. Leaves and dust blew past Dan into the lobby.

'Come in,' Nina said, still baulking at calling Dan by any name and surprised to see him on a Sunday.

Dan stepped inside, taking off his tweed hat.

'Good morning,' he said. 'I came to make sure you were all right after the storm in the night. And I picked up your paper on the way.'

'Oh, that was kind of you,' Nina said. She was glad he had come.

'I'll fetch you in some coal and logs,' he told her. 'You'll be needing them for the study fire.'

'Well – yes. I'd been using the electric heater,' said Nina. Perhaps fetching in fuel was part of his work? It didn't appear on Mrs Blunt's list. 'Though really, with the central heating, it seems extravagant to burn something else,' she added.

'That's a big draughty chimney in there,' said Dan. 'You need a bit extra now winter's coming.'

It seemed natural, when he had brought in the fuel, to offer him coffee. He sat at the kitchen table stirring the sugar round in his cup, his anorak hanging over the back of his chair. He had left his boots in the back lobby and padded across the floor in his thick grey socks. The collar of his cream-coloured shirt, over which he wore a green crew-necked sweater, was spotless. He was not quite the sort of man you expected to find employed as a gardener, Nina thought, sitting opposite him with her own cup of coffee.

'You haven't always done gardening, have you?' she asked.

'Only as a hobby,' said Dan. 'It's my second career, you could say, now I'm retired.'

'I suppose this is my second career, too,' said Nina. 'House-minding, I mean.'

'Do you like it?' he asked.

'It's all right, so far,' said Nina.

'Here, you mean? Or is this the first time you've done it?' said Dan.

'Both,' Nina answered.

'I see. Somehow I thought you were used to it,' said Dan. 'You're not nervous? It's a big place to be in, alone.'

Nina denied any nervousness, but she thought of the telephone calls. Should she mention them to him?

'Are you on the telephone?' she asked, instead.

'No. There's a box at the end of the road, if I need to make a call,' said Dan. 'I've no one wanting to ring me up now. I've lost touch with folk from where I lived before.'

Nina remembered his sad circumstances, described by Mrs Blunt, and felt she had better head the conversation into a safer area. She mentioned the shops, and how many there were.

'It's easier than at home – where I used to live, I mean,' she said. 'We had none at all near.'

She was sorry when he left.

The gale continued to blow all day. In the afternoon, Nina read the paper. A short paragraph reported the discovery of a woman's body the previous day near the Droxton by-pass but gave no more details than she had learned from the television news. Later, she turned the set on and watched a romantic film which made her feel sad; she was glad to have Rory there, lying on the rug in front of the fire that Dan had lit. Rory had no proper walk that day, just a series of runs in the garden.

The telephone rang again that night, at twenty minutes to eleven, and again there was just a single sigh when Nina answered.

7

The body lay on the mortuary table. Little flesh was left on the small bundle of bones.

Police Constable Downes stood by the table, his one aim not to keel over. As the officer who had first seen the body after its discovery, it was his duty to confirm that it was the one found in the copse where, before its removal, it had been photographed from every angle. The area had been staked out and measured, and the surrounding woodland and meadows were still being sifted for evidence as to the identity of the dead woman and the method by which she was killed.

There was no doubt about it being a woman, but at this stage little more was known. The first doctor at the scene had been the police surgeon, whose task was formally to certify death, and to deduce that this was unlikely to have been a natural event. The forensic pathologist who was examining the corpse had been to the scene and made notes before permitting the body's removal. Now, as he worked, he spoke into the tape-recorder nearby, his particular method of noting details as he carefully inspected the remains.

Downes swallowed hard and gazed at the ceiling, trying to ignore the various smells. There was no rule to say you must watch. He thought about going to Spain, maybe, when he had leave, on a package tour, and perhaps finding some juicy young bird. But this body, this mass of bones and fibre, had once been that – a warm, living human being, able to laugh and make love. Whilst he fought his nausea, Downes also knew that he would not be happy until whoever had reduced her to this pitiful state had been found and punished. For there was no doubt at all that she had been killed: the pathologist had found a fracture of the hyoid bone in the neck, a typical injury in a case of strangulation, as if being covered in leaves wasn't enough on its own. She was very young, too; certainly no more than twenty-five and probably nearer sixteen, the experienced doctor remarked. Tests would affirm the exact age more precisely. Some dental work had been done, and was now recorded; if a possible identity for her was discovered, a chart comparison would confirm it one way or the other, but at the moment there was nowhere for the police to start their search. No handbag, purse, jewellery or other personal possessions had yet been found. All that was certain, apart from her age, was that she had fair hair, worn shoulder-length, and was about five foot two. Her clothing, which the doctor had painstakingly removed in fragments, must be analysed and might offer a lead; she was wearing an Indian print cotton dress. She had been dead between two and three months; the doctor hoped to pin that down more accurately later.

Some technicians were watching the postmortem. One of them made a light remark in an aside, and Downes felt his own tension slacken. That was it, he thought; think of something trivial – no disrespect meant to the dead – or you might not be able to take it. There would be more of this sort of thing for him in the future, he knew, and he'd have to be tough, get used to it.

Later that day he told his sergeant he'd like, in time, to put up for the CID.

Nina had decided she must report the mysterious telephone calls to the police. She had slept very badly again, spinning various theories in her mind about the anonymous caller, even imagining it was Martin purposely trying to frighten her, though he didn't know where she was and even if he did, was unlikely to act like this as she was cooperating with his wishes over the divorce and the sale of the house. He was anxious for everything to be settled rapidly, so that he and Miss Kitty-Cat could be married before the birth of their baby.

The gale was still blowing, and heavy rain lashed the windowpanes. The scene outside was grey and depressing and even Rory looked dejected when she greeted him that morning. He was soon back from his run in the garden.

Nina looked up the number of the nearest police station in the directory. There was one at Murford, she saw. She picked up the telephone, to find it dead.

It had been working at ten-forty the previous night, when the caller rang.

The feeling that now she was really cut off from the world outside was frightening. Although it meant no more anonymous calls could be made to her, she could not summon aid if she needed it. She must report the telephone out of order at once. Nina made herself a cup of instant coffee and drank it standing up as she tied on her headscarf and buttoned her coat, not waiting to have any more solid breakfast. She called Rory to her, and, taking her folding umbrella, set off.

Her umbrella blew inside out before she had reached the end of the drive, and she left it there, behind a shrub, to retreive on her return. She should really have taken the car, she supposed, but Rory had to have exercise and he had not had a proper walk the day before. They splashed down the road together, the dog showing little enthusiasm for the expedition. They met the old man with the spaniel whom she had noticed before. The man's head was down as he faced the gale.

In the telephone box by the corner of Chestnut Crescent, she dialled Faults and reported the telephone at the Hall out of order. Faults told her that the gale had brought down numerous lines and seemed gloomy about a speedy repair but promised to do what it could. Then Nina dialled Murford Police Station. A woman answered, and when she said why she was ringing, passed her on to a man. She felt foolish as she described what had happened – the regularity of the calls at twenty minutes to eleven each night and then the silence. The voice at the other end spoke kindly but said it was a matter for the telephone people. Her calls could be intercepted by the exchange; this soon discouraged mischief makers, he said. Nina uttered her theory that the caller might be interested in finding out if the house was empty, to be told thieves rarely made that sort of call at night, only by day. They'd be more likely to come and look themselves, at night, he said, not very reassuringly, Nina thought. Lights on in the house and other signs of occupation were what they would notice, he added. He repeated his advice to ask the telephone exchange to help if the calls continued; the nuisance would soon stop then, he declared.

Nina was disappointed. She'd somehow expected to be told that the line would be bugged and the offender caught, but as he was silent, perhaps that wouldn't be easy. She and Rory turned back, stopping at the newsagent's on the way. Dan had already been in, she was told, and collected her paper.

He'd come in his car. She saw a small green Ford parked by the back door as she approached the house, her collapsed umbrella under her arm. Dan was sitting inside it, and he got out as she drew near. He told her he'd come to fetch in her fuel, but as she was out and the house was locked up, he hadn't been able to do it.

'I never thought you'd go out in this weather,' he said.

Nina explained about the telephone being out of order. She thought of mentioning the calls, but Dan had cut in.

'I never saw you,' he said. 'In the village, I mean. I came right by the box.'

She'd had Rory inside it, with her, lying by her feet.

'Well – thank you for getting my paper,' she said. 'Come in and I'll make some coffee.'

Dan could do nothing outside in such weather, and when he had fetched in the logs and the coal, and had his coffee, he left. Nina took the paper into the study by the fire and read some gossip about the Royal Family and the latest film world romances. On an inside page there was a piece about the by-pass murder, as the paper now called it; the body had not been identified yet. Since the reporter had few facts to use in his story, he was forced to speculate, and drew comparisons between the discovery of other corpses in woods in recent months, and this one. A body had been found in a Sussex wood a year ago, and another in Epping Forest some time later; both victims were young girls, and their killer had never been found. They had been strangled.

Nina turned the page over and started to do the crossword.

Guy Jowett was washing his hands at the kitchen sink. He dried them carefully on a paper towel. Then he washed them again and dried them once more on another piece from the roll suspended near the sink.

He took two cups and saucers from the cupboard, peering at them closely, and ran hot water into the plastic bowl in the sink, squeezing into it a generous amount of Fairy Liquid. He washed the cups and saucers thoroughly, and dried them on paper towels too, then put them on the kitchen table. Then he washed his own hands again before scalding the teapot and replacing it on the Aga beside the simmering kettle. He liked to do what he could to help Heather, who worked so hard and was out now, taking her paintings to a dealer she'd found in Droxton who would sell them. She'd soon be back, bringing scones from Anne's Pantry. Guy, himself, had not been to Droxton for years.

He looked forward to the scones. Heather assured him the shop where she got them was very clean. Heather's own baking produced somewhat leaden results; cooking was not one of her talents.

He heard the car just as he was setting out butter and honey.

Guy moved to the sink again and ran the taps, then, making a big effort, turned them off. He had already, he knew, washed thoroughly.

Heather brought an aura of cold, damp air into the kitchen with her. They moved towards one another and kissed lingeringly.

'It's stopped raining,' said Heather. 'But it's still blowing hard. I passed Nina Crowther out walking with Rory, and asked her in for tea.'

'Who's Nina Crowther?' Guy asked.

'Oh darling, you know! The woman who's looking after the Hall while Priscilla and Leonard are away,' Heather said. 'I've told you about her – I went to see her the day after she arrived.'

'Nina Crowther,' Guy repeated. 'Looking after the Hall?' he added, questioningly.

'While they're in South Africa. You remember,' said Heather. 'Their Spaniards have gone and they don't want to leave the place empty. She's nice – Nina, I mean. I think she's rather shy, so I'll go and meet her. You make the tea.'

As the rain had stopped at last, Nina, out walking with Rory, and curious about the Manor House, had decided to look for it. She was embarrassed when a car coming up the road behind her stopped and she saw Heather inside. Heather had simply wound down the window and said, 'Come in and have a cup of tea – the next house on your left round the bend,' and driven on.

A hundred yards on, Nina came to a gateway. A short drive, gently curving, led to a square house built of mellow brick. It had long sash windows under its slate roof. The proportions were perfect; Nina thought she had rarely seen anything so immediately attractive. It made the Hall seem almost vulgar, by contrast. She started up the rutted drive and saw Heather coming towards her, in the familiar tweed skirt and boots.

'What a beautiful house,' said Nina.

'It's been in Guy's family for ever,' said Heather. 'We're doing our best to preserve it. Come along in.'

'What about Rory?' asked Nina.

'He'll wait for you in the porch,' said Heather. 'Like he does when Priscilla comes round.'

Nina found it odd that Rory was not admitted into the house, and, indeed, that Heather, so much an outdoor person, had no dog of her own. She hoped Rory wouldn't catch a chill.

Heather led her round to the back door, where she took off her boots. Nina wondered if she should do the same, but hers were not in the least muddy. Heather went ahead into the house and Nina, following, wiped her feet well on the mat inside. Heather had gone on into the kitchen, in her stockinged feet, and Nina, behind her, saw a tall old man with silver hair standing near the Aga holding a large brown teapot.

'This is Guy,' Heather introduced them. 'Darling, here's Nina – from the Hall. Remember?' She rested her hand briefly on Guy's arm and the old man set the teapot down.

'How do you do?' he said gravely, and held out his hand.

Nina had pulled off her gloves as she entered the house. She took his proffered hand, thinking the gesture quaint and formal, but agreeable, as she touched his palm. It felt soft and cool.

Guy Jowett wore a beautifully cut tweed jacket with leather patches on the elbows and leather binding round the cuffs. His old brown brogues gleamed.

'Let me take your coat,' he said. His voice was deep and slightly hoarse. Nina thought him the most distinguished-looking man she had ever met. She allowed him to help her off with her coat which he bore away down the passage, leaving Nina alone in the large kitchen. The room had charm, she thought, but was scarcely labour-saving. The sink was an old porcelain one, with wooden draining boards each side. A hod of coke stood by the Aga. The quarry-tiled floor was polished, and on it stood two bright fibre mats, one by the sink and one by the stove. In the centre of the room was a scrubbed deal table with a checked gingham cloth covering one end where tea things were laid.

Heather had vanished in search of some shoes, but Guy soon returned.

'Do be seated,' he said, waving vaguely at a chair by the table, and as Nina obeyed, he said, 'Excuse me,' and went to the sink, where he ran water into a bowl and washed his hands very carefully, soaping them well. Nina watched him dry them on a paper towel. Then he opened a paper bag that rested on the dresser and took from it some scones which he put on a plate and placed in the low oven. All his movements were slow and careful. Then, to Nina's amazement, he washed his hands again.

He was still doing this when Heather returned. She wore flat black shoes, and had brushed her hair.

'Sit down, darling,' said Heather.

She handed the old man a clean towel which she took from a

drawer, and a shadow crossed his face as he accepted it and began drying his hands, paying particular attention to the cuticles, pushing them back, as Nina had noticed he did with the paper towel earlier. His hands were very white; they were narrow, with long, tapering fingers. He turned to Nina and smiled.

'Where did you say you lived?' he asked.

Before Nina could reply, Heather came forward and put the large teapot down on a mat on the table. She set down another cup, saucer and plate, and a knife, then pulled forward a third chair to join the two already at the table.

'Milk and sugar, Nina?' she asked.

'Yes, please,' said Nina. She felt rather light-headed and was bewildered by Guy's behaviour, but as she accepted a scone she remembered that she had forgotten to have any lunch, and now that she thought of it, had had only coffee before going down to telephone that morning. After reading the paper and becoming depressed by its news, she had vacuumed several rooms at the Hall and polished the dining-room furniture. By then the light had begun to fail and she had decided to take Rory out. She had not wanted to sit idly; it still seemed strange not to be centring her day round the time when Martin came home in the evening for dinner.

'You've got two daughters, haven't you?' Heather said, when everyone was settled with tea and scones. 'Tell us about them. What do they do?'

Nina began in a deprecating way, meaning only to speak briefly, but it was as if a dam had burst. Words poured from her as she described Sarah, Jeremy and little Sebastian, and Jenny's college course. Heather smiled and nodded, saying 'Really?' and 'How interesting,' at intervals, and Guy silently ate three scones, smiling at Nina now and then. Nina talked so much that she forgot her own scone, though she paused to drink her tea.

'I'm sorry,' she said at last, suddenly aware that neither of her hosts had uttered more than a few words. 'What about you? Have you a family?' Too late, she remembered the tombstone, and her heart began to beat loudly.

But Heather answered calmly enough.

'Our daughter, Rosemary, is married to a soldier and they're stationed in Germany at the moment. She has a son and a daughter.' She talked a little about her grandchildren, and poured out more tea, smiling at her husband and laying a hand briefly on his shoulder as she passed on her way to refill the teapot. Nina finished her scone and took another when Guy offered her the plate.

'They're delicious,' she said, which was true, though she knew her own were better.

'I bring them from Droxton whenever I'm there,' said Heather. 'They're one of our treats.'

'We have lots of treats,' said Guy. 'We celebrate sunny weather with extra time in the garden. When it rains in the winter, we light the fire early and sometimes have toast for tea.'

'We have sherry on birthdays and anniversaries,' Heather said pouring Nina more tea.

'Extra time in the garden?' Nina asked, puzzled.

'Yes. We have our various tasks, you see – Guy has his painting to do and I have the house and the garden, but we both like sitting at ease in the sun, when there's time.'

'Have you a large garden?' asked Nina. It seemed a safe question.

'We let the fields, as the Blunts do,' Heather said. 'That leaves us about three acres of garden. Much of it's orchard.'

'That's a lot to look after,' said Nina. Surely they had a gardener?

'We manage,' said Heather. 'We let a lot of the grass go to hay and a local girl with a pony comes and takes it away. But we grow a lot of vegetables – we're entirely self-supporting in the matter of fruit and vegetables.'

They were very hard up, Nina realized.

'Of course, Priscilla has the paragon Dan to look after the garden at the Hall,' Heather was saying. 'How are you getting on with him? I imagine you've met?'

'He seems very nice,' Nina said. 'He brought me in coal and logs.'

'Ah,' said Heather, nodding.

'Good, good,' said Guy. 'So he should. Knows his job, doesn't he? An excellent gardener.'

'Indeed he is,' Heather said. 'Are you sure you won't have more tea, Nina?'

Nina sensed she was being gently dismissed. She rose.

'Thank you so much,' she said. 'I must go – poor Rory –'

They lent her a torch, for it was quite dark outside and there were no street lights in this part of the village. Tears fell down Nina's cheeks as she walked home with Rory. She'd talked and talked. They'd never ask her again. She wept on, with shame, as she walked round the Hall drawing the curtains.

In the dining-room, she looked at the sideboard where decanters of sherry and whisky, gin and port, stood arranged. Sherry for birthdays and treats, the Jowetts had said. But it wasn't her birthday, and she mustn't start tippling the Blunts' liquor. She went upstairs and fetched the *gros point* she was working for Sarah, to cover her dining-room chairs, and turned on the television.

At the Manor, Guy said to his wife, 'What a lonely woman. Who did you say she was?'

The telephone at the Hall did not ring that night. It was still out of order.

In Chestnut Crescent, Dan Fenton drew the living-room curtains to shut out the dark evening. He paused by the tank of tropical fish and noticed one specimen motionless among the plants at the bottom: the glass catfish, faking dead again. It constantly did so.

He'd done his housework that day. He had a routine, cleaning all round on a Monday, as Ellen had done, and putting his washing through the machine.

He dusted Ellen's bedroom, never used now. All her frippery things were gone; he'd bundled them off, tied in plastic sacks, to the Oxfam shop in Droxton afterwards. The vicar had wanted to take them for the church jumble sale but Dan wouldn't have that; he didn't want anyone local to wear Ellen's clothes, or a pair of her shoes. Her feet had been pretty and neat, small and high-arched. He liked dainty feet on a woman.

Nina Crowther had small feet too, he'd noticed. He wondered why she had taken on such a lonely sort of job. Was she a widow? Mrs Blunt hadn't said anything about her, except for telling him her name. He'd enjoyed sitting in the kitchen with her over their coffee, though he'd taken care not to stay long.

She was a pretty woman, soft and gentle, he thought, as Ellen had been.

Dan sighed, remembering his wife. The couple next door, the Morrises, had asked him why he didn't take in a lodger; he'd got the large room going spare, they'd said, and it would be company; but Dan was accustomed, now, to his solitude. His days were planned out, his routine rarely varied.

That evening he sat by the fireside, spectacles on, and opened the paper:

GLADE DEATH LINKED WITH WOODLAND MURDERS ran the headline across the centre page. There were grainy photographs of two young girls, previous victims of an untraced killer, and a shot of a police car parked by some trees.

Dan had missed the television report of the body's discovery on Saturday, though he had seen the short paragraph in the Sunday paper. Now he read an expanded version of what Nina had seen in her paper, including the theories of the reporter following the case.

He fetched the kitchen scissors and cut the article out of the paper. Then he took it upstairs to the tiny third bedroom where there was a cheap, scratched desk, an upright chair and an old typewriter, and clipped it into a file which he took from a drawer. The file already held a number of newspaper cuttings.

Dan returned downstairs and sat by the fire, hands folded across his stomach, until it was time for the radio news. There was no mention of the body, nor was it referred to on the television news later.

The girl was unnamed. Her family – her mother, her father – did not yet know she had met a sudden and violent death. Their shock was still to come.

He sat there, motionless, all the evening.

8

After the gale, leaves lay thick on the ground at the Hall. Nina wondered if Dan would come to sweep them up, but by ten o'clock he had not arrived so she decided to go down to the shops in the village. There was the paper to fetch, and she might buy a few things at the grocer's. Little and often for shopping, she thought, not the weekly forays to Sainsbury's that she'd made before: that way, she would talk to someone each day, even if it was only the newsagent or the grocer.

Dogs were denied admittance to the grocer's, a notice on the shop door declared, and quite right too, Nina thought, tying Rory's lead to a railing nearby. Mr Goody, the grocer, was about thirty-six, a pale man with sandy hair and a sallow skin. Nina watched him slice her bacon on to his hand, then lay the slices on some paper beside the machine. With that same hand he took the money she gave him and handed her her change.

Nina walked on to the newsagent's and collected her paper. Now she had spoken to two people today. As she passed the last buildings before the long stretch of road that led to the Hall, she met the old man with the spaniel again; he still gazed at the ground ahead of him, as he always did, the dog pulling at the lead. Nina's pace slowed. She didn't want to go back. Yet at Silverlea, she'd always been glad to get home with her shopping and on with the next task – preparing dinner, sewing, whatever it was. Often someone would come in to coffee, or she would pop round to a neighbour, yet the friendships she had thought were strong had melted away when Martin left and only Felicity seemed to care. People blamed her, Nina thought, for not being able to keep her husband. It did not occur to her that they feared her condition might be infectious.

Near the Hall gates she saw a man coming towards her from the other direction, where she had walked with Heather Jowett on that first morning. He wore a sheepskin coat and a tweed cap and black, not green, wellington boots. Nina soon recognized Guy Jowett. He raised his cap gravely when they met.

'Good morning,' cried Nina, delighted to see him. Three conversations today, she thought: not bad.

'Good morning,' said Guy.

Rory stood wagging his tail but Guy made no move to pat him or speak to him.

'Could you tell me the time?' Guy asked.

Nina looked at her watch.

'It's five past eleven,' she said.

'Oh – not lunch time, then,' said Guy.

'No – not for ages,' said Nina, surprised.

'Thank you,' said Guy, raising his cap once more. 'Good morning,' he added, and walked off.

His boots, Nina noticed were covered in mud; he must have come round by the fields. She had the feeling he didn't remember meeting her before.

She was cleaning the silver coasters from the dining-room when the telephone rang some time later. She was glad to know it was working again and wondered if the caller would be Leonard Blunt's secretary making the regular calls she had been told to expect. But it was Heather, who wanted to know if she had seen Guy.

'I've been to the dentist in Murford,' she said. 'He was in the studio when I left, but now I can't find him anywhere.'

'I met him about an hour ago,' Nina said. 'He asked me the time. He was just near the gates, going towards the village.'

'Oh dear,' said Heather. 'Where can he have got to?'

'He seemed to be out for a walk,' Nina said. 'The weather's much better today – perhaps he just felt like having some exercise.'

'But he's been gone so long, if you met him all that time ago,' said Heather.

'Why are you so worried? Do you think he might have had an accident?' Nina asked. People did fall down dead sometimes, without warning, and very nice for them too, thought Nina, though a shock for their families and whoever found them. Had Guy collapsed somewhere? 'Shall I come down and help you to look for him?' she suggested. It would be nice to have something useful to do.

'Oh, would you, Nina? Would you just come to the house and be here, in case he comes back, while I go and look for him? Would you have a look round the Hall grounds first, in case he's wandering about there? If you find him – if you meet him on your way – bring him back here with you. Be firm. Don't let him fob you off. I'll go towards Stokebourne – as I didn't meet him on the way back from Murford, he must have gone somewhere else. I'll leave the house open, so that if you find him, you can bring him indoors.'

She was talking as though Guy were a child, Nina thought,

and remembered how he had washed his hands several times the day before, and the vague way he had looked at her this morning, forgetting they had met. Was he ill?

She took Rory into the garden to help her search, for if the old man lay unconscious somewhere the dog might see him before she did, but though they traversed every path and looked in all the outbuildings, no one was there.

Nina locked Rory into the house and then got into her car and drove to the Manor, looking out for the tall figure who had walked, she remembered now, rather shamblingly when they had met earlier, but she did not see him. She went slowly up the rutted drive of the Manor and parked at the side of the house, in the yard. The garage doors were open and Heather's Mini had gone. Nina decided to take a look round the garden; he might have returned across the fields, and, apart from that, she was curious to see the garden.

The cultivated section was well kept, but here and there were some weeds or some withered growth that had not been cut back, something not to be seen at the Hall. As Heather had said, a large area was put down to grass but there were rose beds and a mixed border close to the house, and beyond an old brick wall, as mellow as the house, was a vegetable garden planted with cabbages and sprouts, and with a fruit cage well wired round in which were raspberries, currants, strawberries and gooseberry bushes. Fruit trees – peaches, perhaps, or plums, Nina didn't know – were trained against a south-facing wall.

Nina went back to the house. Should she search it, to see if he had come back and was up in the studio? She had, so far, seen only the kitchen, and now she wandered into the front hall. A long-case clock ticked away the minutes. Worn rugs covered the polished floor. Nina opened one of several closed doors and saw the drawing-room, a square room, light and airy, with a threadbare carpet on the floor and chairs and a sofa in faded covers. The room was chilly. A fire was laid in the hearth. She closed the door, and was wondering where to go now when she heard a car outside.

Heather had found Guy. He got out of the passenger seat as Nina came out of the house.

'Oh, good morning,' he said to Nina, and raised his cap, as he had before. 'Have you come to lunch? I'm so sorry we're late.'

He was looking at her again as if they had never met, but this time he smiled, very sweetly. His manners were certainly wonderful, Nina thought; such old-world charm almost made up for his poor memory.

'Nina's just dropped in for a minute,' Heather said briskly, coming round to take his arm. 'Come along, darling.'

She led him indoors. Nina stood aside to let them pass. Guy began taking off his sheepskin coat. Beneath it, he wore his old tweed jacket and a checked shirt with a regimental tie. A worried expression came over his face.

'I've got myself dirty,' he said, looking down at his boots. 'I must bath and change.'

'Just take off your boots and wash your hands, darling,' said Heather. 'That's all you need do. We'll have some sherry. I'll get you some.'

'But it isn't a birthday,' Guy said.

'No, but it's a celebration,' said Heather.

'I'll go, then,' Nina said, but Heather seemed not to hear her. She might have offered me some sherry too, Nina thought, aggrievedly, going back to her car, but Heather had been oblivious of anything except Guy, who had been lost and was found, a cause for rejoicing.

Nina forgot about lunch when she reached the Hall, but she made herself a cup of instant coffee which she drank in the study. The fire took some reviving, though the heap of ashes, which Dan had said need be cleared only once a week or so, was warm. She wondered why he hadn't come that morning.

For a while, sitting there, she looked at the paper. Then she turned on the television, something she had never done in the afternoon at Silverlea except during the Wimbledon tennis fortnight. After a time, in the warmth, she dozed off, and was woken by the back door bell. Perhaps it was Dan?

But it was Heather who stood on the step, in her usual green husky jacket. Her car was parked outside. She looked exhausted, her face grey beneath its network of veins.

'Oh – come in,' Nina said. 'Come and sit down – would you like some tea? Or coffee?' Though really, Nina thought, eyeing the other woman, brandy might be more appropriate.

'Coffee, please,' said Heather. 'But I mustn't be long. Guy's asleep.' She'd given him two tranquillisers today with his lunch, instead of the normal one, the powder extracted from the capsules and mixed up in the mashed potato. They, and the sherry, would ensure that he slept soundly this afternoon. 'I've come to apologize,' Heather went on, following Nina into the kitchen. 'You must have thought me so rude, this morning.'

'Oh – not at all,' said Nina, blushing. She bustled about with cups and the jar of instant coffee.

'Guy's rather forgetful, you see,' Heather said. 'He'd gone some distance down the Stokebourne road before I found him. I'm always afraid he'll get run over. He often can't remember where he is. I try not to let him go out alone, and the mornings are usually safe, when he's painting, but sometimes he gives me the slip.'

'Well, you had to go to the dentist,' Nina pointed out.

'Yes. I should have had an afternoon appointment, though,' Heather said. 'He always has a sleep then. But I'd had toothache, you see, and had to go when the dentist could fit me in.'

Nina had made the coffee. She picked up the tray on which she had set two pretty cups, the milk in a jug, sugar, and some biscuits.

'Let's take this into the study,' she said, standing back for Heather to go first.

'He's been better lately,' Heather went on, when they were sitting by the fire. She put two lumps of sugar in her cup.

'Oh,' said Nina encouragingly, unable to think of a comment.

'You mustn't mind if he doesn't always recognize you,' Heather continued.

Nina remembered the handwashing she had seen. Surely that wasn't just forgetfulness? He'd seemed almost obsessed by the need to be clean. He'd wanted a bath when Heather brought him home. It reminded Nina of something, some character in a play.

'He has dreadful dreams,' Heather was explaining.

Lady Macbeth! That was it! She'd been haunted by dreams and tried to wash blood from her hands. Surely Guy had no evil past like hers?

'It was the war, you see,' Heather said. 'He got over it – he was all right, until we retired. Then he had time to think. It all came back to haunt him.'

'Oh,' said Nina, inadequately. She did not understand. 'What shall I do if I meet him out walking again?' she asked. She had an idea, and added, 'Shall I try to persuade him to go home—pretend I'm walking that way myself and go with him?'

'Oh, would you, Nina? Or bring him in here and settle him down, then let me know – ring up?'

'Of course,' Nina said.

'It's best if he doesn't wander round the village. Some of the new people don't know about him – who he is. A small boy brought him home once.'

A tear trickled slowly down Heather's lined and weather-beaten face.

'He won the DSO during the war,' she said.

Dan had had something more urgent to do that morning than go to the Hall. He backed his small Ford into the road and headed out of the village, past the church towards Stokebourne and on down the Droxton road. When he reached the new roundabout outside the town he took the by-pass, driving down its full three-mile length and parking beyond it in a gateway near the old road which was now fenced off, apart from a small area that was used as a lay-by. Here, a lorry was parked, the driver asleep.

Dan climbed the fence and walked along the old road, his tweed hat pulled firmly down so that the fresh wind which still blew, though the gale had dropped, would not tug it off.

He reached a point from which he could see the copse. Traffic on the by-pass went steadily past, sometimes a group of vehicles boxed behind a slow-moving leader, sometimes just a single car. He had seen a police car parked beside the verge as he drove by himself. *No parking* cones had blocked a track entrance nearby. That would be the direct route to where the girl's body was found, now that this road was closed.

They'd be busy down there, still, Dan knew. As he watched, he saw distant figures moving about and the white of a police car parked by some trees. They'd be hoping to find a handbag, a scarf—something personal that would point to the dead girl's identity.

There would be no such lead, Dan knew. This killer was

74

careful. The other two girls found in woods, his earlier victims, as the papers had surmised, had been identified only by patient detection, the piecing together of evidence about their appearances with facts relating to girls missing from home.

Dan turned and went back to his car. He drove into Droxton, where he went to the pet shop and bought some live food for his fish, as a treat; you couldn't get it in Murford and he usually got some when he came over this way. Then he went to a pub where he had half a pint and a pie for his lunch.

He drove past Chestnut Crescent when he returned to Netherton St Mary, and on to the Hall, for he hadn't taken in any coal or logs that day and he felt a need to make sure that Mrs Crowther was all right. You never knew what might happen to someone living alone if they felt depressed, and besides, he wanted to see her.

Mrs Jowett's old Mini came out through the gateway as he approached. Dan would have liked to help the Jowett's with their garden. He would have done it for nothing, for he knew they could not afford to pay. It was well known in the village that Mrs Jowett only bought the cheapest cuts of meat and no delicacies. But he knew their pride would not permit them to accept his labour for nothing, and besides, if he did not charge them, how could he charge the Blunts? He needed more money than his pension brought in; his trips to London and all they involved were often expensive, and costs were rising all the time.

Mrs Crowther seemed pleased to see him. She said she'd just had a cup of coffee with Mrs Jowett, but she had another with him.

'She's a nice lady, that Mrs Jowett,' said Dan. 'Sad about the son.'

'I've seen his grave,' Nina said. 'What happened?'

'He was killed in a sailing accident,' Dan said. 'He was with Charles Blunt. They were great friends as boys, it's said in the village. There are folk still here who knew them in spite of all the newcomers, like me. The Jowetts were away a lot, though, with the colonel serving overseas and that.'

'How dreadful,' Nina murmured.

'Yes,' Dan agreed.

He liked sitting there, facing her across the table,

domestically. He liked the grave look she now wore, contemplating the Jowett's past.

Today, he'd stop for a second cup, if she offered him one.

9

Nina was settling down. Mr Blunt's secretary had telephoned, showing concern, after the lines had been down, lest she had been perturbed by being incommunicado. Nina had assured her that she was unworried and mentioned that the gardener had been round regularly. The secretary rang again within a few days, with further enquiries; this time, they had quite a chat. A telex had come from the Blunts, now in Johannesburg, and Mr Charles had spoken to his parents on the telephone only yesterday. They were enjoying their trip and the weather was good. Nina did not mention the mystery telephone calls as there had been no more, and the conversation relieved her sense of isolation. The strangeness was wearing off and in the daytime she felt quite at home, but the evenings were drawing in, and were difficult; she was often depressed then, and she kept the radio on continuously, carrying it round the house to whatever room she was in, listening to plays and talks and quizzes, even concerts, but it was the sound of the human voice she really sought. She watched a great deal of television.

Every day, Nina went into each room in the house making sure that all was well, pulling the curtains morning and night and cleaning the rooms in rotation, though that was not officially part of her job. She had realized that Priscilla and Leonard occupied separate bedrooms. A linking door connected them. Priscilla's room had a thick cream carpet, apricot curtains and bedspread, and some beautiful antique furniture – a sofa table used as a dressing table and a regency chaise longue. Leonard's room was blue – dark blue walls and lighter blue carpets, curtains and bedspread. On the walls hung framed photographs of groups of young men at college, a rowing eight, some men in naval uniform. In Priscilla's room there were photographs of a boy in various stages of growth. He was dark-haired and smiling. This must be Charles. Nina inspected one of him as an adult man which stood alone on a walnut tallboy. He looked cheerful. She knew he was the managing director of the firm. No doubt, by now, he was married and had a family, Nina thought, but she had seen no pictures of grandchildren. Mrs Blunt had referred only to his role in the business, not to his private circumstances.

Wondering about the Blunts kept Nina's mind from dwelling on Martin and Caroline, although when she woke every morning she always thought of him, her hand automatically stretching out to find him beside her. Bitter anguish still filled her when she thought of Caroline's cat-like face, the claws clutching at Martin. Did she scratch? Maybe she bit, too. Sometimes Nina dreamed about them, and would wake in the night, crying, but by day it grew easier to control her misery.

What was she to do when the Blunts returned? Panic swept over Nina when she thought of the future, but she tried to be calm. She could advertise for further house-minding posts, or Mrs Blunt had said there was an agency, to whom she could apply. Felicity had pointed out that she would have a reference after this job, a significant one, since the Blunts were people of consequence.

Mr Drew had no news of the money she was due to receive from the sale of Silverlea, but these things always took time. Nina had signed various papers to do with the divorce. As they had agreed – by post, through the lawyers – on so much, it should be straightforward. She stamped her insurance card each week, as instructed by Mr Drew who said she must look ahead, for if Martin were to die, Caroline would receive the widow's pension. Suppose she were ill herself, Nina would think, waking at night, sweating: the girls would see that she was looked after, she consoled herself, but it was another thing to dread.

Almost every day Dan Fenton came. Nina missed him on the days when he did not appear. He seemed to find plenty to do outside, brushing down the yard, digging, and sweeping the leaves which still fell. He came in for coffee every day, prolonging their chats and even helping with the crossword, which she did as a way of sharpening her wits. He always went home at one o'clock. Nina wondered about his lunch. It would be easy to cook him a meal; she'd like to, it would remind her to eat herself. She had little appetite these days and often forgot about meals; she was losing weight and her skirts hung loosely round her.

One day she met Guy Jowett again, this time near the post office. He raised his hat as they passed in the road but did not stop. Nina hurriedly bought her stamps and posted her letters, not stopping for her usual few words with Mrs Fox, the postmistress, aptly named as she had red hair and a sharp pointed face. She hastened up the road behind Guy and followed him all the way back to the Manor, waiting to make sure he had gone right into the house.

She had her own green wellington boots now, bought in Murford, with thermal soles to keep her feet warm, but she had not bought a padded anorak; she still wore her own suede coat unless it was raining hard, when she borrowed Priscilla Blunt's Burberry from the cloakroom. They were much of a size, apart from their feet. Whenever she went to the village she met the two men with their dogs whom she had noticed on the first expedition with Rory. Nina was always ready to say 'Good morning' in the friendly fashion she thought was part of village life, but the men plodded on, heads down, never looking at her. It seemed as if they spent the whole day circling round the village.

She asked Dan about them one day.

'Their wives don't want them hanging about the place, getting in their way,' he said. 'They've been used to having the house to themselves, you see, by day. Then the husband retires and they've lost their castle.'

'Oh,' said Nina. 'That's awful! Is it true? What do they think about, walking around like that?'

'Nothing much, I'd say,' said Dan. 'Maybe they're hoping their number will come up on the pools. They do a bit of gardening in the better weather; it's easier then.'

'You haven't got a dog,' Nina said.

'No, just some tropical fish,' said Dan. 'A good few of the wives go to Bingo. They have meetings in the village hall regularly. Very popular they are, I'm told. I go to the Black Swan now and then, on a Saturday, and hear the news there.'

'Oh yes?' Nina listened with interest.

'Then there's the Silver Club,' Dan went on, sitting back in his chair, his booted feet on a piece of newspaper, the technique he and Nina had evolved so that he did not have to sit intimately with her in his socks.

'The Silver Club? Are they collectors?'

'No. They're the senior citizens – silver hair, you see,' said Dan. 'They play paper games and whist and have talks, and cakes to eat, like a kids' party, really, once a month or so. All old ladies except for three fellows brave enough to join.' He chuckled. 'Some of them come from Stokebourne, and even Cerne St Mary – they're too small to have Silver Groups of their own. It's quite a business getting them here – some good ladies drive them. Two or three of the drivers are older than their passengers, but they're of a different sort, you see – doing good, not having it done to them.'

'It sounds grim,' said Nina.

'It isn't. It's good for them all, whichever kind they are,' Dan said. 'It gets them out, meeting folk. Most of them are alone all day, the rest of the time. They have coach outings, too. Some of them would never get away, otherwise. Off to London to theatres, and to the seaside. Marvellous.'

Nina tried to picture herself in twenty years' time as a member of a Silver Club. Or would she be an elderly ministering angel instead of the recipient of mercy? The idea appalled her, yet she could see what Dan meant about its benefits: she had discovered already the enervating effect of isolation.

When Dan said he would not be coming the next day, her heart sank.

'I'll leave you some extra fuel,' he said. 'And I'll be in on Saturday.'

She wanted to ask where he was going, but did not like to pry.

Her spirits soon improved, however, for that evening Jenny rang to announce she was coming for the weekend. She'd arrive fairly late the next day.

'How will you get here?' asked Nina. 'You're not to hitch-hike.'

'Oh Mum,' came the cry, and Jenny went on, 'I knew you'd say that. I've found out about the trains.'

'Have you enough money?' Nina asked. She and Martin had always insisted that neither girl should ever hitch: money for

79

taxis and buses and trains was money well spent, Martin had always said.

Jenny intimated that she had enough but would not be above accepting a refund.

She planned to catch the last train to Murford, which Nina said she would meet.

With something definite, now, to do, Nina ran upstairs to make up a bed for her in the green room which Mrs Blunt had said she might use. It was near enough to share Nina's bathroom. She put out a towel for Jenny, and as she did so, stuck out her tongue at the smirking pottery cat on the window-sill.

That night, at twenty minutes to eleven the telephone rang, and when she answered, again there was just a sigh. It was nearly two weeks since there had been such a call.

The police in Droxton were continuing their work on the murder case. A sketch of the girl whose body had been found in the copse near the by-pass was prepared. It was based on her skull measurements and the way her teeth were arranged in her jaw and was mainly guesswork, but the victim's hair had been shoulder-length, and fair, and her Indian print dress was described. Her underclothing and tights had come from a multiple store. The likeness was circulated through every division in the country, but Detective Superintendent Wilshaw, head of the division which included Droxton and in charge of the murder investigation, knew that the imagined features might bear only a very slight resemblance to the girl as she was in life, and the chances of it leading to an identification were not high. There was no one missing in the area whom it could be, but the collator, in touch with other forces, might learn of missing women with similar characteristics. Dental records could lead to a positive identification, if that happened; it was the only hope, so far. Forensic tests on the girl's garments might, even after so long, produce traces of her killer; there could be an alien hair, for instance; but without a suspect to match them against, they would be useless, and without a name for the girl, the search for her killer could offer no hope of success.

Meanwhile, he might kill again.

10

The man had come up to Christine as she was leaving the station buffet. She had noticed him earlier, sitting at a table not far from hers and reading a newspaper while he drank his tea. He was quite old, and very respectable-looking.

She and her friend Lynn had left Manchester together rather on the spur of the moment. Originally, their plan had been to come to London in a few weeks' time, when they might be able to get seasonal work over Christmas in one of the big stores. Extra staff were sure to be needed then, and if they seemed bright and willing, as they were, they would be taken on, the girls felt sure, in preference to other applicants for any jobs that were going. They wouldn't be too choosy at first, they had decided, about what jobs they did. Anything would be more exciting than staying on at college, where they were both learning office procedures. Christine was fed up at home; she kept having rows with her stepmother, and trying their luck in London was her idea. They'd start off at a hostel and get a room – even a flat – later. They'd both brought their savings, and Christine had got hold of some other money which she hadn't yet told Lynn about.

On the train, Lynn felt ill. She'd been a bit queasy before leaving home, but once the journey began she grew steadily worse, and spent much of the time in the toilet compartment. When they arrived, she was green.

'I'll have to go back, Christine,' she said, on the platform. 'I really will – I feel awful.'

'You'll be all right when we get to the hostel. They'll give you something, fix you up in no time,' Christine said, but her heart sank at the sight of her friend's face.

Lynn was thinking with dismay of how much the trip had already cost, and what she must now pay to go home, but she held on.

'I can't go through with it, Christine,' she said. 'Not feeling like this. I'll come later. You get fixed up and let me know where you are. I'll only hold you up.'

For a moment Christine thought of turning back too, but that would solve none of her own problems.

'Will you be all right on the train?' she asked.

Lynn nodded. She'd never been as keen on this scheme as Christine, for things were easier for her at home, and indeed, at the prospect of returning to the distracted but effective care of her busy working mother she already felt better. It would take some time to save enough money to come again.

When Lynn had gone, Christine felt very uneasy. In front of her friend she had acted boldly, pretending there was nothing to fear. Now, alone, she must find the way to one of the hostels on the list they'd made in the library at home from the yellow pages of the London telephone directory. Standing on the busy concourse with her suitcase, Christine could not decide which address to try. Which was the nearest to where she was now, she wondered. Who could she ask?

At Euston station there was an advice bureau for just such people as Christine, but she failed to see the sign as she walked towards the exit. The station was bustling with people leaving London for the weekend. Christine turned back, and, to postpone resolute action, went into the nearby buffet where she put her case down by a corner table and lined up to buy a cup of tea and a bun.

He saw her several places ahead of him in the queue and he picked her out at once as a possibility, a lost girl on her own acting big, faking courage. It was almost too easy, he thought, watching Christine eat her bun.

He followed her from the buffet and spoke to her as she hesitated outside, looking at the various direction indicators. He told her he worked at a nearby hostel which was nice and friendly and would have a vacancy for her. Christine had no qualms as she set off with him on the last journey of her life.

Only a few people got off the late train at Murford that Friday night. Jenny was first through the barrier, where her mother was waiting.

'Haven't you any luggage?' were Nina's first words when they had hugged briefly. Unexpected tears pricked her eyes at the contact and her voice was gruff.

'Everything I need's in here,' Jenny said cheerfully, indicating the plastic carrier bag she held. She wore jeans and a duffle coat.

'I hope you've brought a toothbrush,' said Nina, motioning her out to the car.

Jenny tossed her carrier on to the back seat and stretched out her thin legs as Nina started the engine. The beam of her headlights picked up a man who was walking towards the car park.

'Hullo, that's Dan,' said Nina.

'Dan?'

'Dan Fenton, the gardener. I must have told you about him,' said Nina. She pulled up beside him and wound down her window. 'Do you want a lift?' she asked.

'Oh – good evening, Mrs Crowther,' said Dan, and he lifted his hat. 'No, thank you. My car's here.'

'This is my younger daughter, Jenny,' Nina said. 'She's come down for the weekend.'

'Hullo,' Jenny called, across her mother.

'That's nice,' said Dan. 'I'll be along in the morning, Mrs Crowther.'

'Oh good,' Nina said. 'I'll see you then. Good-night.'

'He only just caught the train,' said Jenny as they drove off. 'He was in the same compartment as I was – he came running along as the train was leaving, and just managed to get on.'

'So that's where he goes when he doesn't come to the Hall,' said Nina. 'I wonder what he does in London? Perhaps he's got an old mother, or something.' He was a bit old himself to have a mother still, Nina thought; the 'or something' was much more likely. She vaguely imagined a blowsy woman with jet black hair and carmine lips, hung about with beads and bangles. 'Take notice of Murford, Jenny. We're almost through it.'

'What's Murford got, then?' asked Jenny, peering through the windscreen.

'Not a lot. It's a market town – cattle sales and things. I'm surprised it's still got a station. It connects at Droxton with the main line to the Midlands.'

'Have you turned into a country bumpkin, Mum?' Jenny asked. 'I mean – cattle sales!'

'Well, I haven't been to one, if that's what you're thinking,' Nina said. 'But I've got some green wellies. They're uniform here.'

'That's a start,' Jenny said. 'You could do worse than take up country crafts. You're so good at sewing. You could make patchwork and things. Start a business.'

Nina thought this sounded rather an ambitious scheme. She concentrated on the road, aware of lights behind her, though not too close: probably Dan.

'Shall I drive?' offered Jenny, as they trundled along at forty miles an hour.

'If you do, we'll have to put on the L plates,' said Nina. 'It's not worth stopping now, it isn't far. We'll go out somewhere tomorrow – that would be nice – and you can drive then.'

'OK,' Jenny said. 'When you've paid me my train fare, I'll take you out to lunch in a pub. I bet you haven't been anywhere since you got down here.'

'I've been to tea at the Manor,' said Nina.

'Big deal,' said Jenny. 'I can't wait to hear about it.' But she gave her mother no chance to describe the event, prattling on about her own activities – the societies she had joined and her work. Nina listened with half an ear, concentrating on the road. She felt proud of her busy, confident daughter.

The following lights turned off as they went through Netherton St Mary, and Jenny was silent as they drove on out of the village to the Hall.

'It is a bit out of things, isn't it?' she said.

Nina turned in at the Hall gates.

'A bit,' she agreed. She felt oddly proprietorial as they approached the house. 'You get used to it,' she added.

'Cor, what a heap!' exclaimed Jenny when she saw it. 'Bit gloomy, isn't it? Like a junior cathedral.'

'It's very comfortable inside,' said Nina. 'But I agree, it's not very beautiful.'

Rory was pleased to see them. He snuffed and sniffed round Jenny, wagging his tail and licking her hand.

'I'm starving, Mum,' said Jenny. 'Have you got any food?'

They'd had scrambled eggs the last time they'd had supper

together at Silverlea, Nina remembered. She took the big frying pan out of the cupboard and had just laid some rashers in it when the telephone rang.

'I'll go,' Jenny said. 'Where's the phone?' She rushed from the room pursuing the sound.

'No!' Nina called after her. It was later than his usual time, but she knew who was calling. She hurried out, hoping to stop Jenny from answering, but she was too late.

Jenny, in the hall, was talking crossly into the instrument.

'Who do you want? Who's there? Hullo?' she kept repeating, and then said to Nina, who stood watching her, 'There's no one there.'

'No, there isn't. Hang up,' ordered Nina.

Jenny stared at her, surprised at her peremptory tone, but she obeyed. Nina went to the telephone and put her hand on the receiver. She waited a few seconds, then lifted it and listened. When she heard the dialling tone, she laid it on the table. Her hand shook.

'Mum!' Jenny cried. 'What are you doing?'

'I've been getting these calls,' Nina said, trying to keep her voice steady. 'Calls with no one there. Some fault in the exchange, I expect, but anyway, if it's off the hook, we can't get any more.'

'No obscene remarks?' said Jenny.

'No.'

'Breathing, though. I heard that,' Jenny said.

'Yes,' admitted Nina.

'How long has this been going on?' Jenny demanded.

'Oh – it only happens now and then,' Nina said. 'Not very often.'

'What have you done about it?'

Nina told her what the police had said.

'I haven't reported it to the exchange yet,' she said. 'He hasn't rung for a bit.' But there had been a call the night before. Did it come in cycles, this madness?

'I'll fix him,' said Jenny. 'Just leave your nutty caller to me.'

'What do you mean?'

'All you need is a whistle. We'll get one tomorrow. I expect there's a sports shop in Murford or somewhere that sells them. All you do, when he rings again, is blow very loudly. That'll finish his nasty little game. With luck, it'll give him a headache, and it might even burst an eardrum,' said Jenny with relish.

'That seems a bit drastic,' Nina suggested.

'Well, it serves him right,' Jenny said. 'He's not ringing from a callbox, is he? No pips.'

'No,' said Nina. It was odd to think of someone, somewhere, standing in a building dialling the number of the Hall, perhaps from a living-room, or a deserted office.

'Poor Mum, with a weirdo to deal with,' said Jenny. 'It's a good thing I'm here, isn't it?'

'Yes, dear, very,' said Nina. 'Heavens – your bacon. It'll be cinders.'

But all was well. Nina pulled the pan to the side to cool it before breaking the eggs into it.

'I think I'll have some too,' she said, adding a third egg to the two she had put out for Jenny. She fetched two more rashers, laying them alongside the others.

'Good idea,' said Jenny. 'You've lost weight, haven't you? Mind you, it's an improvement,' she added. 'You were getting a bit of middle-aged spread.'

Tears pricked Nina's eyes again. Children set you up and then put you down sharply, without a pang, she thought, but they told you the truth. Sitting down at the table with Jenny she found it hard to remember when she had last eaten a proper meal.

Having Jenny there was wonderful, but she must not say so too effusively; neither of the girls favoured displays of emotion. And she'd better not get too accustomed to her company, Nina thought: it would make letting her go at the end of her visit so painful.

In the morning, Nina had been up some time before, wearing a loose, shaggy sweater over her nightdress, Jenny appeared. She came into the kitchen yawning and stretching, her fair, silky hair unbrushed and her face still shiny with sleep. To Nina, she looked about fourteen.

Nina was making pastry. Jenny loved treacle tart.

'Kettle's on the boil, and coffee's in that cupboard,' Nina said, pointing.

'Oh mum, things haven't changed. That's what you always said at home,' Jenny said.

'Well, this is home now,' said Nina. 'But take care. None of the things are ours.'

'Except that frightful cat in the bathroom,' said Jenny. 'That's yours, isn't it?' She'd seen it at Silverlea. 'Wherever did it come from? It's not your style at all.'

Nina was tempted to tell her the truth. They'd laugh, and Jenny would say 'Let's blow whistles in its ears and Caroline will go deaf,' or something like that. But Caroline would soon be married to Jenny's father, and Jenny would have to get on with her.

'It's a sort of joke mascot,' she said. At any time she could smash the cat, boil it in a pan, harm it somehow and vicariously torment her supplanter, Nina told herself. 'Would you like some porridge?'

'Just toast, thanks,' said Jenny. She wandered about the kitchen assembling her breakfast, pouring milk into her coffee, making herself several slices of toast which she loaded with butter and marmalade. She sat at the table to eat, watching her mother rolling the pastry.

'You enjoy cooking don't you?' she said.

'Yes – when I'm not in a rush and when there's someone to cook for,' said Nina.

'But you're never in a rush,' Jenny said. 'You're always so well organized. Dad's mad. I bet that Caroline can't cook for peanuts. She's as thin as a lath – well, I suppose she isn't by now,' she amended.

'I bored him,' Nina said flatly.

Maybe she had, after twenty-four years, Jenny thought, uneasily, but there must be more to it than that.

'Well –' words like loyalty, duty, came into her head, but they were not part of her everyday language and she would have been embarrassed to say them aloud. 'I think it's rough,' she said.

Nina decided to change the subject.

'When Dan comes, I thought we'd ask him to lunch,' she said, trimming pastry from the rim of the tin. 'There's plenty of food and he may be glad of something hot.'

'We were going to go to a pub,' said Jenny.

'Well, we can go out to tea instead,' Nina replied. 'I haven't asked Dan before,' she added. 'It never seemed a very good idea, somehow – just the two of us – though he's only the gardener.'

'Very prudent, Mum. You don't want to give him ideas, do you?' said Jenny. 'Stick to your middle-class values.'

'Don't be silly, Jenny,' Nina rebuked her. 'And you'd better get some clothes on. He'll be in soon for his coffee and you're not decent.'

'Yes, I am,' said Jenny. 'I'm covered all over.'

'Well – he may not be used to young girls,' said Nina.

'Hasn't he got a family?'

Nina told her what she knew of Dan's sad history. Jenny was shocked.

'What a thing,' she said. 'Poor bloke. Are you sure he won't do for you, Mum?'

'You're outrageous,' said Nina, but she laughed.

'You mean because he's just the gardener?'

'No, of course not, and anyway he was something else first, I'm not sure what,' said Nina.

'Your prejudices are showing,' said Jenny.

'Not at all,' said Nina. 'There never could be anything like that between us. It's out of the question.'

'You mean, you don't fancy him,' said Jenny bluntly.

'Exactly,' said Nina. 'Since you put it so crudely.'

Dan wouldn't stay to lunch, although he was grateful for the invitation. He accepted a slice of hot treacle tart and bore it away on a plate wrapped in foil, which he put in his bicycle basket.

'Nice old boy, but I see what you mean,' said Jenny, when he had gone. 'And he is a bit old for you, Mum.'

They took Rory out in the afternoon. Jenny was surprised by the modern buildings in the village, the explosion of houses.

'Before long the village and the Hall will join up,' she said.

'I doubt it. The land in between belongs to the Blunts, and they won't need to sell it,' said Nina. 'They let it to a farmer.'

'And these Jowetts – the flower-planting person – where do they live?' asked Jenny.

'We'll go past their house,' said Nina.

Thin sunlight shone on the Manor as they reached the big

gates. One hinge was broken, and the open gate sagged; dead leaves lay at the sides of the drive, waiting, presumably for Heather to sweep them up. Didn't Guy help her at all, wondered Nina.

'It's lovely,' said Jenny. 'Big, though. What happens after they're dead?'

'Jenny!'

'Well, what does? Will a film star buy it, or something?'

'I've no idea,' said Nina. 'They've got a daughter – their son died. It would be a pity if it went out of the family – they've had it for generations. But they won't be dying just yet; they're not even seventy – well, he may be, but she's not, though she looks it. People quite often live to be ninety or more, these days.'

'Two old dears rattling round in there,' said Jenny. 'I bet they don't keep it properly.'

'It needs a few things done to bring it up to date, certainly,' Nina said. 'But they do keep it properly – the garden is beautiful and the house is very clean. I hope you don't think they should be turfed out and the place given over to a bunch of drug-taking drop-outs?'

'No, no. Cool down,' Jenny soothed her. 'I just thought it was a bit pathetic.'

'It isn't,' said Nina, but there was something in what Jenny said. Though there was much to admire in the way the Jowetts hung on to the place, with, she assumed, Guy's army pension their main source of income, it must be an exhausting struggle. 'The house is their whole life,' she said, with more conviction.

'You said the old boy paints. Have you seen any of his pictures?' asked Jenny as they turned back.

'No. He sells them, though, so they must be good,' said Nina.

Walking back, they passed the chapel, with fresh texts now framed, one showing an apple cut through to reveal the core rotting. The legend said *God sees the inside*.

'Ugh,' said Jenny. 'How beastly. I hate the idea of a Prying One up above.'

Nina thought anyone who might be up above had long since washed their hands of the problems below.

Jenny hadn't forgotten about the telephone call, and after their walk they went to Murford to buy the whistle, leaving Rory in the house. Jenny watched as Nina carefully carried out the locking ritual. A mixture of pity and admiration filled her; her mother must be lonely in this huge place with only the dog for company – and she'd never been keen on dogs. The telephone calls were a worrying complication, yet she hadn't complained and, Jenny guessed, would not have mentioned them had it not been for Jenny answering one of the calls herself. She was showing spirit and mettle Jenny had not realized she possessed. She remembered a fall she had had as a child, when she had cut her leg very badly. Blood had poured from the wound, frightening her more than the pain. Her mother had been utterly calm, bathing the injury, then deciding it needed stitching and taking her off to have it done. When they reached home afterwards, the wound dressed, Nina had vanished upstairs, reappearing later ashen white. She had been very sick, she'd admitted. What would happen when this job ended? Would there be some sort of collapse then? The patchwork idea she'd suggested so lightly wasn't so far out, Jenny thought; her mother should have work of some kind. Apart from the independence it would bring, it would give her an identity of her own, even if Daddy did go on paying up. Jenny didn't trust Caroline not to make him find an excuse to cut off funds; she'd think the past years of marriage counted for nothing, but that wasn't right, not after so long, and when you remembered that women of her mother's age often lacked training. It wasn't enough to hope that Mum might, in time, meet some nice widower who would look after her. That wasn't the answer, not any more: a woman must be able to stand on her own feet.

They fixed the L-plates on the Metro and Jenny drove them to Murford.

'You must have some more proper lessons,' said Nina. 'I'll give you some for Christmas if you like. You should be able to take your test before long.'

Daddy had sent her a cheque for a course; conscience money, Jenny had thought, banking it. She didn't tell Nina about it.

They found a shop that sold sports gear; it stocked whistles. After buying one, they went to the Primrose Café for tea, where they each ate a large toasted teacake with strawberry jam. Nina had not eaten so much in so few hours since she came to the Hall. She felt better, though whether that was due to food or the company, she didn't know; perhaps it was both. When they returned to the Hall she got out of the car and waited while Jenny put it away in one of the several spare garages. They were both walking round to the back door, over which a light shone, when a tall figure suddenly loomed before them.

Jenny gave a startled shriek, but Nina managed to swallow hers, for she recognized Guy Jowett almost at once.

'Oh!' she gasped. 'Good evening.'

'Good evening, madam,' said Guy. 'Are you visiting Mrs Blunt?'

Nina sensed Jenny tense beside her. She put out a hand and pressed her daughter's arm warningly.

'The Blunts are away,' she said. 'But won't you come in for a glass of sherry? I'll telephone your wife and invite her to join us.'

'Oh – very well. Away, did you say?' said Guy. 'Are you sure? How long for?'

'Some weeks,' replied Nina. She walked on towards the house, the keys already in her hand.

Jenny stared curiously at the tall old man in the light that shone from above the back door as her mother undid it. Whoever was this?

'Come in,' said Nina, opening the door. 'This is my daughter, Jenny. Jenny, this is Colonel Jowett from the Manor.' Nina was grateful to Dan for supplying her with this detail of martial rank, not disclosed by Heather, so that she made a correct introduction. She turned to the old man. 'Do come in,' she repeated. 'Jenny, you'll find glasses and a decanter of sherry in the dining-room. Please bring them to the study – four glasses.' Then she turned to Guy. 'Let me take your coat,' she said.

Guy allowed her to help him remove it, and gave it to her, with his cap.

'I must wash,' he said abruptly, and he headed along the passage to the cloakroom. Of course, he would be familiar with the house, Nina realized; he must often come here. She was recovering from her fright. She went into the study and stirred up the fire which had died down while they were out.

Jenny soon came in with the drinks tray.

'He's in the cloakroom,' Nina said. 'We'll get him settled, then I'll ring Heather and she'll come to collect him.'

'Is he quite gaga?' asked Jenny.

The use of so brutal a word shocked Nina.

'I think he's ill,' she said. 'He's rather a dear. I like him.'

They waited ten minutes for Guy to return. Jenny was sure he had collapsed in the lavatory, but Nina had remembered his elaborate handwashing ritual at their first meeting.

Jenny had to admit that he was a handsome old man as he smiled at her, accepting his sherry. Now, he seemed to know who Nina was, calling her by name and understanding that Jenny was her daughter. Nina left them together while she telephoned Heather, and Guy began to ask Jenny about her university course with apparent comprehension of her replies. When Nina returned, they were discussing *Hamlet*. Jenny was sitting on the floor in front of the fire and Guy was leaning back in a deep armchair, completely relaxed.

'He wasn't mad,' he was saying. 'It was a pretence, to get away with murder. Not such a bad idea.' Then he added, 'I've got a grand-daughter much your age. A little younger, perhaps. She isn't at university – doesn't plan to go there. She's mad on horses. It's not surprising, I suppose. Her mother was just the same.'

'I grew out of them,' said Jenny gravely.

'Her mother hasn't,' said Guy.

It seemed quite an interruption when Heather arrived. She'd been on the point of going out in the car to seek her wandering spouse when Nina had rung. Her relief at finding him was evident; she eagerly took the glass of sherry Nina gave her.

Sherry was one of their treats, Nina remembered.

11

'He is rather an old charmer,' said Jenny, when Heather had taken her husband away. 'There's something about men of that generation – that type. I can see why you're taken with him, Mum.'

'Don't be ridiculous, Jenny,' said Nina. 'I'm not taken with him, as you put it. I'm sorry for him. He must have been a fine, active man, once.'

'He seemed perfectly sensible, once we were indoors and he'd got his drink,' said Jenny. 'It's pretty awful for her, though, if she has to keep chasing round after him all over the place.'

'I suppose he can't stray very far, if he's on foot,' said Nina. 'But it's getting dark early now – he might have an accident.'

After their supper they sat in the study with the television turned on to an old, indifferent film. Nina did her *gros point*, paying little attention to the screen, and after a time Jenny grew bored and began to examine the bookshelves.

'Golly, look! Here they all are when they were young!' she exclaimed.

'Who?'

'The Jowetts, and it must be the Blunts too. Fascinating! Come and see, Mum. Lots of old snaps,' said Jenny.

She was sitting on the floor inspecting a photograph album.

'Where did you get that?' Nina asked. 'Put it back.'

'Why? It's not private,' said Jenny. 'It was on the shelf, beside Thackeray. Just look at their clothes! Those skirts! Here, Mum,' and she got up and put the open album on her mother's lap, on top of the embroidery canvas. 'It's pure Noel Coward!'

Nina saw a print of some young people standing in a row, smiling self-consciously. The women's hair was waved, and their straight skirts were worn well below the knee. In some photographs they held tennis rackets. On most pages their names were neatly printed beneath, so that it was easy to learn that Guy was the slim young man with thick, dark hair, and Heather the tall, pretty girl beside him, her features strong even in youth.

'Don't they look happy?' said Nina, intrigued despite her words to Jenny. 'Here's Mrs Blunt – and this must be him – Leonard. He doesn't seem to come into many – I suppose he was the photographer.'

Priscilla Blunt, when young, had a soft, warm expression as she gazed at the camera. She had worn that look in Fortnum and Mason's as she listened to Nina's sorry tale, though her face had lost is smoothness and she was elegant now, rather than pretty.

There were pictures of the Hall, with a pre-war Austin saloon parked outside the front door. Jenny went on looking through the albums, while Nina returned to her sewing.

'Here are the children,' said Jenny suddenly. 'Look, Mum. The Jowetts and the Blunts, with two boys and a girl.' She read out the names. 'Robin, Charles and Rosemary.'

Nina, who was threading her needle with sage-green wool, became interested again and looked at the album. Three small children sat on a rug with a toy horse on wheels beside them. In the black-and-white photograph, slightly faded now, all wore pale clothes and looked excessively neat.

'Robin Jowett died when he was only twenty-one,' said Nina. 'His grave's in the churchyard.'

'How awful,' said Jenny. 'What happened?'

'A sailing accident, I believe,' said Nina.

Jenny did not ask her how she had learned this.

'Rosemary must be the horsey daughter,' she said, turning a page. 'What about Charles? I suppose he makes buns, like his dad.'

'Yes.'

'Nice to walk into such rich shoes,' said Jenny.

'I'm sure his father worked hard to acquire them,' Nina said, somewhat tartly.

'Yes – well,' Jenny inspected further snapshots. 'They are rather fun,' she said. 'Here are the children getting older. Look at those caps the boys are wearing!' She tittered at the sight of the two small boys in large tweed caps.

Nina could remember her own brother in one like that.

At last Jenny put the albums away, saying that she felt sleepy.

'It's all the country air,' she said. 'Don't forget the whistle, Mum, if your funny friend rings up tonight. It's here by the telephone. Just blow it as hard as you can.'

Nina said that she would. She sat on for some time after Jenny had gone upstairs, expecting the telephone to ring, but it didn't. At last she, too, decided to go to bed. She folded her sewing away inside its bag, plumped up the cushions and glanced round the room before switching out the light. The fire had burned right down, but she put the guard across.

Jenny had replaced the photograph albums, but one of them

stuck out from the shelf, breaking the neat line. Nina went to push it back, but instead, she removed it, and began looking through it. In the centre of this one were some wedding photographs of Leonard and Priscilla, in 1938. 'Peace in our Time!' was written below. Those were the Prime Minister's words, said after Munich. Nina had seen Neville Chamberlain on television so often, when old news reels were shown, that she thought she remembered the original occasion, but as she was only a year old at the time, that was hardly likely.

She leafed on through the album and soon saw photographs of Guy and Leonard in uniform, one an army officer, the other in naval uniform with the words Sub-Lieutenant Leonard Blunt, R.N.V.R., printed below. There were prints of Priscilla in uniform, too; she was a Red Cross nurse; but after that, apart from a few snapshots of Rosemary Jowett, at first in a pram and then as a toddler, there was a gap which covered most of the war years. The history continued with the photographs Nina had already seen. She moved on to another album, her attention caught. Had Jenny noticed what she now saw? Surely not, or she would have said so. Nina felt, still, that in a sense she was prying, but as Jenny had said, the albums were kept openly on the shelf, and certainly photographs were not as private as letters.

There were a number of prints of the three children, Charles, Robin and Rosemary. Nina scrutinized them. She had not imagined the likeness between the two boys; it was pronounced, and it persisted through the years. There they were as young men, standing beside an old Morris Minor, both of them grinning. By now, Robin was taller than Charles, just as Guy was taller than Leonard, but they were still very alike.

The sequence of albums ended after 1963, as though with Robin's death photography had ceased to be a hobby, but there were earlier albums here, which Jenny had not opened. They went back another generation, and Nina saw women in long skirts, with wide, shady hats, standing outside the Hall. There were ancient cars, a chauffeur in leggings, a pony and trap. So the Blunts had been here a long time: that was a surprise to Nina; perhaps they had built the house. She picked out Leonard's parents, and some brothers and sisters. What had become of them, she wondered: were they still in the firm?

Families were larger then. The ink beneath the entries had faded, and often it was hard to read the names.

It was getting late when she came to the last album. Nina glanced through it, intrigued by the history it revealed. She looked at her watch when she returned the book to the shelf and saw that it was after half-past eleven. He had never rung so late; she felt sure it would be all right tonight.

In the morning it rained.

On Sunday morning, while Nina was busy preparing vegetables for lunch, Jenny slipped off to the study where, if she used the telephone, she could not be overheard. She had promised to ring Alec, to pronounce on her mother's condition. If she seemed all right, Alec would come over to collect Jenny. He was aware that there might be problems; Jenny might even have to find a callbox to use; but he had promised to wait near the telephone until half-past ten. After that, he'd give up.

While the number rang, Jenny idly turned the pages of the telephone directory. There were the Jowetts – Lt. Col. G.R., she read, The Manor House.

Someone answered the telephone and went off to fetch Alec, who had been standing nearby only minutes before. Jenny turned back through the directory, and the name Fenton suddenly stood out from the page. Fenton, D.E., she read, and a Netherton St Mary number. Then Alec came to the telephone and she closed the directory.

The shining whistle glinted at her throughout her conversation.

Jenny found her mother receptive to the idea of one extra for lunch even though he might be late; she was glad that Jenny would have a lift back.

'I'll bring him next time I come,' said Jenny. 'If that's OK. I thought I'd better not, the first time, as it isn't our house and all that.'

Nina gave permission. She'd clear it with Leonard Blunt's secretary on the telephone, and another time, if she took such a post, it would have to be part of the deal.

'Tell me about Alec,' she added.

'Oh – it's not serious,' said Jenny lightly. 'He's a biologist.'

'Oh – he can talk, then,' said Nina.

This made Jenny laugh. She'd been out for some time with a budding mathematician who was by nature morose. Neither Nina nor Martin had managed to extract more than monosyllabic replies from him when he came to Silverlea.

Nina wanted to beg Jenny not to stick exclusively to Alec, but she knew the modern way was to cling to a partner, once found, or you were considered a social outcast. It seemed to her that, paired in this fashion, it was almost as difficult to break away as to leave a marriage. The so-called freedom of this generation was a myth.

Alec turned out to be short and merry; he had a mop of curly hair which, if he'd been a girl, Nina would have thought was permed. Perhaps it was. He wore corduroy trousers, not jeans, and a tie.

Nina saw by the tie that he had made an effort, wanting her to approve of him. She warmed to him instantly. He'd brought a bottle of wine, and he stood up when she entered the room. Without being asked, he revealed that his father was a farmer who had five hundred acres in Cornwall on the edge of a real village, not a developing one like Netherton St Mary.

When the young people departed that evening, Nina felt bleak. The house seemed so silent. She called Rory to her, and he, who had been wandering round looking melancholy after the car had gone, laid his head on her knee and made a sad howling sound.

Nina, at this, could not hold back her tears any longer. She wept for ten minutes while the dog looked at her sadly.

At last she was able to make an effort to pull herself together. She went off to wash her face, then tried to settle with the paper, but she could not concentrate. There were only the God-spots on television and she did not want to watch them. She went over to the bookshelves and took down one of the later photograph albums, spreading it open at a page showing the two boys, Charles and Robin, aged about twenty. Then she hunted back through the earlier ones to the first photographs showing Guy Jowett as a young man.

Robin Jowett resembled his father. He had dark hair, straight, well-defined eyebrows and deep-set eyes. Charles Blunt, though shorter and more sturdily built, was also dark.

He had the same thick, straight brows over deep-set eyes.

It's chance, Nina thought: the figures in the photographs were, after all, small. She looked again at the Blunts' black-and-white wedding photographs, taken when they were young. Leonard's hair, which she remembered as thin and sandy, looked fair. Both of them had gently arched brows.

It proved nothing. Even so, she could not stop thinking about it.

That night the telephone rang at twenty minutes to eleven, and she heard the soft sigh of her unknown caller.

The whistle, placed by Jenny near the telephone, winked up at her. Nina picked it up, took a deep breath, hesitated for a moment, for it seemed a ridiculous action, then took another deep breath and blew hard. She put the receiver back without waiting for any reaction and went up to bed feeling extremely shaky. But Jenny would be pleased and if it worked she need not ask the telephone exchange to intervene.

12

Lynn felt better as her train drew in to the station, but her stomach had started churning again by the time she got off the bus at the corner near her home. If her parents had found the note she had left in her room, there'd be a row.

Her parents owned a newsagent and tobacconist's shop on the edge of the city. It was a lucrative business, with low overheads as both her mother and father worked there full time, and there was a flat above, where they had lived years ago, which was let at a good rent. Their day, however, was long, and both were always tired in the evenings.

Lynn and her friend Christine had both left school that summer and had enrolled on the same business course, but Christine had dropped out after the first week. She spent her days in coffee bars, and most afternoons met Lynn in time for the two girls to go home together. Lynn was not enjoying her course, which had been her parents' idea; they thought a knowledge of book-keeping would help her when she started to work in the shop. Lynn didn't look forward to that; she wanted to do something more exciting – be a model, work in a dress shop – and she had let Christine talk her into their escapade. She had planned to telephone her parents that night, when she and Christine were installed in their hostel, to spare them worry. She often went out in the evenings, to a disco with Christine or to the home of some other girl, but her parents always knew where she went and she was never late home.

Christine's was a different case. Her mother was dead, and her older brother and sister were married. Her father had recently married again and his wife, Iris, was young. Christine felt Iris usurped her mother's place, and the girl was incapable of responding to her new stepmother's friendly overtures. She was rude and uncooperative. Her mother had been a good cook and home-maker, but Iris was not, and the meals she prepared were mainly fry-ups or came out of tins. The house, once neat, was neglected and grubby. Christine had taken a pride in looking after her father and keeping the place clean after her mother's death. Now she was not needed. Lynn had sympathized with her wish to start a new life.

Walking up the path to the house where she lived with her parents and younger brother, Lynn planned to accept whatever scolding, and even punishment, she received without complaint. She'd think hard before running away again.

As she entered the house – she had her own key – she heard the radio playing. Lights were on in several rooms, but there was no one at home. Lynn went upstairs at once to her own bedroom. The note was still there, on her pillow, where she had left it. Heart thumping, she tore it into tiny pieces and flushed them away down the lavatory. In the kitchen, propped by the bread bin, was a note with her name on it. It said that her grandmother had had a bad fall and broken her leg. Her mother and father had gone to the hospital and might not be back till late.

She'd been reprieved! Lynn couldn't believe her luck, though she was sorry about her grandmother, of whom she was fond. Never had the house felt so safe and welcoming! She even felt hungry. She made herself scrambled eggs on toast and a cup of tea, went upstairs and had a bath, and was in bed when her brother, Neil, came back from the neighbour's where he had spent the evening.

In the morning, Christine's father came round to see if by any chance his daughter had spent the night at Lynn's, as she sometimes did. He was not on the telephone, so she couldn't have rung to say that she wouldn't be home.

Lynn was asked if she knew where Christine was.

She knew she was safe, for she'd seen her arrive in London, but she didn't know where she was; not exactly. She barely hesitated before giving her answer, for she could still save herself.

'I don't know where she is,' said Lynn.

'Christine's got other friends besides Lynn,' said Iris Potter when her husband returned after seeing Lynn's parents.

'She's never stayed away without telling us,' said Frank.

'Maybe she's doing it on purpose to make us worry,' said Iris.

'Now, why would she want to do that?'

'Well, Frank, she doesn't go much on me, does she? You can't deny that.'

'She'll come round,' Frank said, uncomfortably, but he found Iris's theory credible, though it angered him. They were both nice girls. Why couldn't they get on? He'd often heard Christine make hurtful remarks to Iris, and, in private, he'd scolded her for it. If Iris was right, she'd be back in a day or two. She'd want money, for one thing.

Iris discovered her money had gone from the tin where she kept what Frank gave her that afternoon, which was her Saturday off. She'd planned to buy a new dress from La Boutique, but she couldn't do that anyway, with Frank so upset; it wouldn't be right. She didn't tell him about the money. When Christine came back, she'd ask her about it and make her repay it. She'd enough of her own to manage with, meanwhile.

Frank was sure Christine would return on Sunday; she'd want to get ready for college next day – wash her hair, all that. Over the weekend he'd been to see several of her school friends to find out if anyone knew where she was, but no one could tell him. It was not pleasant, admitting to the parents of other youngsters that she'd gone off without a word. People went 'Tch, tch,' and looked sympathetic, but Frank was sure they blamed him for her disappearance. If he hadn't remarried – and a girl young enough to be his daughter – it wouldn't have happened, he inferred. None of the youngsters told him that Christine had dropped out of college, though several of them knew.

He searched for a note in her room, and saw that the suitcase he'd bought her for a school trip to France a few years ago had gone. He could find no washing things, nor a hairbrush. In a way these discoveries were a relief for this meant her departure was planned; she hadn't been whisked by magic from the streets, or so he thought then.

He took Monday morning off from work and went to the college to confront her himself. He was there for over an hour, for when she did not appear he made enquiries, and soon found that she had not been in for some time.

What had she been doing? What did it all mean? He didn't know where to start looking for her now. Perhaps, he thought hopefully, she'd gone to her married sister or brother? He should have thought of that before. Both lived some distance away. He couldn't get hold of them till the evening, since both couples were out at work all day, so he went back to his own job, meanwhile. That evening he rang both families from a telephone box. When neither had any news, he went to the police.

Police Constable Young came round to the Potters' house to collect a photograph of Christine and to find out what she had been wearing when she left home. At the police station, Frank had not been able to give a certain description of her clothes, though she usually wore jeans and an anorak unless she was off to the disco, and sometimes even then. Iris might know which of her clothes were missing, he thought.

'That will be Christine's mother,' said Young. He was a big, slow-moving man with a high bald forehead and pale eyes. Facing him, Frank was glad they were both on the same side; he thought it would be hard to get past that penetrating gaze with a lie.

He explained about his new wife.

'And did they get on? Her and Christine?' Young asked.

'Well,' said Frank, and was silent. His tone was a reply, and Young, who had heard this sort of story before, prodded him gently.

'It's quite usual to have trouble with kids, when a parent marries again,' he said. He'd been married twice himself. His first wife hadn't been able to accept the demands of the job, with its unsocial hours and sudden spells of overtime. She'd taken the kids, when she left.

Frank admitted that Christine had not taken kindly to Iris.

'Mind you, Iris has been very good – very patient,' he said. 'But she's not like Christine's own mum.'

When Young saw Iris, he felt a twinge of envy, quickly suppressed as disloyal. His own second wife was a tough, sturdy woman his own age who had been married before to a soldier who was killed in Northern Ireland. She had grown strong herself, while alone with her two children, and she was a good sort of wife for a policeman; he'd been lucky to meet her. But she hadn't the looks of Iris.

Young noticed a pile of ironing on the kitchen dresser, the unwashed dishes heaped in the sink. Well, it didn't do to set too much store by that; he'd seen a lot worse. He went up to Christine's room with Frank and Iris. Iris looked among Christine's clothes and said that a lot had gone, including a green wool skirt and the mock fur jacket Frank had bought her for her sixteenth birthday.

'So she's planning to be away some time,' said Young. 'What about money?'

Frank thought she spent most of her pocket money on clothes and cosmetics, though there were her fares to college, of course, and her meals. He gave her as much as he could, but she wasn't likely to have a lot put by.

'How will she manage, if she's skint?' he asked, his worried face sagging. 'She'll be –' he couldn't bring himself to say what she might be forced to do.

Iris put a hand on his arm.

'She's got some money, love,' she said. 'There was some in the dresser drawer. I keep a bit there. It's gone. There was nearly a hundred pounds.'

Frank was furious.

'She stole it – she took your money,' he said, and as he rubbed his hands across his face Iris saw him through new eyes. He looked really old.

'I expect she felt it was yours. She knew it came from you,' Iris said. 'That wasn't like stealing.'

'It was stealing,' Frank insisted.

'Let's have a list of her friends,' said Young. 'She may have told someone her plans.'

Frank said he'd already asked them, but Young said they must be asked again. He began writing down their names. He told Frank that most youngsters who went missing turned up quite soon; they learned their lesson and came back home. Only a few were never heard of again.

Lynn couldn't think why Christine hadn't phoned on Sunday. She couldn't be job-hunting on a Sunday. Had she already found new friends and was too busy with them to remember her old ones?

Lynn went to college on Monday. If she worked hard, she thought guiltily, her grandmother, who was still very ill, would get better. She bent industriously to her studies that day, but during breaks her thoughts returned to Christine. Was she already at work in a shop? Christine had said that a job in a shop, or even as a waitress, could lead to all sorts of things. An agent passing through might notice you as just the type he was wanting, and sign you up. Such a case had been written about in a book she'd read. In Christine's vocabulary, books and magazines were synonymous. She'd read a good few in her truant hours.

Lynn saw Christine's father at the college that morning. She expected to be sent for and questioned about her friend, but that did not happen.

On Monday evening she and Neil were at home watching television. Their parents had gone to the hospital after closing the shop – her mother had been there for most of the day – for her grandmother's condition had deteriorated. When the doorbell rang, Neil went to open it. They had been told to be careful when alone in the house; although the area was a quiet, respectable suburb, break-ins could happen anywhere, and at any hour.

A uniformed woman police officer stood on the step, and at first Neil thought she brought news about their grandmother, but Lynn knew why Woman Police Constable Dixon had called as soon as she entered the house, and her stomach lurched.

After years of working at the same level as her male colleagues on cases of drunken disorder, theft, and even riot control, WPC Dixon was now, like other women police officers, specializing in work with children, assaults on women, and domestic problems, as had been typically the woman police officer's role for years until the Equal Opportunities Act decreed that there were no differences between male and female officers. First she established why Lynn and Neil's parents were not at home. As Lynn explained, Beryl Dixon perceived her unease, and suggested that Neil might care to make them all a cup of tea while she and Lynn had a chat.

'What do you want to talk to her about?' Neil asked, squaring his shoulders and looking tough. 'She's not done nothing wrong.'

'No, I'm sure she hasn't,' said WPC Dixon. 'I'm not here about anything like that. I want to talk to her about Christine Potter. You're close friends, aren't you, Lynn?' she added, and when Lynn nodded, continued to Neil, 'Lynn probably knows a good deal about where she spent her time and who her friends were. She's missing from home, you know. You do know that, don't you?'

'Yes. Mr Potter came round,' said Neil. Reassured that his sister was not about to be arrested, he went off to the kitchen, and WPC Dixon suggested to Lynn that they might sit down while the kettle boiled. In the living room, she sat on the sofa and watched Lynn turn off the television and subside into a chair as far away as possible.

'Now, Lynn, you do know something, don't you?' said WPC Dixon. 'Did Christine go off with a boyfriend?'

Lynne's mouth had gone dry.

'No.'

'But you do know where she went?'

Lynn looked anywhere but at the policewoman.

'Well? I suggest you tell me before your brother comes back,' said WPC Dixon. 'All we want to do is find her, Lynn. Make certain she's safe. If she is, there's no need to worry.'

This made sense.

'She went to London,' said Lynn, in hoarse tones.

'I see. You know that for certain, do you?'

Lynn nodded.

'Do you know when? Was it on Friday, the day she didn't go home? She didn't go somewhere else first?'

'No – it was Friday,' said Lynn.

'But you didn't tell Mr Potter when he came asking?' said WPC Dixon. 'Why not?'

Lynn swallowed.

'He said, did I know where she was. I didn't, exactly. She said she'd phone up, but she hasn't,' she said.

'Did you know her plans? Had she any friends in London? Somewhere to stay?' asked WPC Dixon.

'She'd got some addresses of hostels. She wrote them down from the yellow pages in the library,' said Lynn.

'Do you know which ones she meant to try?'

'Not really. She just wrote them all down,' said Lynn. 'We – she said there were plenty.'

WPC Dixon noticed the slip. Lynn knew more about Christine's disappearance than she was willing to say, but she may have made a pact with her friend to keep her secret. Antagonizing the girl would not help to trace Christine.

'You can't tell me any more?' the policewoman asked as Neil came in with the tea. 'Do you know which train she caught, for instance?'

Lynn told her.

WPC Dixon noted it mentally. In the absence of the girl's parents, she had written nothing down. She stayed for a cup of tea; a few more minutes would make little difference in the hunt for Christine, who was probably safely installed in a hostel in London while her father made himself ill with worry. It was important to establish a friendly feeling between herself and these two young people.

When she had gone, Lynn rounded on Neil.

'Don't say anything,' she warned him. 'Don't tell Mum and Dad she was here.'

'But it was about Christine,' said Neil.

'Never mind. You're too young to understand,' said Lynn. 'No one likes the police at their house.'

Neil thought it would be bad tactics to say that, even though it was dark, a neighbour might have noticed the police car outside. If he told, Lynn would get back at him, he knew. There were lots of ways she could do it, like telling her mother that he came home from school by the canal path, which he was forbidden to do in case he got into a fight and fell in, as had happened to one of his friends. There were plenty of ways in which he transgressed against parental rules and which Lynn had discovered.

He agreed to keep quiet.

13

Nina received a letter from Mr Drew, the solicitor, on Monday morning. Though bearing a first class stamp, and postmarked with Friday's date, it had taken the whole weekend to make its way to Netherton St Mary. It contained hard news, and Nina knew it would have spoiled her time with Jenny if she had read it sooner. The sale of Silverlea was not going ahead: Martin intended to live there himself and was moving in quite soon. Nina couldn't help wondering if this had been his plan all along, but he must have discovered that she was no longer there and perhaps that had influenced him. He had, through his own solicitor, agreed to release capital to her; indeed, if he did not, the court would order him to do so and he could be forced to disclose his assets in order to arrange a fair sum. Unless there was a quick, satisfactory response, Mr Drew would take the matter to court, but some delay was inevitable and much depended on how Martin planned to raise the money.

Nina had to concede that Mr Drew's doubts about Martin's intentions had been justified, but what she minded most was the thought of Caroline occupying the house which had been her own home for so many years.

When she took Rory out, she walked glumly along with her head down, just like the old men she met daily walking their dogs. She almost collided with Heather Jowett outside the grocer's, where most days now Nina went for some small purchase. She and Mr Goody were quite friendly by this time. She had grown used to his hand going straight from the cheese and the ham to the till.

'Sorry,' said Nina, who had been about to tether Rory to the railings outside the shop.

'My fault,' said Heather. 'I wasn't looking where I was going. Nina, thank you for retrieving Guy the other night. I was going to ring you. Has your daughter gone?'

'Yes.'

'You'll be missing her. Come and have tea this afternoon,' said Heather. 'I can't stop now – Guy hasn't settled this morning, I don't know why. You didn't meet him, did you?'

'No.'

'He's in an odd mood. Perhaps he caught a chill that night. Anyway, it would be nice if you came. We don't see many people.'

Nina accepted. Since the Jowetts regarded shop-bought scones as a treat, how would they react if she made them a cake and took it round, she wondered. She'd love to do it, but perhaps it would be wrongly interpreted. It would be dreadful to offend them, and really she hardly knew them.

Perhaps, after all, she didn't need to buy anything from Mr Goody today, she thought, turning away. There was food left over from the weekend, and Rory's tinned supply of Blunt's branded dogfood stretched along a whole shelf in the larder. Her purpose had really been to exchange a few words with another person.

Dan had brought her paper. When she got back, she sat in the kitchen reading it. By coincidence, there was an article on the woman's page by a bright thirty-year-old journalist advising divorced women – of whom the journalist was one – to retrain for a career. But what was the good of such counsel to her, Nina thought. With so much unemployment, who would take on an older woman? And train for what? Was she capable of going to college now? Could she live like Jenny while she learned something or other? What could she usefully study?

Dan found her sitting there when he came in for his coffee.

'Well, now,' he said, feeling embarrassed, for he saw that she had been crying.

Nina jumped up, dabbing away at her face with a handkerchief.

'Oh – sorry, Dan, I'd forgotten the time,' she said.

'You'll be missing Jenny,' he stated.

Nina accepted this excuse for her tears.

'Yes,' she said.

'She'll be back to see you soon,' said Dan.

He wanted to comfort her. He wanted to put his arms round her, draw her close, feel her softness, her hair brushing his cheek.

Instead, he sat down with his cup of coffee.

Guy's paintings were so bad.

Nina stood in the small attic room which he used as a studio trying to think of a kindly comment. She had small confidence in her own artistic judgement, but these scenes, with the crude colours, the trees and buildings geometrically arranged like sentinels, offended her eye. If she had not been standing beside the artist as she looked at the work on the easel, Nina would have thought it had been done by an eight-year-old child. Vivid blue sky surmounted a landscape dotted with dark trees; there was an orange-coloured church in the centre of the picture, with a donkey, its limbs stick-like, its ears exaggeratedly large, standing nearby. Looking round the room, Nina saw other paintings stacked against the walls, presumably waiting for Heather to take them away for sale. All were vivid scenes with the same sort of dark trees, harsh orange or terra-cotta buildings with scarlet roofs, and overhead, always, the brilliant sky.

'Where is it?' she asked, of the work on the easel. Surely this wasn't England?

'It's Italy,' said Guy, standing back to squint critically at his masterpiece. 'The camp was over in this direction,' and he pointed away from the canvas.

'The camp?' said Nina.

'Guy was a prisoner in Italy during the war,' said Heather.

'I began painting then,' said Guy. 'Several of us took it up to while away the time between escapes. Others studied for degrees. Painting's a relaxing occupation. I decided to take it up again when I retired. Now it pays the bills.'

Who on earth would want these paintings, Nina wondered.

'How long does a picture take you?' she asked.

'Oh – a week or two. It depends,' said Guy.

'Do you use photographs?'

'The photographs are in here,' said Guy, tapping his head.

Nina nodded, and searched her wits for further comment. She was saved by Heather, who said it was time for tea as the kettle would have boiled by now. Asking to see Guy's work had seemed an obvious request to make in a conversational lull after she arrived. She had been taken to the drawing room, where a smoky fire burned in the grate, so her advent was being treated as an occasion. The room was cold, however; draughts whistled in through the windows and past the long curtains. Guy had seemed pleased with Nina's interest; he had led the way up the stairs, along an icy passage whose floor was covered in threadbare brown Wilton carpet, and up a further flight of stairs, lino-covered, to the top floor and this north-facing room which must once have been, Nina supposed, a maid's bedroom. Would the children have slept up here too, she wondered, in a nursery suite under the eaves, cut off from their parents, banished with a nanny? Guy's studio contained nothing except his bench, easel, a high stool and other equipment, and a calor gas stove.

As they left the room to go downstairs, Guy stood back by the door, holding it for the two women. He followed them out, closing the door. There was something about him that touched Nina's heart. He had no idea that his work was worthless. Yet it couldn't be, she reminded herself: it sold.

'I must wash,' said Guy abruptly, in the hall. He turned off into what must be the cloakroom.

'Can I help you?' Nina asked Heather.

'No. You go and sit down,' said Heather. 'I won't be a minute with tea – I must just get Guy a clean towel.'

Nina wandered back to the drawing room, where she rescued the ailing fire by judiciously moving some of the logs into better positions. There were radiators in the room; she touched one and found it stone-cold. Heating oil was very expensive; perhaps having the central heating on was another Jowett treat, Nina thought, and sat down in an armchair. It sagged, badly in need of re-upholstering.

Minutes passed.

Nina remembered Guy's elaborate washing ritual as she had witnessed it at their first meeting; she thought of the time he had spent in the cloakroom at the Hall on Saturday. What was behind this obsession with washing?

She had almost decided to go in search of her hostess when she heard a clunking sound outside and Heather came in, pushing an ancient tea-trolley. Nina sprang to help her before the milk spilled and, between them, they steered it to harbour in front of the fire.

'Ah – that's burned up well,' said Heather. 'I knew it would,' and she looked with satisfaction at the fire. Much of the heat was disappearing up the wide chimney. 'Sit down, Nina. Guy's just coming.'

He entered as she spoke, smiled vaguely at Nina, and sat in an armchair at one side of the hearth.

Heather had made some hard little rock buns. Guy, balancing his plate on his bony knee, cut his bun exactly in half, then split it. He spread it carefully with a minuscule amount of butter and cut it again, this time into bite-sized pieces suitable for a small infant. Then he frowned, laid his knife down on the plate and put the plate on the small table beside him, where Heather had placed his tea. He looked at his hands, holding them out before him, pale and long-fingered. He started to rise.

Heather got up and pushed him gently back into his chair. 'It's all right, darling,' she said. 'You've washed.'

'Oh – yes,' said Guy. He sat back, and then, as if nothing unusual had happened, suddenly began to talk. He described hiding in Italy, in the Apennines in the snow; visits from partisans who brought food; the intense cold; finally, with the improved weather, the hopeful though ill-advised southerly trudge towards the advancing armies.

Nina listened, amazed. His voice grew stronger as he talked, and, animated, he seemed younger. All of a sudden, as suddenly as he had begun, he stopped talking and began to eat his bun.

'More tea, Nina?' said Heather calmly, and asked about Jenny's plans. They discussed the disillusionment young people must feel when, after having high hopes, they failed to find jobs at all, much less any post worthy of higher education and qualifications.

'It was different when we were young,' Heather said. 'We weren't brought up to have careers outside the home, and the war, when it came, channelled our energies – gave us a cause in which we believed. You're younger, of course, Nina,' she added. 'But you must have regarded marriage as a career too.'

Nina agreed that she had, but did not add that this thinking had been the biggest mistake of her life.

Guy had finished his bun. He stood up.

'I'm a little tired,' he said. 'Please excuse me,' and he turned to Nina, bowing slightly as he looked at her vaguely. 'I'll go up and lie down, now,' he said, rubbing a hand over his forehead. He had gone very pale.

'Very well, darling,' said Heather, also rising. 'I'll come up with you.'

Nina stood, too.

'I'll go,' she said. She was horrified at the sudden change in Guy. He had talked sensibly, compellingly, about his war experiences and now, once again, he had become a lost soul; moreover, he looked it.

'No – stay. Have another bun. I won't be long,' said Heather. She took Guy by the arm and led him from the room.

There were only two buns left: one each for Guy and Heather tomorrow, thought Nina. They were not very nice, but to Guy and Heather they counted, no doubt, as a treat. She collected up the china, wheeled, with difficulty, the heavy old trolley out to the kitchen, and by the time Heather returned had washed everything up, put it away, wiped down the sink and the top of the stove and rinsed out a milk bottle.

She had just dried her own hands – there were no rubber gloves – when Heather came into the room. She took the towel from Nina, folded it up and put it in the drawer from which Nina had seen her take one and hand it to Guy on her first visit.

'But it's damp – I've just used it,' said Nina.

'Doesn't matter. He won't notice – he'll think it's clean,' Heather said, 'I have to do things like that all the time.'

Nina could think of no reply.

'You like him, don't you?' said Heather. 'I know you do.'

'Yes – of course,' Nina was shocked by the question but her answer was prompt.

'Everyone does,' said Heather.

'I didn't know he'd been a prisoner of war,' Nina said, tentatively.

'He was recaptured trying to get through to our armies,' said Heather. 'He was sent to Germany. He had an awful time there. He's never really got over it – a long forced march, friends shot. Even I don't know the whole story. He has nightmares about it, still. It's strange, Nina. Things that happen when you're young – that you think you've forgotten, or at least have come to terms with – like someone's death, for instance – can come back years later, as a sort of haunt.'

Was she haunted by her dead son, wondered Nina.

'I dream about my father, sometimes,' she said. 'He died years ago.' It was all she could offer as comment.

'Guy's sleeping now,' Heather said. 'He didn't sleep much last night. When he talks like that – which he hardly ever does – he gets tired.'

'Is it good for him to dwell on the past so much?' Nina asked. She was thinking of the paintings.

'I think it is. He didn't live through all his hurt and grief – fear, too – at the time. He's doing it now,' said Heather. 'He had to pick up the pieces – go on with his active life after the war. He pushed it away then and he's having to face it now. One can't always run away from uncomfortable thoughts.'

'Will he sleep long?' asked Nina.

'Yes. He's had some pills,' Heather said. 'He missed his after-lunch nap today.' He hadn't eaten the baked custard in which she'd dissolved his tranquillizers. When she saw his mood, she'd popped them into his tea, with the sugar. She'd put the powder in his cup before bringing in the trolley, stacking another cup on it as concealment.

'How do you manage?' The words burst from Nina and as soon as they were uttered she wished them unsaid.

Heather looked surprised.

'We've had a wonderful marriage,' she said. 'Sorrows, of course, but one can't escape those. So much joy, too.' Her face softened. 'He wasn't always forgetful and ill. What worries me is, how would he cope if I was ill, or if I died first? Rosemary

112

wouldn't be patient enough to look after him. Still, I'm tough –
I keep well,' she added, and smiled.

And you do the garden, and plant your bulbs and scatter
wild flowers round the countryside, Nina thought. Some people might call you dotty too.

'I expect you miss Mrs Blunt,' she said.

'In a way,' said Heather. 'I don't know many people in the
village now that it's got so large. They seem to come and go so
fast. Their jobs change. We used to have friends all over the
county, but with petrol so expensive and so on, one can't keep
up the social round now. Anyway, there isn't time, and it's not
easy for Guy. He can't adjust – he can't get used to the village
being full of modern houses with people rushing off to their
offices in Slough, or wherever they go, leaving those estates
almost deserted. I meet a few of them. I still manage one or two
committees.'

'Please let me know if there's anything at all I can do, the rest
of the time I'm here,' Nina said earnestly. 'I can shop, or be here
in the house, if you have to go out,' she added. 'I've plenty of
time.'

'Thank you,' said Heather, but she knew there was nothing
anyone could do.

Departing in her car, Nina felt that her own problems were
comparatively straightforward. She had only herself to worry
about, and now she knew she would survive.

14

The Metropolitan Police searched for Christine Potter at every
hostel listed in the yellow pages. No girl of that name had
asked for a bed. When her photograph was shown, no
member of staff at any hostel recognized her as having
booked in under a different name. As the weeks wore on,
Christine Potter was still missing.

The police enquired at Euston station, where the train she
was on, according to Lynn, had ended its run. It was unlikely

that she had left it before her intended destination, although she might have met someone persuasive during the journey. The ticket collector who was on the barrier could neither confirm nor deny that she had passed through. In a mass of travellers leaving the platform, who would recognize a particular girl unless there was something unusual about her? In the station buffet, however, the enquiring constable was luckier. A cleaner could not be sure which day it was, but he had seen a girl like the one in the photograph. He added, however, that one young girl, these days, was much like another. You often saw these girls on their own, in their furry coats, with their bags. The cleaner, whose job was to wipe the tables and clear the crockery, had an idea the girl may have left with a man. Perhaps it was not the same girl, the cleaner added, but there was a man who came there often, and talked to girls. He was able to describe this elderly man.

The collator had come up with a possible name for Detective Superintendent Wilshaw's unidentified body. One Maureen Betts, aged sixteen, had left Newcastle last August and had never been heard of again. She had worn, when last seen, an Indian print dress; she was fair-haired, and five foot two inches tall. At the time of her disappearance railway staff at Newcastle had seen a girl resembling Maureen, wearing an Indian dress and high-heeled sandals, waiting for the London train.

Her dental records were sent for comparison with the chart of the teeth of the girl found near Droxton.

The other two girls who had been found in woodland graves and whose killer had not yet been caught, had both run away from home, one after a row with her parents, the other as the result of some whim. It seemed as if the Droxton body was that of a girl who had run away too, and now a fourth girl, Christine Potter, had vanished after leaving home. The chance that all these cases were linked was high, and fears for Christine increased. Every police force in the country had her photograph, and patrolling officers were asked to display extra vigilance in searching for her. In woodland areas, it was stressed, unusual activity should be noted. Christine's photograph was shown on television in an appeal for information, and it appeared in the newspapers under the headline: HAVE YOU SEEN THIS GIRL? Details about her were added, and the girl herself was asked to come forward if she was safe.

Her father and Iris were scarcely able to speak to each other, so far apart had they become since she disappeared. Frank, unable to sleep, was drinking to keep himself going. Iris, sure that he blamed her for Christine's flight, was frightened and miserable.

Marrying Frank had, to Iris, meant security. He was even-tempered and kind, with a good job, and they'd had a lovely fortnight in Spain for their honeymoon. Iris had wanted to settle down. She worked in a supermarket where most of the female staff were married. Shopping there was easy. Her own mother had fed the family from tins and on convenience food and it had not occurred to Iris that there were other ways, though Frank had once or twice wistfully asked if they couldn't have a roast on a Sunday, and what about apple pie? She produced the apple pie, from the supermarket; it only needed warming through; but a roast was beyond her. They'd had a frozen *lasagne*, though, as a change.

She'd learn, Frank had thought. She was still very young. They'd met at the supermarket, where he was a regular customer on late-night shopping Fridays, and he often went to her till. Iris, at the time, had a boyfriend who was giving her the run-around. Finally he dropped her, and Iris, vulnerable, had become interested in Frank who was always so pleasant, paying his bill from a wad of notes drawn out of his pocket. She'd begun to wonder why he did the household shopping.

Iris was pretty, and Frank looked forward to his weekly meetings with her at the check-out. Once, when she wasn't there, he felt quite let down, and the next week he waited outside for her until the store closed, then invited her to the Bull for a drink. She accepted, and it went on from there. In her company, Frank was rejuvenated. Neither had looked very hard at all that was involved, and Frank had wanted to make sure of her before a younger man cut him out. He had expected Iris to have the household skills of his dead wife, and he hadn't foreseen the trouble with Christine.

While the television screen displayed the missing girl's

photograph, Frank sat drinking in front of the set and Iris didn't know what to do. He'd suddenly turned into an angry, elderly stranger. She went up to bed alone, and lay curled in a ball beneath her new printed apricot sheets, weeping with guilt and fear.

'There's another young girl missing, I see,' said Nina to Dan on Friday. 'I wonder if there's a connection with that poor girl they found near Droxton. The police seem to have found out who she was.' She had been looking at the paper while she waited for the kettle to boil for their coffee. 'Maureen Betts, she was called. Only sixteen. How horrible.'

Dan was not making his usual Friday visit to London this week. While the hunt for Christine Potter went on, the railway stations would be staked out, and any girls planning to leave home might be postponing their departure.

'They get it into their heads that the streets of London are paved with gold,' said Dan. 'Coming up thinking glamour jobs grow on trees, even these days.'

'What happens?' Nina asked. 'I suppose they meet a – a pimp, or something.'

'Oh, somebody sweet-talks them,' said Dan. 'Offers them a nice place to stay and when they get there it's a brothel – something like that. They know no better than to go along, though they must all have been warned of the dangers dozens of times.'

'This Christine has probably been killed too,' said Nina. 'Otherwise, surely she'd have come forward. It's dreadful – such a waste.'

Dan was stirring his coffee and crumbling his digestive biscuit. Normally, he ate it quickly.

'Yes,' he said. 'They never think harm will come to them. People always think violence happens to others.'

'Dan, I'm sorry, I shouldn't have brought the subject up. I'm sure you'd much rather not talk about these things,' said Nina. 'It must be painful for you.'

'No, no, Mrs Crowther,' said Dan, who still addressed her like this, although Nina had been using his first name for some time. 'Facts are facts,' he added.

'Even so –' Nina made a gesture with her hand as she tried to think of the right response.

'It's all right. Everyone's afraid of mentioning Susie,' said Dan. 'No one ever does. Perhaps I should talk about it to someone.'

Nina remembered Heather's words about facing the past.

'Susie,' she repeated. 'A nice name. Was she like you?'

Dan took a worn leather wallet from his pocket and from it extracted a faded snapshot. Silently he handed it to Nina. A smiling teenager looked at her from the scuffed print. She had curly hair and a small, straight nose. Nina thought she did look like Dan, and said so.

He was pleased.

'People said they could see it,' he admitted. 'I've other pictures at home. Better ones. There's one taken a month before it happened. She'd been a bridesmaid.'

'I'd love to see them,' said Nina warmly.

'Would you?' Dan brightened. 'Would you come round, Mrs Crowther? Come to tea, perhaps? Or even –' he paused, summoning courage, 'to supper?'

Nina was startled. She'd meant him to bring his photographs with him one day, to the Hall. How should she answer? She didn't want to snub him.

'Tea would be lovely,' she said. 'Thank you. May Rory come to your house?'

'Oh yes,' said Dan. 'Of course.'

Visions were flashing through his mind, superimposing themselves rapidly one upon the other. In the first, Nina sat in the chair that once had been Ellen's, her soft fair hair haloed by the nearby lamp, a glass of sweet sherry beside her. This was succeeded by a scene at the dining-table, places laid for two, roast chicken before them, or even, he thought, growing bold, a pheasant – the butcher in Murford sold them and Dan was sure he could cook one with the aid of his cookery encyclopaedia. They'd talk, and he'd show her the photographs. She'd notice his tank of fish and he'd tell her about them. Then he'd bring her home in his Ford – he forgot that she would probably have come in her own car – and he'd ask her to come again. Next time, she'd say that she would be cook; she'd wear his big apron and he'd see her soft arms – fair-skinned they'd be, for she was

117

so fair – bare to the elbow, for she'd roll up her sleeves to protect them as she worked.

The shutter closed on this fantasy, to be followed by one where she sat drinking tea and eating a slice of cake with Rory at her feet. Her hair would still touch the back of the chair, and he'd still be able to ask her again.

'Will you come on Sunday?' he asked. 'Your daughter won't be here again so soon?'

'No,' said Nina. 'Not just yet. I'd love to come. Thank you.'

She needn't stay long, she thought, clearing away his cup while he went back to prolong his work in the garden on the chance of another chat with her before leaving. He was mending a fence that the gale had damaged. There was always something to do in a garden.

A farmer near Bedford noticed some tyre marks when he was walking along a track on his land that afternoon. It was a public footpath, but at that time of year was not used a great deal. It was not suitable for cars, yet a vehicle had been along there recently. The tyre marks showed distinctly where the ground was damp and muddy. They ended abruptly. The car had reversed out, he thought. There had been very little rain since the previous week when there were gales and storms, but even so the driver was lucky not to get stuck.

Broken twigs at the side of the path caught his eye. The undergrowth was beaten down where someone had blundered through it to the spinney beyond. Cursing under his breath, imagining at best empty beer tins deposited among the small trees and bushes, but more likely larger items of rubbish, for people thought nothing of using your land as a tip, he followed the trail of damage.

He saw the piles of leaves heaped up higher than the surrounding area. Because he was expecting to find an old cooker, a chair, or a broken bicycle, his reactions were slow, and at first he did not connect what he saw with the recent appeals in the press. He took little notice of missing girls. He bent and moved some of the leaves from the long, low mound. There was freshly turned earth beneath.

He still thought only of rubbish, dumped by someone tidier

than usual who'd taken the trouble to bury it, but he burrowed a little at the side of the mound. He touched something cold, and moved more earth away. His fingers felt other fingers, the cold, dead touch of a human hand.

15

On Sunday morning the Jowetts set out to church. When Matins were held in Netherton St Mary they never missed, but they did not attend family services, where children ran freely about the aisles and played in the chancel, and strange, jolly hymns were sung. The vicar was shepherd of a far-flung flock, for the parish had been combined with Stokebourne and Cerne St Mary, and, on his motor-bike, he travelled from one to the other. He was a short, sturdy man, a youthful forty, keen on cricket, and he mortified himself by playing it a great deal during the summer for various village teams he had helped to organize. The mortification came from being unable to watch better matches on television when obliged to field long-stop on the village pitch.

Guy couldn't get on with the fellow, as he grumblingly put it, and had given up reading the lesson, a duty he and before him his forebears had undertaken, with rare breaks during wars and the like, for generations.

Heather endured the services. At least, during them, she knew where Guy was, and could let her mind stray, even doze unobtrusively during the long, uncompelling sermons. Sometimes she gazed at the commemorative plates on the wall, several referring to the Jowetts from long ago, and she would think of the grave outside, where Robin lay. Occasionally, she would yearn to lie there too, tranquil at last, but she must survive Guy, for his fate, if she were not there to protect him, would be grim.

As the vicar exhorted them to be like little children and trust their troubles to the One Above, Heather, seated beside her own elderly child who was fidgeting restlessly, turned her thoughts to the greenhouse, where, although she could not afford heat, she raised seedlings, and rehearsed in her mind what must be done with the plants wintering there.

Most of the congregation came to church by car, but unless it was wet, Guy and Heather walked.

'This generation will lose the use of its legs,' said Guy testily as they left, Heather in her old camel coat and green felt hat, Guy in his British warm. He made this remark every time they went. On the way back they kept to the side of the road while the cars of worshippers who were not going on to the pub dashed past.

'Why do we go to church?' Heather said suddenly as they turned down their lane. She put her hand through Guy's arm.

'To set an example,' said Guy firmly.

It's habit, thought Heather. Neither of us believes in all that any more, but Guy still sees himself as the squire, with a role to perform. She sighed.

'I don't suppose anyone notices,' she said. 'Not even the vicar.'

There was sherry, however, when they got home, and hand of pork, already in the oven. Afterwards, Heather sent Guy off for his rest while she sat down in the drawing room with the paper. They lit the fire early on Sundays, and today it was drawing well. With her chair pulled close to the hearth, she was warm. Soon, she slept.

When she woke, the light was fading. She got up and went to see if Guy was still sleeping. Their bedroom was above the kitchen and was warmed by the Aga.

She must wake him, or he wouldn't sleep tonight.

Heather opened the bedroom door and went in.

Guy was not there, and the bed was undisturbed. It looked as if he had not rested at all. But he'd had his pills; she'd mixed them into his sprouts. The familiar dread swept over her as she rushed upstairs to see if he had gone to the studio, but it was empty. Heather hunted all over the house. Sometimes he went to Robin's room, and would sit there in the cold, gazing at nothing.

He was not there today. He was nowhere to be found. She ran round the garden, hair blowing wildly, calling his name, seeking him in the dusk, but without success. Before going out in the car to search for him, she telephoned Nina, as she would have telephoned Priscilla, in case he had gone to the Hall, but there was no reply.

Walking up the path to Dan's front door, Nina felt self-conscious. The young man from the adjoining house was washing his car and looked at her curiously as she and Rory arrived.

'Good afternoon,' said Nina, nodding austerely.

'Hullo,' said the young man. He smiled pleasantly. Nina was sure he was wondering what lay behind her visit. He'd tell his wife about her, she thought uncomfortably, and they'd laugh. It didn't matter, she told herself; she knew few people in the village, and she would be leaving in a few weeks.

Dan was watching for her, and the door opened before she could ring. He was wearing a suit. It was a good suit, dark grey and well cut, and with it he wore a pale blue shirt and a narrow maroon tie. He looked quite unlike the handyman who fetched coal every day at the Hall and brought logs in to pile by the hearth. Nina was taken aback; her gracious condescension was, perhaps, misplaced.

He took her coat and put it on a hanger which he hung in a cupboard under the stairs.

'I noticed your neighbour washing his car,' said Nina, unable to think of a better opening remark.

'Ah yes – young Tom. They're a nice couple,' said Dan. 'Sometimes I baby-sit for them.'

'Do you?'

'Why not? It's only next door. I watch their television instead of my own,' said Dan. 'They're good to me – they give me cakes and puddings.'

They were standing close together in the narrow hall. A faint, fresh scent came from Dan: aftershave, Nina recognized, with a pang.

'Come along,' Dan said, quite masterfully, ushering her into the long, narrow living-room which ran the whole width of the house. A large tank of fish occupied a table at one side of the room, and a bright fire blazed in the hearth. Rory wandered

121

about looking for a spot for himself and finally slumped down on the hearthrug. Nina, not yet at ease, had already walked past the fish so she looked through the french window at the garden. She saw a neatly pared lawn, tidy beds planted with a few rose bushes but mainly given over to fruit and vegetables. Bright green netting was draped over the winter greens to protect them from marauding wood pigeons.

'What a model garden,' she said.

'Yes. It doesn't take long to keep neat,' said Dan. 'Now you can see why I was pleased to have the chance of looking after the Hall garden. I've plenty of time. It's a pleasant second career.'

'What was your first one?' asked Nina, genuinely curious.

'I was a civil servant,' he replied. 'Do sit down.'

What sort of civil servant, Nina wondered, taking the wing armchair he was indicating. She decided that it would be impertinent to ask.

The tea things were laid on a long coffee table. There were pretty bone china cups and saucers, decorated with delicate flowers. When Dan went out to make the tea, Nina looked at the bottom of one cup; it was Spode. He soon returned, carrying a plate of hot scones as well as the teapot. Rory was given part of a scone, though Nina said she didn't give him titbits at meals. She found herself telling Dan how anxious she had been about undertaking the care of him, but how fond of him she had grown.

'I've never really lived in the country before,' she said. 'We called it the country, in Surrey, where I used to live. There are lots of nice houses with big gardens, and there are woods and common land, but not many real villages.'

'Netherton St Mary used to be an agricultural village,' said Dan. 'I mean, the old cottages were the homes of farm workers and so on. Not now. Most of them have been done up for commuters. There aren't too many of the real village folk left. Still, I like to see the youngsters about, like the Morrises next door. But they come and go. They change their jobs.' He stopped talking while he poured out the tea gravely, with concentration, then asked her about Jenny and Sarah. After that, conversation faltered. Nina had eaten a slice of excellent fruit cake as well as a scone. He had made both, it transpired.

He was a better cook than Heather Jowett seemed to be, she thought wryly. Now it was time to get to the purpose of her visit, and then she could leave.

'Your daughter,' she said. 'You were going to show me some photographs.'

He had been waiting for it; the albums were ready on the sideboard. At his suggestion, they moved to the sofa, where they could sit side by side as he turned the pages. Nina remembered the other albums she had looked at the week before, the likeness she thought she had seen, as she admired photographs of Susie as a baby; as a solemn, plump toddler with bucket and spade on a beach; as a serious schoolgirl; and as a bridesmaid in a long yellow dress. She saw pictures of Dan's wife, Ellen, a round-faced woman with a mild expression.

'I've got a lot of newspaper clippings, too,' Dan said. 'From when she died, you know.'

Nina feared he meant her to see them. She had run out of comment – 'Oh, what a sweet little girl', and 'Where was this taken?' and so on, and felt unequal to the change of emotion the grim newspaper reports must evoke.

'I'm sure it must upset you to look at them,' she said.

'It does,' Dan agreed. 'But I have to, sometimes. I can never forget.'

He wanted to show them to Nina; he wanted to tell her the whole story. She was so calm and sympathetic, so soft and feminine, sitting there beside him. But now she was standing up, speaking to Rory, saying that she must go home. The moment had passed.

Nina, however, was not going home. She was returning to a large, empty house where she constantly answered the telephone to a ghost who never spoke.

Dan wanted to drive her back; he didn't mind Rory in his car at all, he said, but Nina replied that the walk would be good for them. It wasn't raining, and Rory needed the exercise. He'd see her home, then, Dan suggested: walk with her. But Nina said this wasn't necessary. She had brought a torch, which she'd need for the last part of the way, where there were no street lights. She left, thanking him for the tea, fearing he would insist, hurrying off before he could put on his coat, her footsteps echoing as she hastened away.

Dan felt flat, let down, as he turned back to the house. It seemed empty, now she had gone. A cushion on the sofa was crushed where she had leaned against it, and he imagined her scent hung on the air. He left the cushion as it was to remind him that she had really been there, in the room. Slowly he set about clearing away the tea things and washing them up, putting away the good china he never used when alone.

Nina met a few people on their way to chapel as she hurried back to the Hall. She didn't like the last part of the journey. In Surrey she would never have walked home from anywhere, except Felicity's or one of the other close neighbours. She drove to the shops and the houses of friends, and never went out of Silverlea's grounds on foot after dark. She liked lighted ways and people about unless she was in her own safe home. But her home had, in the end, turned out not to be safe after all and was no longer hers. Walking along, Nina thought of Caroline, who would be heavy, now, with her pregnancy. Did Martin still love her, desire her? Would she, perhaps, have a son?

I smothered him, Nina thought suddenly. I made him everything – there were the girls, of course, but Martin was really the centre, to me. What a burden I must have been! One human being can't be the whole of life to another, it's asking too much. She felt tears rise to her eyes as she walked on with her troublesome thoughts. She was doing a lot of weeping these days. Rory seemed to sense her distress and he snuffled beside her, pressing against her leg. A few cars passed, and one cyclist who made her jump, coming up behind her and pedalling past in the dark. She'd been silly not to let Dan come with her, she thought. The truth was that she hadn't wanted to be seen walking along with him. She hadn't even wanted her car to be noticed outside his house, which was why she had walked there.

Why not, she asked herself, and knew that the answer lay in some difference she perceived between them. Yet what did it matter, even if it existed? And hardly anyone in the village knew who she was, anyway. Besides, what, precisely, was her own status? She was a house-minder and Dan was a gardener, but he had been a civil servant and he possessed good china and a well-cut suit, and used after-shave.

With Martin appearances had mattered; they had mattered among their friends, too. Possessions had been important. One had to watch one's figure, and it was essential to give elegant parties. When all that was torn away, what was left? Who cared, now, if she wore the knitted two-piece that was three years old? All you needed as a house-minder in Netherton St Mary were a padded anorak, slacks and green wellies, she thought, turning in at the Hall gate.

She had left lights burning, but she was relieved to let herself into the house at last. Because she came in by the back door she did not find Heather's note for over an hour, for she went straight to the study to stoke up the fire. Then she turned on the television for company. She went upstairs at last, to hang up her coat and wash her face, for she had done some more crying sitting in front of the television. In the bathroom, she looked at the pottery cat, still smirking on the sill, and called it a few names aloud, the worst she could think of. If she dropped it in a river or pond, perhaps Caroline would fall into the canal near her flat or meet some other watery fate. In her mind, she rehearsed the doorbell ringing, and Martin revealed on the step, returned to his senses, begging forgiveness. Part of her, in this dream, cast herself eagerly into his arms; but another part, the emerging cold, independent part, stood back and slammed the door.

Walking downstairs again, planning to have a glass of the Blunts' sherry to cheer herself up, Nina noticed the square of paper on the mat by the front door.

4.40 p.m. Guy missing again, she read. *Please ring if you've seen him. Have looked round outside. Heather.*

Oh dear, Nina thought. Then she felt a spurt of excitement. There was something urgent to do, if he were still lost, for she must help to find him. But Heather's note was written some time ago and by now he might have turned up. The first thing to do was to find out.

There was no reply when she telephoned the Manor. Did that mean that Heather was still out searching for him? Nina hadn't noticed her car as she walked back from Dan's, and surely, if Heather had recognized her in the darkness – and she might, because Rory was with her – she would have stopped. She may have been searching further afield. Nina stood by the telephone wondering what was the most effective help she could give. Then she decided. She fed Rory and told him to guard the house, locked him in, and went out to the garage, leaving a great many lights on in the house as well as those outside.

She drove straight to the Manor. Lights were on there, too, but no one came when she pressed the bell. She tried the door and found it unlocked. Nina went in to the house and called out, but there was no reply. She called several times and looked in the downstairs rooms, but the place was deserted. Heather had abandoned thoughts of security, Nina thought, for she must often have to leave the place open like this while she went off searching for Guy in case he came back on his own. Presumably she knew his favourite spots, and if he liked a particular walk she would search there. Was she combing the bridle paths in the dark?

Nina had brought a torch. She walked round the side of the house to the yard where Heather kept her Mini in a garage which must once have been part of the stables. Nina saw that the doors stood open and the car was out. As at the Hall, there were considerable outbuildings here, and these were really old. She felt curious. Besides, she thought, justifying the exploration she wanted to make, Guy might have wandered back and be in one of the sheds or whatever they were: dairies, perhaps, or still-rooms. She opened a door and looked in, shining her torch.

The room revealed was long and narrow, with whitewashed walls. There was a saddle horse at one side of it, with three saddles on it, a small felt child's one and an old, worn leather one with knee rolls. The third was a strong, well-arched one. Nina touched them. The leather was dry. Wasn't saddlery very expensive these days? Why didn't the Jowetts sell them? Even a few pounds for the three would be a help, buy some treats, several bottles of sherry at least. But the daughter was keen on horses, she remembered, and the grand-daughter too. She saw some bridles, with rusting bits and curb-chains, hanging from hooks on the wall. At the rear of the room a staircase ascended to some sort of loft beyond. Nina, so nervous at the Hall, felt no fear here; she was too much intrigued by the Jowetts and their lives. She mounted the stairs. A door at the top was locked, but the key was there. Nina turned it and went into the room, shining her torch around. She saw a light switch by the door. It would hardly be working, she thought, but when she pressed it, the light came on, a single low bulb hanging from the raftered roof.

Nina saw a row of galvanized bins. They were for corn, of course, she thought, and opened one, expecting it to be empty. She peered in, her body coming between the light and the bin, and, not believing what she was seeing, she shone her torch inside.

The bin was filled with canvases. Nina reached in and lifted one out. It was a landscape with dark, rod-like trees protruding from a vivid background. Next to it, a smaller grey painting depicted tiny human figures standing in groups with huts in the background and, to the front, rolls of what was meant, she supposed, to be barbed wire. There were more of the same, and some English landscapes with fields of cut corn standing in stooks. How old-fashioned, thought Nina; today, it was instantly harvested by those monster machines you met on the road in the summer.

All the bins were filled with paintings. There were several trunks and boxes in the loft too, and they also contained paintings. A door in the far wall opened into a further loft. There was no light in here. Nina shone her torch round and saw some more pictures covered in sacks and black polythene bags. There were a few bales of straw here, and some musty hay, and in one wall was a solid door secured by a strong wooden bar that dropped into sockets. Slowly Nina worked out its function: when open, hay or straw could be dropped directly into the yard below, or conversely, pitched up from a cart, to be stored.

She went back the way she had come, turning off the light and locking the door at the top of the stairs. She walked past the dry, cobwebby tack. Heather didn't sell the paintings at all, for no one would buy them. She hid them here, so that Guy wouldn't know. Meanwhile, he went on buying expensive canvas and paints, and Heather somehow deceived him into believing that he had been paid. She must fiddle the housekeeping to do it, unless he left all the budgeting to her. Nina felt stunned by what she had discovered.

She crossed the yard and returned to the house. Heather had not come back, and neither, it seemed, had Guy. What could she do? Perhaps Guy had been hurt or was ill, and Heather had taken him to the doctor, or even to hospital? She might even, Nina supposed, have asked the police to find him, but would they bother much about an old man? They couldn't do a lot in the dark, whoever was lost, she thought, old man, child or young girl.

She went into the house and searched for some paper so that she could leave Heather a note. In the kitchen, she found a pad and a stubby pencil on the window.

Sorry to miss you. Found your note and called in 7.30 but no one at home. Telephone if I can do anything. Nina, she wrote. That would do, even if Guy was the one to find it. She left it on the kitchen table.

She drove slowly back to the Hall, looking carefully along the road in case the tall figure was somewhere about, but she met no one.

16

The whistle had proved effective; Nina's mystery caller had not telephoned since she blew it a week ago. But that evening Nina wished the telephone would ring; she wanted to hear from Heather that Guy had returned. Unable to bear the uncertainty any longer, at half-past nine she dialled the Manor, but there was no reply. After that she rang again at half-hourly intervals, but when there was still no answer at eleven o'clock, she decided there was no point in staying up, for Heather, unless in real trouble, would be unlikely to ring so late. Guy had doubtless returned, and Heather was probably too busy looking after him to answer the telephone.

Before she went to bed, Nina took down one of the old photograph albums and glanced through it again. There were the boys, as like as the brothers she felt convinced they must be.

There was Guy, a dark, handsome, smiling man. Odd things had happened during the war and contraception had been uncertain before the Pill. Men had been away for years, but it was Guy who had been the prisoner of war. Where was Leonard Blunt then? Had he been at sea? What form had his naval career taken? The albums provided no answer to that. Marriage was a strange, private affair which no outsider could understand. When the Jowetts and Blunts were young, people divorced less easily than today. What had happened between the two couples then? They all seemed to be close friends now, and Heather and Guy appeared to be devoted to one another. Heather must love Guy dearly to deceive him over the paintings, and there was no doubt that he was utterly dependent upon her. Apart from a wish to understand, Nina felt great concern for them.

As she got ready for bed, she thought about her own future. She must decide where to go when the Blunts returned. She could put an advertisement in the *Lady*, seeking another house-minding post. Now that the telephone calls had stopped, she was sleeping better; it was not a demanding job, and one lived in comfort, since those willing to pay for the service had well-equipped homes, but it was solitary, and offered no great challenge. As a career for the rest of her life, it lacked allure, but it might see her through for a while. She didn't want to plant herself on Sarah and Jeremy for more than a night or two; and with Martin and Caroline due to move into Silverlea, she couldn't visit Felicity or any other friends in the area; it would be painful for her, and embarrassing for those who now had to accept Caroline – as they would, and quickly, Nina knew. Turning it round in her mind, Nina switched out her light and snuggled under the bedclothes, drifting towards sleep.

Some time later a small sound made her start up, wide awake, heart thumping. She clutched the blankets round her. What had she heard? It couldn't be Rory; he was shut into the back lobby by the boiler, where he spent every night, and it wasn't a barking noise. He'd bark, wouldn't he, if an intruder had entered the house? She could hear her own alarmed, rapid pulse pounding in her ears. Were there burglars downstairs? She was here to defend the house, so she ought to find out, but what she had read about robberies came into her mind. She'd be mugged, if she surprised them. Let them take the silver and Meissen, she thought. It was certain to be insured.

But the craven nature of these thoughts made her ashamed. How could she face the Blunts and say she had done nothing to protect their possessions? She could slip along the passage to their bedroom and ring up the police from that extension, then lock herself in until help came.

She'd better not put on her bedroom light in case there was someone outside, even now, on the landing, although the sound she thought she had heard had seemed to come from somewhere deep in the house, not near. She always kept a torch on the bedside table, and she switched it on, waiting tensely for her bedroom door to burst open and masked raiders appear. Nothing happened. She got out of bed, put on her dressing gown and slippers, then moved quietly to the door. Gingerly, she turned the handle and opened it, peering cautiously out. There wasn't a sound. Had she imagined the noise? She would look pretty silly if she called the police and it was a false alarm. But perhaps what she heard had been the burglars departing? Although, if so, they'd been quick; she hadn't been in bed very long – less than an hour.

The landing and hall lights were on, as she left them every night. Nina went down the wide front stairs clutching the torch, which would be a weapon of sorts, if required. She listened outside the dining-room door and could hear no sound from within. Greatly daring, she opened the door. The room was in darkness and she switched on the light. All was tranquil. No thieves were there and the silver was still on the sideboard. The drawing room was empty, too, and undisturbed. She must have imagined the sound.

At the end of the passage was the study. A burglar would surely make off with the valuable objects in the dining-room and the drawing-room before trying his luck in here, she thought, but she had better make certain. She turned the handle of the study door.

The first surprise she received was the fact that the light was on. Because the passage was lit, she had not seen the bar of light under the door. She must have forgotten to turn it off when she went to bed, she decided, reaching out for the switch. Her heart seemed to stop as a figure, invisible when she opened the door because the high back of the wing armchair, where he sat, was turned towards her, rose as she entered the room.

'Where is he?' asked Guy, advancing towards Nina with arms outstretched. 'Where is our son?'

Nina felt sick with shock as Guy approached, but she knew there was no need to be afraid of him. She took a step forward round the side of the chair. In the soft light from the shaded wall fixtures, her fair hair shone round her small head like a halo.

'Hold me again, my darling,' said Guy.

His mind must have snapped completely. Did he think she was Heather? Nina concentrated on taking some deep breaths to steady her racing heart. What could she say to him? Robin, his son, was dead.

Now Guy was close to her, arms wide. Nina hesitated, then took a small step backwards.

'Oh, don't go away again,' said Guy. 'Please.'

In a detached way, Nina had already recognized in Guy the wreck of a once sexually attractive man who was still handsome. Now, as he reached for her, she made a conscious decision not to retreat for fear of confusing him even further. To her own astonishment she felt a faint, half-forgotten physical flutter as he touched her. It was not difficult to let him put his arms round her, enfold her against him. He was so tall that the top of her head came level with his chin. She felt soft kisses on her hair, and a gentle hand stroked it.

'You were always such a little thing,' he said. 'Such a naughty little thing.'

He thought she was Priscilla! Nina's heart thundered as she tried to think how Priscilla would answer.

'It was so long ago,' she said. 'Sit down, Guy.'

'Charles has to be told,' said Guy. 'There are things I must ask him to do. Duties to the future.'

'Yes, my dear,' said Nina. 'We'll talk about it.' Though her pulse was still racing, she felt calm. She must avoid disturbing him even further. She took his two hands in hers. They felt very thin and soft as she moved them away from her body. 'Sit down, Guy,' she repeated.

'Yes,' said Guy, and drew her back with him towards the

sofa. His hands were still linked with Nina's as he subsided into it, pulling her with him.

'I'm too heavy,' she protested, as he held her so that she sat on his lap.

'You never used to be,' said Guy. 'Please stay, my darling.'

Nina thought his old thigh bones might crack. She felt ridiculous and had a wild urge to giggle. She had never sat on any man's knee since her father died; such a posture had not been part of her life with Martin. As the impulse to laugh died, she felt a wave of panic. Surely he wouldn't want – ? Her mind refused to pursue this thought.

But Guy had drawn her to him. He tucked her head against his shoulder. She felt light, passionless kisses on her hair.

'Charles,' he said. 'Where is Charles? I must talk to him. It's important. I keep ringing up and some strange woman answers the phone – never you, never Charles. Not even Leonard.'

Now Nina's poor, overstrained heart began battering away again in her chest.

'You've been ringing up?' she gasped.

'Yes. When poor Heather is having her bath. Then some strange thing happened – my ears – I had a headache,' said Guy. 'I forget.'

Guy was the phantom caller! And she, with the whistle, had made an assault upon him – this poor, foolish, harmless old man. Aghast, Nina made a fractional move towards him.

'Why do you want to speak to Charles?' she asked softly.

'It's Heather. He must take care of Heather,' said Guy. 'And the house. I want it to stay in the family.'

'I'll tell him,' said Nina. 'Don't worry, Guy.'

'Promise?'

'Yes,' Nina said.

'Ah,' said Guy. 'Good.'

She felt him relax as she lay there against him, keeping very still, letting him hold her. Gradually her own tension eased and she felt oddly comforted, though she began to fear that he would get cramp. His grasp round her slackened and his breathing grew slower. He had fallen asleep.

Nina must somehow get herself off his lap without waking him. Heather must be told he was safe; she would be frantic with worry by now. But what if he went rambling on like this, about Charles, when he went home? And the telephone calls – if only she'd known! At least she could somehow have humoured him; she wouldn't have been afraid, and she wouldn't have blasted his ears with the whistle.

Very gently she moved his arm, limp now, and heavy, from around her, and slid her own body down sideways, on to the sofa away from him. He stirred slightly, turning his head, and gave a little moan, but he did not wake. He must have been wandering about for hours, she supposed, and was exhausted. Where had he been? Hiding here, in the house, while she was out and while Heather was searching for him? How had he got in? She knew she had locked up properly. Had he loved Priscilla all these years, continuing their affair under Heather's nose? That was an awful thought, but such things happened. Yet his present concern seemed to be for his wife – and, she remembered, the Manor.

It was Heather who mattered now. Nina got to her feet and stood looking down at Guy. He had moved a little, resting more on his side, and she bent and lifted his long legs, laying them on the sofa. He did not wake. Nina went upstairs and fetched two blankets which she brought down to the study. He had not stirred. Gently, she unlaced his heavy brogues and slid them off. He grunted, but slept on. Nina draped the blankets over him, tucking them round him, her hand lingering a little, caressingly, as a mother would with a child.

Then she went upstairs to telephone Heather from the bedroom extension where she would not disturb Guy.

What if Heather were still out, searching? As she dialled the number, Nina worried about the course to take, but the telephone was answered after a single ring.

'Oh, thank God,' Heather said, 'I'll come round at once and collect him.'

Nina had said she had woken up and come downstairs, thinking she heard a noise, and that Guy was asleep in the study, implying that she had found him like that. She couldn't begin to relate their conversation to Heather.

'Why don't you leave him?' she said now. 'He looks as if he'll sleep all night.' If Guy were to be woken suddenly, what might he not say? He might become more disturbed than ever. Nina had a strong desire to protect Heather from discovering what she was sure had, so far, been kept secret from her. 'I've already put some blankets over him,' Nina went on. 'His clothes are quite dry and the room is warm. You must be exhausted, yourself. Why don't you go to bed now and come round in the morning?'

'He mustn't be left,' Heather said. 'I'll come round and stay in the study with him.'

'I'll do that,' Nina said. 'I can make a bed from the two armchairs – you're too tall to do that comfortably. I'll be all right. You'd do better to have a good night's sleep yourself in case he's a bit confused tomorrow, when he finds where he is.'

'It's not your responsibility,' said Heather.

'It won't hurt me,' Nina said.

'Oh Nina – you tempt me,' said Heather. 'I'm so cold and tired – I've been out over the fields with a torch. God knows where he's been. How did he get into the Hall?'

'I've no idea,' said Nina truthfully.

'Perhaps you left something unlocked,' Heather said.

This was no time to insist that she knew she had not. Nina let it pass.

'You have a bath and a good hot drink,' she advised. 'Take some pills, if you've got any. You needn't worry about Guy – I won't let him escape.' Her own firm, authoritative tone amazed Nina, who had seldom before, in her life, taken a lead.

Heather gave in.

'Very well. I'll be round first thing if you don't ring before,' she said. 'You will ring, if he wakes?'

Nina crossed her fingers.

'Yes, of course,' she said.

'I don't know how to thank you,' said Heather.

As she hung up, Nina thought that Heather might feel less grateful if she knew that a blast from a whistle blown by Nina had given Guy a headache and led – for surely it must have done – to this increased deterioration.

She fetched a pillow and blankets from her own bed and took them downstairs. Before turning out the study light she made up the fire, quietly, blessing Dan for leaving such a good supply of fuel in the house. Nina looked at Guy as he lay shrouded in blankets, a bundle on the large sofa. A lock of his hair had fallen over his face. He looked stripped, defenceless. An immense pity surged in Nina. It was hard to picture him as a bold adulterer, yet he was. She remembered Priscilla Blunt at their three meetings: neat, petite, composed – kind, too, showing sympathy for Nina. Was it the sympathy that sprang from her own guilt? Nina saw that she and Priscilla could be described as physically alike. Perhaps her arrival had disturbed Guy – revived old memories. Yet the first telephone call was made before they had met. He might have had an emotional parting from Priscilla Blunt before she left on her trip. Nina thought she would never learn all the answers. She turned out the light and clambered into her makeshift bed, which was snug and comfortable. The flickering firelight cast shadows round the room. In an odd way, it was nice not to be alone.

She woke to find Guy gazing at her. He was sitting up straight at one end of the sofa, his hair brushed, the blankets she had arranged over him tidily folded, his feet neatly together. The curtains had been drawn back, and the morning light poured in.

Nina blinked at him, surfacing, remembering.

'Mrs Crowther, please don't be alarmed,' Guy said when he saw that she was awake. He struggled to his feet, and then, fearing his height might make him appear to loom threateningly over her, sat down again. 'I seem to have been here some time,' he added.

'Er – yes,' agreed Nina. 'All night, really.'

She put her hands to her hair, patting it, trying to make it lie down, and he smiled at her.

'Your hair looks nice. In fact, you look charming,' he said, and an almost impish expression crossed his face, so that he seemed to shed years.

'Yes, well, thank you,' said Nina. How to extract herself in a seemly manner from the nest made by the two chairs was her immediate problem. She felt with her toe, under the blankets, for the edge of the chair on which her legs rested, and gave it a kick. It moved away, and she stood up in a smooth movement, making sure her dressing-gown was effectively fastened across her, a hand at her throat.

Now an alarmed look had come over Guy's face.

'I hope I didn't – I hope nothing –' he floundered.

'You don't remember?' asked Nina.

'No,' said Guy. Then he asked, hesitantly, 'Was I looking for my son?'

'Yes,' said Nina.

'How foolish of me. He's dead,' Guy stated firmly. 'Robin died in a sailing accident when he was a young man.' He gazed steadily at Nina as he said this.

'I know,' she said. 'It's very sad.' Could he really have forgotten their interlude in the night?

'Heather will be anxious,' he said. 'I must go home, but I didn't want to leave without an apology to you for whatever –' he waved a vague hand.

'I telephoned her last night,' Nina said. 'She had been out looking for you and was very tired. We arranged that she would come round and collect you this morning. I promised to stay with you, in case you woke during the night.'

He accepted this explanation without comment.

'You're sure I haven't – I didn't – that my conduct – ?' Guy wanted reassurance.

'Nothing improper happened,' said Nina primly, but well might he ask, the bad old man.

'I slept well,' he said. 'So did you, I think. You looked enchanting, when I woke up. You still do, in your pretty dressing-gown.'

Nina was suddenly aware of her bare feet. She looked round for her slippers, kicked off last night.

'I went upstairs and had a bath in Leonard's bathroom,' said Guy. 'I found a spare razor.'

'Oh – did you? I didn't hear you go,' Nina said.

'I tried to be quiet,' Guy said.

She'd been certain she'd wake if he stirred. What if he'd left the house? He might have got lost again.

She found her slippers and put them on.

'Breakfast,' she said. 'What do you normally have? An egg?' Perhaps an egg, like a scone, was a treat?

'A boiled egg would be nice,' said Guy. 'I'll prepare it, and one for you, too, while you dress. I know where everything is in this house.' He paused, and went on, 'Including a spare set of keys.' He took them from his pocket and showed them to her. 'I'll let Rory out,' he added.

He'd lapse again, Nina felt sure as she went upstairs. This sharp grasp of events must be just temporary; perhaps, after a sort of collapse, he improved – a seesaw effect. She had the feeling that he had not totally forgotten what had happened during the night. Did he remember the promise he had extracted from her?

They had slept late, she discovered. It was after nine by the time they were eating their eggs and drinking their coffee. Guy had capably laid the table in the kitchen, and made toast. They were just finishing their breakfast when Dan arrived with the paper. He looked very surprised when he came into the kitchen and found them both there, and the eager expression he had on his face died away.

He can't imagine we slept together, thought Nina. But we did, literally, she told herself, almost giggling aloud.

It was none of Dan's business.

17

It was after ten o'clock when Heather arrived. She came racing up the drive, scattering gravel on either side and watched disapprovingly by Dan, who had lit a bonfire at the end of the garden and was out fiercely raking up stray loose twigs and rubbish. Flames crackled and sparks soared into the sky as he added the withered tops of michaelmas daisies and hardy chrysanthemums to his pyre. His first shock at seeing Guy in the kitchen began to disperse as he recognized the probable innocence behind his presence in the house. The colonel was known to be vague and forgetful. Perhaps Mrs Jowett had been away for the night and Mrs Crowther had been looking after him, as a child would have to be cared for in its mother's absence.

The night before, after Nina's call, Heather had taken two of Guy's tranquillizers and a hot whisky. Only then had her shivering stopped. She had been severely shocked by Guy's prolonged disappearance; always, before, if he had not returned home on his own, she had managed to find him fairly soon. She had confidence in Nina's efficiency, and knew that after one of his escapades Guy always slept soundly for hours, exhausted by whatever demon had driven him out to roam around. It made sense to get what rest she could, Heather had decided. The drug, to which she was not accustomed, and the whisky, took effect, and she slept heavily, waking late. Automatically, Heather reached out for Guy in the morning, but she was alone in the large four-poster bed. Her head was muzzy. It took her some minutes to wake up properly and recall what had happened. Then, in haste, she swung her thin, muscular legs out of the bed and scurried along the landing to the chilly bathroom to splash cold water on to her face. She brushed her teeth, dressed quickly in her shapeless everyday skirt and sweater, thick patterned tights and stout shoes, and went out to the car.

She entered the Hall without ringing, by the back door, and found Guy and Nina sitting together in the study in peaceful silence. Guy was reading the paper and Nina was working at some embroidery. When Heather burst into the room, Nina slipped out to let them get their reunion over in privacy.

She went upstairs to fetch Guy's coat, which she had found that morning when she went round the house drawing back the curtains. It was lying on Priscilla's bed. The cushions on the chaise longue in her bedroom were crushed. Guy must have waited there for the house to be quiet before going down to the study. Nina had drawn the curtains early that afternoon because she was going out to tea, otherwise she might have found him sooner. He must have been up there while she ate her solitary supper, had her bath, thought herself alone. Though she wasn't afraid of Guy, it was alarming to know that he had been there all that time. She wondered about the set of keys he had shown her, unnerved to think they existed. No doubt he used them to visit Priscilla when Leonard was up in the London flat. Had the Spanish couple known what was going on? Probably not, in their remote flat at the top of the house.

She watched the Jowetts drive off; both seemed calm. What

would happen now? Would Guy paint more useless pictures for Heather to conceal? As he left, he had taken Nina's hand and pressed it, gazing into her eyes, nothing feeble or confused in either his touch or his direct regard. Replaying the moment in her mind, Nina recognized his charm. This was the man who had terrified her with his telephone calls.

When they had gone, Nina found it hard to settle down for the rest of the day. Dan was silent when he came in for his coffee; she had to call him from the garden, though now he usually came in promptly at eleven without being summoned.

Offering him a digestive biscuit, Nina said, 'I enjoyed coming to tea with you yesterday,' in an effort to mollify him.

Dan had spent the evening before weaving a plan to invite her to the cinema. There was a good film on in Droxton, one that had had acclaim and seemed suitable to watch with someone you didn't know well: so many films, these days, could be embarrassing under such circumstances. They could have a meal first, at the Star Hotel, which was staidly respectable and had a reputation for good food. Now, he would not risk a rebuff. An intimate of the Jowetts, she had moved away from him.

He made no reply to Nina's remark, so she asked a question about something that was, to her, more important.

'Does Charles Blunt come down here much?' She couldn't find out from anyone else in the village.

'Not a lot, no,' said Dan.

'What's he like?' Nina pursued.

'Pleasant enough.' Dan made an effort. 'He's been married twice,' he said. 'There was a divorce. It was all in the paper. Sandra, next door, was quite interested – gossip, you know. His new wife's half his age. They haven't been married long.'

A chip off the old block, thought Nina.

'Any children?' she asked.

'I don't think so,' said Dan, and went on abruptly, 'I'm going to London tomorrow. I'll bring you in plenty of fuel today.'

'Isn't Friday your usual day?' Nina asked.

'Yes, but I didn't go up last week,' said Dan. 'I suppose I can please myself, go when I like.' He'd decided to go to the bus station at Victoria to avoid the police. Plenty of people travelled long distances by coach as well as by train, and he'd found young girls at the terminal there, before.

'Of course – I'm sorry,' said Nina.

But her apology did not placate him.

'You can always go down to the Manor for company,' he said.

How prickly he had become, Nina thought. She shrugged. What did it matter? She'd soon be leaving here anyway; a few ruffled feathers were of no account. She made no reply, turning away from him, taking her cup to the sink. On her mind was the problem of Charles, and what to do about the promise Guy had extracted from her on Sunday night. He'd probably forgotten all about it by now, but if not, what was to prevent him from getting in touch with Charles himself? Couldn't he write? Or did Heather intercept his mail?

There was no need, she decided, for any immediate action.

In the car going home, both Jowetts behaved as though nothing out of the ordinary had occurred. They discussed the weather. The sun was out, filtering palely through the trees to which, since the recent gales, only a few leaves still clung.

'We'll have a treat today,' Heather said, stopping at the newsagent's. 'I'll see if they've got a *Times* left.' They couldn't afford it now, and took a paper only on Sundays, relying on the television and the radio for the news.

Guy waited while she went into the shop and took her turn to be served. People were buying their magazines and paying accounts. Heather kept glancing anxiously out to make sure he was still in the car. There was no spare *Times*. Heather rejected the *Sun*, which was all that remained, so the newsagent rummaged about in a pile of papers at the back of the shop and produced a *Mail* he'd intended to read himself, which she took. It might help to keep Guy quiet for a couple of hours.

She expected him, when they reached the Manor, to go straight to the cloakroom or to the kitchen sink to wash, but he did not. He took off his coat, hung it up, and then went into the drawing-room where he sat in his usual chair. The room was cold, with the heating off and the fire unlit, and to go there at this hour was never part of the weekly routine. This was painting time. However, Heather stopped by the grate and began to clean out the ashes.

'You shouldn't be doing that my dear,' Guy said. 'Why haven't we got some help in the house? What happened to that woman – what was her name?'

'Oh Guy, you know she had to leave and we decided to manage without,' said Heather.

'Well, it's not right. You ought to have help,' Guy said.

Protesting would be useless. Heather couldn't have anyone in the house who might discover how vague Guy had become, but she promised to look about for someone. He'd soon forget.

'That's a nice woman Priscilla's found,' Guy said. 'Pretty, too. Why isn't she with her husband?'

'They've parted, I think,' said Heather. 'Surely I told you?'

'Hmph,' said Guy. Perhaps she had. He forgot such a lot these days, but oddly, today, his memory was sharp.

Heather went out of the room to fetch kindling. When she returned, he had put on his glasses and was glancing at the paper, though he had already read Nina's. He looked up as she stooped to her task, briefly seeing not a tall, scrawny woman in an ill-fitting skirt and loose, slightly matted sweater, with untidy grey hair framing a weatherbeaten face, but a thin, leggy girl, full of spirit but shy, whom he had met when he went to a ball in that perilous time just before the war. No young person, now, could understand the mood of those days: the excitement; the danger; the challenge.

'We were brave,' he said aloud.

'Brave? Who?' asked Heather.

'Our generation, when we were young,' said Guy. 'I'm sorry, Heather.'

'Whatever for?' said Heather. 'Darling, don't talk like this. We've been wonderfully happy.' She stood up, rather stiffly, and went over to perch on the arm of his chair, laying her hand on his knee. 'I've never loved anyone else,' she said. 'You know that.'

He did. He wished he could say as much.

He'd met Priscilla at the same ball. Leonard, whom Guy had known all his life, was also there and it all began then, for the four had often met at the same social functions after that night.

Guy had enjoyed watching Heather's shyness dissolve as she felt his charm. He had tried its effect on Priscilla, too, but she had soon seen which of the young men was the better prospect. Leonard already had his foot on a high rung of the ladder to his father's position; Guy, in the army, seemed to have no great ambition. Priscilla turned Guy down and married Leonard; three months later, Heather and Guy were married.

'We might get a dog,' Guy said, as Heather rose from the chair and returned to the grate. 'That labrador of Leonard's seems to give no trouble. It would be company for you, on your walks.'

'But Guy –' Heather felt the pulse in her throat flutter with fear. They'd had dogs in the past, and a cat too, who was intended to deal with the mice in the stables but spent most of his time in the house. When Guy developed his passion for cleanliness, he had refused to allow an animal into the house. 'They cost a lot to feed,' said Heather lamely. It would not do to remind him of his earlier attitudes.

She went out to the kitchen to see about lunch. He was, though apparently calm, in a mood she did not recognize. Would he go wandering off again? Could she find some excuse to hide his shoes? She didn't want to consult the doctor, who had years ago prescribed tranquillizers and renewed the prescription without any trouble when she telephoned, for she feared what he might say.

As always, she must just take each day as it came, she decided. He'd refused to take the pills the doctor had ordered. 'Quack's nonsense,' he'd said. So Heather had evolved her own method of seeing that they were swallowed, and ensuring, at the same time, an hour or two free from worry herself, while he slept.

Though relieved to have a name for the body found buried near the Droxton by-pass, Detective Superintendent Wilshaw was pessimistic about finding whoever had put her in her leafy grave. But now there was a new and similar victim, one whose body had been discovered only a week after she left home and disappeared. This time, clues might be found which would lead to the killer. There could be a connection between the two cases, and Wilshaw made contact with his opposite number in charge of the other case. If the police investigating Christine Potter's death made an arrest, it might be possible to prove the same person had killed Maureen Betts.

Frank Potter had been taken to the mortuary to identify his daughter. He had seen the sad little corpse, tidied up now, doll-like. He felt numb, totally unable to accept the fact of her death. No one said, in his presence, that girls of her age should not travel alone to London without having somewhere to stay. No one suggested that Frank had provoked her flight. Girls did these things, said the police officer who showed him the body. They made mountains from problems that could be resolved if only the girl and her parents could discuss them; perhaps they existed only in the young person's head, products of a too-active youthful imagination.

She had been strangled. The hyoid bone in her neck was fractured. At this stage, no one was going to volunteer the information that she had been sexually assaulted, but when Frank asked, he was given the answer.

The pathologist had learned a lot from the body. More information would follow when his report was complete but already the police knew that it had been moved after death. Hypostasis showed that it had lain on its side, probably with the legs drawn close to the chest. The theory was that Christine had been taken from the place of her death to the copse in a van or the boot of a car. If the vehicle could be found, it might reveal traces of Christine's presence – fragments of clothing, hair.

Enquiries in the area where she was found had brought results and the police were investigating every report of cars seen near the spot at the approximate time when she may have been taken there. Quite a lot of cars had travelled that way, and some had parked. A blue Cortina, the easiest type of car to steal, had been seen in a lay-by near the place on the night of Christine's disappearance, and a blue Cortina had been stolen from a street not far from Euston that same afternoon. Eventually, if necessary, all blue Cortinas registered on the computer would be tracked down and their owners questioned, but the stolen car might be found first.

There was another lead for the police to pursue: the man who had been seen at the station talking to young girls so regularly. His photofit picture had been prepared with the help of several witnesses and would be circulated to the police forces throughout the country. It would be issued to the media too. The police had something to go on now: the scent had not had time to grow cold.

Frank was taken home in a police car. When he arrived, the house was empty. Iris had taken all her clothes from the bedroom; her washing things were gone from the bathroom. Most strange of all, the place had been cleaned and polished from top to bottom until it shone, and there were flowers, a great mass of small pink chrysanthemums, in the lounge.

18

Nina had grown used to Dan's early arrival with the paper and she missed him on Tuesday morning. Later, she took Rory down to fetch it, and went on to the Manor. She was concerned about the Jowetts.

The house lay in a pool of winter sunlight as Nina walked up the drive between the potholes. Rory flopped down in his usual spot in the porch as she rang the bell. When Heather opened the door, she wore a flowered apron over her skirt and sweater, and looked harassed.

'Oh – Nina – I'm just doing out the kitchen,' she said. 'Come in.'

'I came to see if everything was all right,' Nina explained, following Heather through the hall to the kitchen, where the chairs were upended on the table. A tin of red polish, a kneeling mat and some rags lay on the floor.

'Goodness – what a job,' said Nina, who remembered this chore from her childhood but not since, when cork or lino tiles, cleaned with a squeezy mop, had been her own experience. 'How often do you do it?'

'Once a week,' Heather said. 'I was going to come round to

see you later today, Nina, to thank you for what you did. It was so good of you. You must have been very frightened when you found Guy. I suppose he stayed in some other room, while you were still up and about.'

'I suppose he did,' Nina agreed.

'Of course, he's known the house all his life,' Heather said. 'Perhaps, he had a sleep in one of the bedrooms – like Goldilocks.'

'Yes,' said Nina. 'I didn't think of searching the house.'

'Why should you?' said Heather. 'He's been very quiet, ever since we got back. Quite rational – very thoughtful – not that he wasn't before,' she added quickly.

Nina thought that there was no great difference between Martin's betrayal of her, and Guy's conduct. But Guy had not left Heather; he had not broken her life. He had implied that Heather had no idea of the truth about Charles. To discover it now would be devastating for her, Nina knew; more so, even, than Martin's defection had been to her. Yet, for the rest of Heather's life, the risk of finding out would exist. Did Leonard know the truth? It might be something he did not want to admit, even if he suspected it, Nina thought, and knew that she would join their conspiracy of silence.

She gave Priscilla's bedroom a really good cleaning that afternoon to remove any trace of the visitor.

Dan still seemed to be sulking on Wednesday, so Nina decided not to ask him about his day in London. She could think of nothing at all to say as they drank their coffee together. She was feeling depressed herself, for she had received a letter from Felicity which disclosed that Martin and Caroline had already moved into Silverlea. Felicity was refusing to invite them to her house, but most of the rest of their circle were welcoming them, and someone had given a party for them. No one seemed to know that they weren't married yet, except Felicity, but anyway, that sort of thing didn't matter these days. Felicity's husband said that they would have to accept the position, but Felicity meant to hold out.

Nina was grateful for Felicity's partisan stance, but knew that it could not last. It was as if she had died, she thought.

145

Caroline had won it all now: Martin, the house, and Nina's former position in the district.

Jenny seldom saw television. She was usually at a meeting or working in the evenings. She did not read newspapers very often, either, in her university life, except those concerned with campus affairs and run by the students. On Wednesday, she found a copy of the evening paper on a chair in a café where she was waiting for Alec, and glanced at it idly. On the front page she saw a photofit picture of a man the police wanted to trace.

His face reminded Jenny of someone, but she could not think who it was. Those made-up pictures were weird, not really like the person at all. Different people gave different descriptions of the same person.

Alec arrived and she forgot about it, tossing the paper down on the bench beside her as he sat down opposite her, his new infant beard giving his face, in her opinion, an air of distinction.

The blue Cortina stolen from the street near Euston the day Christine Potter disappeared had been found in a parking lot in Luton. Before it could be reunited with its owner, it was taken away for examination by police forensic scientists. Even before their tests began, a long, light brown hair had been seen on the floor of the boot. This would be matched with the dead girl's hair, and the police hoped they would find further clues. There might be fingerprints not belonging to the owner or anyone else with a legitimate right to be in the car. More probably, careful inspection might produce a thread from the driver's clothing, or, on the floor by the pedals, earth from the area where Christine's body had been found. Soil particles might cling to the tyres or the car's underside. However, even if such evidence were to be found, tracing the man who had stolen the car, unless there was a fingerprint and he had a record, would be difficult. They needed a name, a man they could bring in to question, whose clothes could be examined for traces from Christine. It might require more than a photofit picture to identify him.

Extra vigilance would be enforced at the big London railway terminals. Plain clothes officers would mingle with the crowds.

Meanwhile, the photofit pictures had been widely circulated. Somebody, somewhere, would recognize the man.

Three years ago, on her sixtieth birthday, Heather had received a most generous gift from Priscilla. It was a large chest freezer, into which she could put her fruit and vegetables grown during the summer. Until then, Heather had still bottled fruit and salted beans.

'I don't know how you exist without one,' Priscilla had said, waving away Heather's thanks.

For the same celebration, Rosemary had given her a food processor. Guy's gift had been a painting of the garden; she had hung it in their bedroom.

On Thursday, for a treat, Heather took some raspberries out of the freezer, and some mince, which she bought in bulk from a butcher in Murford. That afternoon she was going to a charity committee meeting in the village. She was the president of the association, and today she intended to resign. She had, until now, felt it her duty to make this effort for the welfare of others, and she enjoyed the brief escape from her normal routine. She liked meeting the brisk women, some her own age, but most of them younger, who worked more actively for the cause. She had been chosen as figurehead years ago, because she lived in the Manor. That had less significance these days, particularly since functions had ceased to be held there. Guy no longer wanted people even to use the garden for fêtes, though once he had thought it an obligation to open the grounds.

Guy ate all his lunch. The pills were in his helping of the mashed potato on top of the shepherd's pie which Heather had made from the mince. He went off to bed for his nap, and Heather, in her old maroon tweed suit, drove off in the Mini. It was making a most disturbing noise, a rattle from somewhere deep inside. It would be very serious indeed if the Mini needed some costly new part. Well, she couldn't worry about that now, Heather decided, parking outside the large, comfortable modern house where lived the committee chairman who would take the meeting after she, Heather, had graciously asked her to do so. She'd resign at the end, when the business had been concluded.

147

There would be tea, later. Heather would have some before going home. There were always delicious cakes on these occasions. She longed to smuggle some into her handbag to take back to Guy, but hadn't the nerve.

Guy was soon asleep. The room was warm, the bed his familiar one, and he had eaten a filling, if not very exciting lunch. The raspberries had been a pleasant surprise. Heather made most of the crop into jam and tended to reserve the ones she froze until after Christmas when, she said, everyone needed a tonic.

Then the dreams began. There were shots, screams, terror; and somehow Robin was there, in the prison camp. Guy started awake, but as he struggled to surface from the drugged muzziness, the past would not retreat. He saw Robin and Charles in the water, the upturned boat hitting Robin's head, the boy going under. Why Robin? What fate had decreed which boy should survive?

Guy sat up in bed seeing again the cottage near Amesbury where he and Heather, with Rosemary, then a baby, had lived while Guy was stationed nearby. Leonard was away at sea, and Priscilla had come to stay for a few days' leave from her London hospital. One afternoon Guy came home unexpectedly early to find her alone, asleep in the garden. Heather and Rosemary had gone to another child's birthday party in the village. That chance was all that they needed.

Leonard had leave some weeks later, but when Charles was born, allegedly prematurely, was again at sea. He did not see the baby until Charles was six months old, by now a sturdy child. Leonard, a robust man himself, would expect his son to be strong, even if he had arrived early.

Guy, by now in North Africa, heard of the baby's birth from Heather but did not think much about it. A few months later Robin was born, and within a year Guy had been wounded and captured. His parents still lived at the Manor, and Heather and the children spent the rest of the war there. Priscilla and her son joined Leonard in Scotland when he had a spell there ashore, and remained there for the rest of the war.

Guy continued in the army after the war, apparently none

the worse for his experiences. At first the family were based at
the Manor, and when Guy was posted abroad Heather and the
children followed. During the years they had a number of
overseas postings, but in between would return to the village.
Guy's father died not long after the war, and soon his mother
decided that she could not cope with the place any longer. She
went to live with a widowed sister, but she died a year later.
Two sets of death duties in such a short space of time seriously
depleted the Jowetts' estate, and Guy let the Manor whenever
the family was not using it. Meanwhile, Leonard had returned
to the firm as soon as he left the navy. He was responsible for its
rapid expansion when conditions improved. At first he and
Priscilla lived, with the small boy Charles, a few miles outside
Slough, where the firm's offices were at that time. Then old Mrs
Blunt died, and Leonard's father, who was still working, had no
heart to remain at the Hall. He found a flat in Datchet, and the
young family took over the house in the country. There were
long spells when the Jowetts were away from Netherton St
Mary, but in between, the two households saw a great deal of
each other, and the friendship between Charles and Robin
developed.

Guy, the would-be painter, noticed the likeness, and hoped
earnestly that no one else would do the same. His suspicion that
Charles was his son was confirmed one evening during dinner
at the Hall. Heather was pregnant again, and this was, to the
Jowetts, dismaying. Money was tight, and they had not planned a third child. Rosemary was due to go to Heather's old
school, where she and Priscilla had met, Robin to Guy's; the
expense of a third set of fees was daunting.

'It's you and Leonard who should be having the big family,'
Heather had said. 'You've got this big place and you can afford
it – you should have four or five.'

'I wish we could,' Leonard said, 'we seem to have lost the
knack.'

At that moment, Guy had felt Priscilla's gaze on him. Over
the years, she had become more assured, developed an elegant
style and transformed herself into an effective wife for a
dynamic tycoon, as Leonard was proving to be. Now, Guy met
her stare. It was hard, steady, and told him the truth.

Well, he had thought at the time, but for their interlude

Leonard would have no heir. Later, Heather miscarried, and much later still, Robin had drowned.

Now, Guy remembered all this, struggling against the muzziness induced by his pills, fighting the fear of his dreams. You pay, he thought, and not only you, but others, innocent people who don't deserve to suffer. Heather had lost her son, and her third child, also a boy. Since his retirement, he'd thought about it all a great deal. It had preyed on his mind and lately he had become obsessed with the need to make sure that Charles would look after Heather, and preserve the house that had meant so much to the Jowetts for so many years. He could buy it – he had plenty of money now – and live there till his parents died. It and the Hall could become – as in fact they had been for years, in a way – interdependent. That woman at the Hall had said she would get in touch with Charles, but she might forget her promise. Guy decided that he must do it himself, since his attempts to get hold of Priscilla on the telephone had failed. She, after all, should bear some responsibility.

Guy got out of bed and padded across the floor in his socks to the chair where his neatly folded trousers were laid. He put them on, and took his tweed jacket with its leather patches from its hanger. He had put on no weight since it was made by his Savile Row tailor fifteen years before. Guy brushed his white hair, opened the door and went out of the room.

'Heather?' he called when he reached the foot of the stairs. If he was going to use the telephone to ring up Charles in his office, he must make sure Heather would not find out. She would query the bill, when it came, he knew. He'd think up some story – say he'd rung the bank – the Jowetts banked at Coutts – find an excuse. She often went out in the afternoons, if only into the garden to work. He must help her more – give up these afternoon sleeps; he was, after all, only a year or two older than Leonard, who was still so active.

Guy went round the garden looking for Heather. She wasn't there. Perhaps she'd gone out in the car. He walked on to the yard and saw the garage doors were open, the car gone.

The fresh air had cleared his head and he remembered now that she'd gone to a meeting. There was plenty of time to telephone London. Committees always talked for hours. Guy paused in the yard, the ghosts from the past still with him.

Years ago, there had been horses here in the stables. He and his sister, a widow now and living in Edinburgh, had ridden; Rosemary and Robin had had a pony. Guy's father had hunted, and so had Guy, long ago. His father's horse was a big chestnut with a temper that matched his colour. Here, in the tackroom, Joe, the groom, had once worked, cleaning the saddles, rubbing in saddle soap, telling Guy tales of the past.

Guy opened the tackroom door. He hadn't been in it for years; the hay in the loft had made him sneeze and he kept away.

There were the saddles, the soft one he'd used as a boy, the felt one for the children when they were tiny, and wasn't that the one he had used on Bimbo, a grey who could jump any fence? Guy ran his hand over the dry leather. What a state they were in! He was shocked. Some tattered rosettes, trophies from shows, hung on the wall near the bridles. Guy moved across to the stairs at the back of the tackroom and slowly began to climb them. At the top, he saw the key in the door, and unlocked it.

Here, in the loft, he had had his first sexual experience with Kitty, a girl from the village who worked in the house as a maid. They were both about seventeen. She'd laughed when he had an attack of sneezing. Kitty had later married the gardener and they'd emigrated to Canada. Guy smiled, remembering her plump, eager body and laughing face. There had been no harm in it; it was natural, he thought, a happy initiation.

Guy walked across to the row of bins where once oats and bran had been stored. He lifted a galvanized lid.

He saw the paintings inside the bin.

19

Jenny was finding it hard to attend to the lecture. Her mind strayed away from the subject of Milton and she started to think of the weekend ahead. She had decided to visit her mother. Had there been any more telephone calls? Was her mother all right, alone in that huge house? Jenny was worrying about her. She'd lost so much weight – what if she were ill? Jenny found the idea frightening.

Alec wanted to drive her to Netherton St Mary and it would be fun to be there together. They hadn't however, got round to letting Nina know their intentions, and now something was wrong with Alec's car. It needed a new part, he'd said, which he'd fit on Saturday; they'd go down then, if that was all right with her mother.

It was while she was thinking about this that Jenny remembered who the photofit pictures she had seen in the evening paper the previous day reminded her of: Dan Fenton. Jenny felt quite cold, sitting there in the lecture hall on her functional chair.

As soon as the power to move returned to her limbs, she gathered up her possessions and scrambled her way out of the room, mumbling excuses but earning frowns from the lecturer. She hurried along the corridors to the vestibule where there was a pay-phone for the students' use, rummaging in her purse as she went for some money. Then she couldn't remember the Hall's number, and had to find her diary, submerged in the depths of her bag, where it was written.

The number rang and rang, but there was no reply.

So she could not warn her mother. What should she do now?

Jenny replaced the receiver and went to get her coat, dragging it on as she hurried out of the building, her bag of books trailing from her arm. There was no time to look for Alec, whose support would have been a help.

There was a police station less than a mile away; she'd been past it often enough on her bike. Going there to report the matter in person would be better than dialling 999. She was terrified. The fact that the man went after young girls wouldn't protect her mother; the telephone calls proved that. She pedalled swiftly off.

That afternoon, Nina prepared for her walk with Rory. In spite of buying her green wellington boots, she had not been over the fields since that first day with Heather. She decided to go that way today, since it hadn't rained for several days and the ground would be reasonably dry. She must justify owning a pair of uniform boots.

Rory was pleased at their choice of route, running on ahead, but not far, looking up now and then to make sure she was near. They passed the spot where Heather had planted the snow-drops. The sun was sinking now in the short winter day. From the spot where she and Heather had parted on that first morning, Nina looked down at the Manor.

She saw a plume of smoke billowing into the air, drifting away from the house. It rose from the source close to the hedge at the end of the garden. This was the bonfire season; Heather must be having a bonfire worthy of Guy Fawkes himself. Guy Fawkes: Guy. The connection made Nina somehow uneasy. Surely it was a massive amount of smoke for a garden bonfire?

She walked towards it, putting on speed, going as fast as she could over the springy turf, and soon she could smell the smoke, an acrid smell, not the pleasant, soft smell of an ordinary bonfire.

Approaching the garden, Nina saw a gate in the fence. These were the Jowetts' fields, she supposed; the ones they let. She turned towards the gate. It would take her into the garden, and if Heather was, after all, simply burning her rubbish, Nina would say she had seen the fire and come over.

The gate led into the vegetable garden. Nina followed a path that ran along near the hedge towards the fire. She could hear it crackling now, and flames leaped up high in the sky. Nina turned a corner and saw a figure who stoked the fire, his long legs taking scissor strides as, his back towards her, Guy Jowett gathered together the canvases on the pyre. It was a weird, satanic spectacle, the tall man, pitchfork in hand, raking stray fragments up from the edge of the fire and adding them to the blazing mass. As she drew near, Nina saw him cast an entire canvas on to the fire. She realized, then, what he was doing. Somehow he had discovered what Heather had done with his work, and was destroying it. Did Heather know? Had she helped?

This was some private rite. Nina had no place here, as a witness. She had put Rory on the lead as they entered the Manor grounds, and now she drew him towards the house, hoping to slip away with him, unobserved. She walked quickly through the yard and saw the garage empty, its doors wide. The loft doors, above, appeared to be closed.

Nina felt rather disturbed to think that Heather was out while the incineration went on. Didn't Guy sleep in the afternoons? She walked down the drive and out into the lane, where she turned left, away from the Hall. She'd walk on for a bit, she decided, take a turn round the village and then come back to the Manor to see if Heather was there. There had been something wild, demoniac, about that figure, capless, just in a jacket, stirring the flames. Yet he couldn't hurt himself, surely? And there was no risk of the house catching fire, though the flames had been leaping high: the bonfire was well away from the house and the outbuildings. Guy had the right to do as he chose with his own creations.

Nevertheless, Nina felt uneasy as she walked towards the village. She turned at the end of the lane into a road which would, she thought, take her back to the Black Swan. Then she could circle round again, past the Manor.

She thought she knew where all the village roads went, but to her surprise Nina found that this one, along which she had not walked before, led into Chestnut Crescent, where Dan lived. This was rather annoying. The last thing she wanted, now, was to meet Dan. She hurried on, Rory padding beside her, and round a bend in the road saw ahead, parked outside Dan's house, a police car. As she walked towards it the door of Dan's house opened and two policemen came out. With them was Dan. They got in the car together and drove away. Nina, who had slowed down as they appeared, stared after them. Her first thought was that she hoped Dan hadn't seen her; her second was to wonder what reason the police could possibly have for taking Dan off in the car.

She slowed up, passing his house, looking at it curiously. Had it been burgled, his precious fish stolen, perhaps? As she hesitated on the pavement outside, the door of the next house opened and a young girl came out, holding a baby. This was the neighbour Dan baby-sat for, Nina supposed, moving on.

'Excuse me – Mrs Crowther – Mrs Crowther,' the girl called after her, and Nina stopped. The girl came hurrying down the path, though she wore no coat, and the baby was clad simply in a pink stretch suit. 'You are Mrs Crowther from the Hall, aren't you?' the girl said at the gate.

'Yes,' Nina acknowledged.

'I thought so – I saw you the other day – Sunday – when you came to tea. Dan often talks about you – he thinks the world of you,' said the girl.

'Oh,' said Nina, not certain how to take this.

'The police took him away,' said the girl. 'Did you see? Just now. Oh, I do hope he's not in some trouble.'

'Why should he be?' asked Nina. 'I expect it's about something quite simple – I thought perhaps his house had been broken into.'

'They wouldn't take him away, if it had,' said the girl. 'At least, I don't think so. Oh, Mrs Crowther, I'm dreadfully worried about him – I'm so glad you came by. Would you come in for a minute?'

Nina saw that she must, if the girl and her baby were not to catch cold. She urged the girl back to the house and went up the path behind her.

'What about Rory?' she asked, at the door.

'Oh, bring him in,' said the girl. 'He's a love isn't he?'

Nina followed her into the house, the mirror-twin of Dan's. The living-room, like his, looked over the garden, but across this one, in the fading light, flapped a line of washing, mainly nappies. The girl laid her baby in an armchair, propping her up with a cushion. The infant smiled round benignly.

'Thank goodness she's still young enough to be dumped,' said the child's mother, and picked up the newspaper which lay on another chair. 'Have you seen this?' she asked.

Nina had not looked at the paper that day. She took it from the girl. Across the page were photofit pictures of a man wanted by the police in connection with the killing of Christine Potter. She stared at them, slow to see the implication.

'It is like Dan, isn't it?' said the girl. 'That one.' She pointed. There were three versions, and one, Nina had to concede, did resemble Dan. She stared at it, and then at the girl; then back at the paper again. 'It can't be him,' said the girl, her voice shaking a little. 'He's so kind and gentle. You should see him with Amanda.' This was the baby, obviously. 'It must be some awful coincidence,' the girl insisted.

The mysterious trips to London, thought Nina; the sulkiness which she, in her vanity, had attributed to Guy's presence at the Hall on Monday. She felt sick.

'But his own daughter was killed,' she told the girl. 'Shot in a bank raid.' She tried to speak calmly.

'It could have made him flip, I suppose,' said Sandra Morris sadly. 'Couldn't it?'

Heather hummed under her breath as she drove home. She had had one tea at the committee meeting and would be in time for another with Guy. She had enjoyed her sojourn in the luxurious, warm home of the chairman. The women reminded her of the army wives she used to know. They had displayed regret at her resignation, which was nice. She could not know that earlier there had been lobbying aimed at applying pressure to get her to go: someone should, it had been suggested, voice the thought that it was wonderful of Mrs Jowett to find the time to come when she had so much to cope with at home, and that she mustn't hesitate to say if she wanted a rest. An active faction of the committee wanted Priscilla Blunt to become the president; she was rich, on the ball, had better contacts, and, moreover, would allow the Hall to be used for various functions.

'You must admit Mrs Jowett's pretty eccentric, wandering around planting flowers all over the place, and her husband's completely dotty,' said the leader of this group.

'I like Heather Jowett,' said a dissenter. 'And I think planting flowers is a good idea. If you ease her out, I go too.'

As the rebel was the treasurer, her loss would be grave. It had been decided to leave the subject for the moment, and now Heather herself had taken the initiative. When she had gone, most of the committee expressed their delight, and resolved to invite Priscilla Blunt to take her place.

The treasurer went angrily home, where she exploded to her husband as soon as he came back from his office. She might still resign, she said; it was disgusting.

Unaware of all this, Heather drove into the garage and turned off the ignition. She got out, and closed the garage doors. It was dusk now, almost dark. As she walked towards the house she smelled smoke, a strong, odd smell, not like an ordinary fire. She sniffed. It must come from somewhere nearby, yet the Manor had no close neighbours. No one else's bonfire ever blew their way.

She dropped her handbag on the ground and began running down the garden. She saw smoke spiralling up from a heap of ashes on her bonfire spot.

Who could have set the fire but Guy? She called him, but there was no reply, and she couldn't see him in the garden. What had he been burning?

She knew the answer before she looked down and saw, on the edge of the dying fire, a last curling wisp of singed canvas and a fragment of stretcher from a frame, but she had to confirm it. She turned and ran back to the yard, a lanky, ungainly figure loping along in her maroon suit and the lacy tights Rosemary had sent her last Christmas. She opened the tackroom door and ran up the stairs. Because Guy never came up here, she no longer removed the key unless her family were visiting, and now the door was open. Heather rushed into the first loft, which was in darkness. She turned on the light and saw that the lids of the bins were raised. The door beyond, leading into the hayloft, was closed. Heather was very frightened as she opened it.

At first she did not see Guy there, in the dark. He was sitting on a straw bale on the far side of the loft, and, as she burst in he stood up, taking a step away from the sudden interruption. Guy had pulled the outer doors to, but he had not secured them. When he stepped heedlessly back, they parted behind him, and with one loud cry he fell to the ground below.

20

'Did you tell the police about Dan?' Nina asked the girl.

'No. I didn't look at the paper until after Tom had gone to work,' she said. 'And he only glanced at the sports page, so he didn't see it. I thought it must be just a coincidence.'

Nina was rallying.

'It probably is,' she said. 'The police must have come about something else.' She thought of her pleasant sessions with Dan at the Hall over coffee, his courtly good manners when she had tea at his house. It couldn't be true. Yet weren't some of the most vicious murderers mild and quiet at home? 'He'll be able to tell the police where he was when that girl was killed,' she said. 'An alibi,' she added, remembering Felicity's diet of thrillers.

Sandra, shocked by the episode, was reluctant to let Nina go. Apart from anything else, she had trusted Dan with her precious infant. Nina stayed until she was calmer, but she refused a cup of tea. She was still anxious about Guy and wanted to make sure things were all right at the Manor.

Nina had no torch as she approached the Manor for the second time, and it was getting dark, but her eyes had adjusted and she could see well as she reached the gate. Lights shone from the lower windows of the house, and she almost turned back then, but there was something about them – the number that were on, the fact that the curtains were not drawn, that made her uneasy. She went a little way up the drive, and soon saw that the front door was open.

Nina hurried on, then, and when she reached the house, stepped inside, loudly calling Heather. No one answered. Were they both down at the bonfire? She'd smelled it on the air as she came down the drive.

Nina hurried out again and round the side of the house to the yard. The exterior lights were on, and she found them there, both in the yard, Heather crouched over Guy's inert form, holding his hand and stroking his hair and murmuring to him.

Nina dropped on her knees beside them, releasing Rory's lead. The dog gave a small keening sound and stood off at a distance. Nina laid a hand gently on Heather's arm, not wanting to startle her.

'Heather – it's me – Nina,' she said. 'What happened?'

Heather turned a ravaged face towards her.

'He fell,' she said, and looked upwards.

Above their heads, the loft doors stood open.

'Is an ambulance coming?' Nina asked. 'Have you telephoned?'

Heather nodded. She'd run in to call it, turning on all the lights as she rushed through the house to the telephone. Then, coming back to him, she had put her own jacket over the upper part of his body and was shivering herself, both from shock and the night air.

The cobbles Guy lay on must be so cold, Nina thought, but moving him might make his injuries worse. He was deeply unconscious, and now she saw, with a sinking heart, that his head was turned at an odd angle. One arm was twisted beneath him. She took her own coat off and put it over his legs.

'I'll go and get some blankets,' she said. 'The ambulance might be a few minutes getting here.'

'Oh – good thinking,' said Heather, her voice steady. 'No – I'll go – I'll be quicker. Stay with him, Nina.' She relinquished his hand and lumbered away.

The keys, Nina thought suddenly: the keys to the Hall. What if Heather were to find them? Quickly she felt in Guy's jacket pockets, hardly expecting that they would still be there, but they were, wrapped up in a handkerchief. Nina dropped them into her own pocket before Heather returned.

She stayed with them both till the ambulance came, and when it had driven away, with the two of them inside it, Nina went into the house to close it up. She'd get her own car and follow them to the hospital for they would need help. The daughter must be got hold of, and someone must look after Heather.

She forgot about Dan, his plight driven from her mind by the more immediate claims of the Jowetts.

Later that evening Jenny and Alec arrived at the Hall in a car they had borrowed, an aged Hillman Imp. Its maximum speed was sedate, and Jenny had been steadily growing frantic as they ground up hills in low gear.

'Don't worry, Jenny. I'm sure everything's all right,' Alec kept saying, as he had from the moment she told him her fears and described her interview with a police constable who was, at first, unbelieving, but soon decided to shift the responsibility for action on to the sergeant's more experienced shoulders. After that, she had tried to ring her mother again, but got no reply. In the end, because she was so worried, Alec suggested they should abandon their lectures for the rest of the week and go to Netherton St Mary at once, assuming he could borrow a car as his own was not roadworthy.

'We'll have to tell the police Mum's missing,' Jenny said, as they went down the Droxton by-pass.

The loss of her normal cool self-possession was having a powerful effect on Alec. He wanted to scoop her into his arms and apply masculine comfort. Instead, he must coax the rest of the distance out of the Imp.

'She's not missing,' he said. 'She's probably gone out to tea, or to the Women's Institute – it's all go in these villages, you'd be surprised. You don't have to worry about this Dan – the police took what you said seriously. They won't hang about. It's a murder case, after all.'

'You don't have to tell me,' said Jenny, shuddering.

The old car ground up the drive of the Hall at last, and Jenny was reassured by seeing lights on, the ones outside and a thin line beside some of the curtains, but there was no reply when they rang the bell except for some barking within the house.

They went round to try the back door, and here the barking was louder.

'Rory, good boy, where's she gone?' Jenny asked the dog through the stout wood of the door. A few snuffling sounds answered her, and another bark.

Alec had wandered away to the garage.

'Her car's out,' he reported. 'So you can calm down, Jenny. She hasn't been abducted – she's probably gone out to dinner. Now, who are her friends?'

'I only know about the Jowetts,' said Jenny.

'Well, let's go to their place and see if she's there,' said Alec.

Jenny agreed to this sensible plan and they returned to their elderly car, turned it round and set off again.

'You wouldn't think bad things could happen in a place like this, would you?' said Jenny. 'I mean, a peaceful old village.'

'I guess you would,' said Alec. 'Witches being burned, that sort of thing. Human nature doesn't change much – it just demonstrates differently.'

This was not a soothing response, and Jenny did not speak again except to direct him to the Manor. Here, also, lights were on, both outside the front and back doors, in the yard, and in the house, where Nina, so security-conscious, had drawn the curtains and left some lights burning to discourage prowlers.

But her Metro was not parked outside and there was no reply to their repeated knocking and ringing.

Alec went into the yard and tried the garage doors. They were not locked and he saw the battered Mini inside. He shut the doors and sniffed the air.

'They've been burning rubbish,' he said. 'Old tyres or something. Smells a bit weird.'

Jenny had no time for any thoughts not relating to her mother's disappearance.

'Never mind about that,' she said. 'What shall we do?'

'The only other person you know of here is this Dan Fenton, right?' said Alec. 'Where does he live.'

Jenny shivered.

'He won't be there – he'll be in prison, I hope,' she said.

'We'd better make sure,' said Alec. 'Where's his house?'

'I don't know,' said Jenny.

'Well, you know he's on the telephone. There'll be a callbox somewhere, for sure. Let's look him up,' he said.

A few minutes later they parked the Imp by the callbox on the corner of Chestnut Crescent. They had no torch, so Alec removed the tattered local directory and took it to the car. They turned the pages and there was the entry: Fenton, D. E. with the Netherton St Mary number.

'Jenny, this D. E. Fenton doesn't live in Netherton St Mary. It's a Stokebourne address,' said Alec. 'I expect there's one telephone exchange for several of these villages. It's like that at home.'

Jenny stared. She read the line above his pointing finger. Fenton, D. E., 18 Hill View, Stokebourne.

'Oh, Alec, what have I done?' she gasped.

'The right thing,' said Alec robustly. 'You thought the photograph in the paper was like the man and your mother told you he pops up to London quite a bit. But he can't have been your mother's mystery telephone caller.'

He got out of the car and returned the directory to the box.

'We'll go and ask where he lives at the pub,' he said. 'They may know. Perhaps he's a regular.'

They drove back to the Black Swan, where the publican described how to find Dan's house and they realized how close to it they had just been. The publican was not sure which number it was in Chestnut Crescent, but they would know it by the green gate and the neat rosebeds in the front garden, he said.

Alec was longing for a beer and a sandwich, but he knew Jenny was in no mood for delay. They drove back the way they had come.

Dan's house was the only one in the Crescent with no lights on. For form's sake, though very relieved, Alec walked up the path and rang the bell. Jenny followed, loitering behind him, telling herself things like this didn't happen in England: your mother didn't just vanish.

Alec, who had been wondering how to phrase his request for information about where Nina might be to Dan, if he were at home, now felt a keen desire to know what had happened here today.

'I'll ask next door if they know anything,' he said, walking up the path and through the nearest gate – luckily, and quite by chance, choosing the Morrises and not the neighbours on the other side, who had seen nothing of the afternoon's events.

Tom Morris opened the door, and Alec asked if he knew where Dan was.

'Well,' said Tom. 'That depends.'

He had expected the press to be outside, after what Sandra had told him. It could only be a matter of time before television crews and reporters were there with their cameras and microphones, wanting the villagers' opinions about their neighbour, and the prospect appalled him. This young man with his wiry curls and wispy beard might well be a journalist.

'It's my mother we really want to know about,' Jenny said, stepping forward. 'Mrs Crowther – Nina. She's living at the Hall at the moment.'

'Oh – my wife saw her today,' said Tom, his defensive manner dispersing at once. 'Come in and she'll tell you.'

Twenty minutes later eggs and bacon were being cooked for Alec and Jenny by their new friends, and Jenny was relaxing in the knowledge that her mother had been in this very house minutes after Dan was driven off in a police car.

While they were eating their meal, having described their search round the village, Tom told them that Colonel Jowett had been badly hurt in some sort of accident. He'd met the ambulance hurrying through the village, siren wailing and blue light flashing, on his way home from work. Such a sight was rare in Netherton St Mary. One of their neighbours knew it had been to the Manor.

'Mum will be helping, if she can,' said Jenny. 'She likes the old colonel. So do I, come to that.'

'Well, let's find out,' said Tom. He understood Jenny's anxiety, even though she knew, now, that her mother had not been strangled. If Dan Fenton had been somehow mixed up with that murder, the thought that he had lived next door, visited them, been alone with the baby, was terrifying. Reassurance all round was needed, and he dialled the hospital's number.

After some delay, Nina was traced and brought to the telephone. Jenny almost burst into tears at hearing her voice.

'I was so worried – Dan Fenton – those photographs in the paper,' she said, incoherently. 'They're just like him.'

Nina had quite forgotten Dan.

'I know,' she said. 'It must be a mistake. He's not that sort of man at all.'

How did one know, wondered Jenny. She saw that this was no time to confess her own possible part in his detention. Her mother, meanwhile, was turning her mind to practical matters.

'You'll be wanting beds, you and Alec,' she said. 'And you can't get into the Hall. I don't know how long I'll be here, Jenny. Things aren't too good and I can't leave Heather. You could come and collect the keys.'

'Hang on for a tick,' said Jenny, and turned to Alec. 'We're to go and get the keys and let ourselves in,' she said.

'You're not,' said Tom firmly. 'Your mother may be at the hospital all night, and you're staying here. We've got a spare room. Only one,' he added, grinning.

'Are they sure?' Nina said, when the invitation was relayed. 'Oh, how kind. There's going to be rather a lot to do here, Jenny. The daughter to ring in Germany – that sort of thing. I'm afraid there's not much hope.'

Alec was smiling away to himself as the conversation was concluded. He would have his chance to comfort Jenny, at last.

21

Though she had slept for only a few hours, Nina woke the next morning charged with energy. There were tasks ahead, but they were the kind she knew she could manage, concerned mainly with domestic organization.

In a room along the passage lay Heather Jowett. Guy had died just after midnight, without regaining consciousness, and Heather, after shedding about five tears, had allowed Nina to bring her back to the Hall. She had accepted a mug of hot milk and one of Nina's sleeping pills, laughing shakily and saying she'd soon be a junkie, since this was the second time in a week she'd gone to bed doped.

The hospital had warned Nina that there would have to be an inquest. She must let Charles Blunt know what had happened, and someone must decide whether his parents should be told of the death of their friend. Heather, when she woke, might think of this herself, Nina realized.

What a thing to learn of the death of your lover while you were sunning yourself in South Africa, Nina thought. What a shock.

Would Priscilla mind very much?

Heather woke when Nina drew back the bedroom curtains. She stirred and stretched in the unfamiliar, very soft bed. She was in a strange room, and daylight was filtering in through heavily latticed windows.

Guy was dead. She remembered at once, and experienced a dreadful sense of total desolation.

'You've slept, that's good,' Nina was saying. 'I've brought you some breakfast. Please try to eat something.'

Like a capable nurse, she helped Heather to sit up in bed, propped up her pillows and offered her a peach bedjacket which she had found in a drawer in Priscilla's bedroom.

'Oh – Nina –' Heather fought for her self-control.

She looked so old, Nina was thinking, with pity.

'Come along,' she said aloud. 'Look – there's just some toast. I didn't think you'd want much more.'

On the bedside table rested a tray. It was laid with delicate china on a linen traycloth. There was a shining silver spoon in the saucer, and a small silver toastrack with crustless slices cut into triangles. Heather had seen nothing like it for years as the tray was laid across her knees.

'I hope you like coffee,' said Nina.

'Yes,' said Heather. 'Perhaps it will wake me up. I feel so stupid.'

Nina poured out a cup of coffee and added hot milk. There was sugar in a small bowl. Heather took some sips. Then she began spreading butter on to a slice of toast. The tiny silver knife felt, in her inept grasp, as heavy as a small shovel; all her strength seemed to have gone. There were two little pots, one filled with honey, the other with marmalade, each with its miniature spoon. Nina had enjoyed setting a tempting tray.

'How lucky for me that you were here, Nina,' said Heather. 'You've been so kind.'

'Mrs Blunt would have been more help,' said Nina.

'She wouldn't have done so much,' said Heather. 'She'd have told me to pull myself together.'

'You don't need to,' said Nina. 'You haven't collapsed. Perhaps you should, but not just yet, not till I've told you about Rosemary and when she arrives, that sort of thing. Now, eat some toast and when you've finished your breakfast, why don't you have a bath? It will refresh you. There's loads of hot water. Would you like me to fetch you some clothes from the Manor?'

'Oh no, Nina. What I had on yesterday will do,' said Heather. 'Once I'm dressed, I must go. There will be people I should ring. Guy's sister in Scotland. And others.'

'Well, of course. We'll see about all that later on,' said Nina. 'Your daughter will be here this afternoon and you'll want to be on your own then.'

'She'll be very upset,' said Heather. 'She hadn't realized how he'd been failing.'

During the night, Nina had spoken on the telephone twice to Rosemary, once with the news of the accident, later to say that

Guy was dead. Her husband had rung the Hall early this morning giving the arrival time of Rosemary's plane.

'There are things I must do before she comes,' said Heather. 'I must clear up –' her voice trailed away. She meant that she wanted to make sure no evidence remained of Guy's destruction of his work.

Nina was wondering if Rosemary knew her father's paintings were hidden away and decided that she did not. She thought of the wild figure she had seen by the bonfire, the frantic piling of canvas on canvas. If she had come forward then, made her presence known, could she have persuaded him to go into the house, have managed to calm him? Could she have prevented the accident? Nina knew she would often have to face this thought. But now her mystery telephone caller was dead and she would never let anyone know that he had frightened her in such a manner. She would tell Jenny that the whistle had ended the nuisance – as it had. It was after that episode that Guy had grown quiet, less confused: the lull before the final storm, and again Nina wondered how much she was to blame. Had the whistle triggered off the final tragedy?

'He loved you so much,' she said abruptly, not good at expressing emotion. 'He told me so, on Sunday night when he stayed here.' It wasn't a lie; Guy's main concern had been for his wife's protection after his death.

'I wish you'd met him when he was young,' said Heather. 'He was so handsome – so gay, in the old sense of the word – there's no other word with quite that meaning. He could dance divinely, and he rode so well. The war changed everything. Afterwards, he didn't get on well in the army. The carefree part of him seemed to shrivel up and it had quite gone by the time he retired. Then, at first, he helped in the garden and so on, and he was on the District Council, but he lost his seat and that upset him, and a few years ago he got this obsession about keeping clean. You must have noticed, Nina. Odd – he'd stopped that in the last few days. Though he was so quiet, he was much more like his old self.' She did not mention his paintings.

Nina saw that she must be careful not to let slip that she knew the nature of the rubbish Guy had been burning. At the hospital, Heather had simply said that he'd been clearing the loft and must have forgotten to fasten the outer door when he went up to make sure he'd brought it all down. She'd gone up there to look for him; he hadn't heard her coming and, startled, had stepped backwards.

'He was still a fine-looking man,' Nina said. 'I liked him so much, and I'll never forget him. Jenny liked him too,' she added, and went on smoothly. 'She's here now – Jenny. She's come for the weekend with her boyfriend.'

The two had arrived at the Hall while she was preparing Heather's tray. Their overnight hosts had given them one breakfast already, but now they were having more coffee and toast in the kitchen. Alec had offered to meet the Jowetts' daughter at Heathrow. Rosemary's husband was to follow as soon as he could. Alec thought Mrs Jowett should get in touch with her solicitor promptly for the police would want to find out just how the accident had happened. When Nina said he seemed to know a lot about this sort of thing, he replied that a fatal tractor accident had happened on a farm owned by a friend of his father's, and he remembered that the unavoidable formalities which followed had been very distressing to the family. Nina thought how sensible Alec was, and was grateful for his support.

She left Heather to finish her breakfast and went downstairs to the kitchen to tell the young people that it looked as if she would cope with the day ahead fairly well. When she entered the kitchen there was a small scuffle as Jenny and Alec sprang apart. Both looked happy and beaming. Nina felt an odd lurch in her stomach, part a pang, because Jenny was adult now and experiencing feelings appropriate to her age, part a sort of envy because one aspect of her own life seemed to be over, and yet she sensed that there was a whole area of it she had never properly understood.

'Don't mind me, you two,' she said, with a smile.

'You've got a super daughter, Mrs Crowther,' said Alec. 'Takes after you, doesn't she?'

'I'm not such a good cook,' said Jenny, and added, 'yet.'

At this light-hearted moment, the back door opened. In came Dan, carrying the paper.

His appearance startled them all, and he was the one who spoke first.

'I'm sorry to be later than usual. I hope you weren't waiting for the paper. There were things I had to see to before I came,' he said.

The astonished silence in the kitchen seemed to last for minutes before Nina managed to say, in her usual calm voice, 'Well, I'm so glad you're here, Dan. We're busy today. Mrs Jowett stayed here last night – she isn't up yet. I don't know if you've heard, but Colonel Jowett had an accident yesterday and I'm afraid he died during the night in Murford Hospital.'

Dan hadn't heard. Talking about it carried them over the awkwardness of Dan's recent predicament – presumably, since he was here, now resolved – and soon he was sitting at the table having toast and coffee too. Breakfast at Droxton Police Station had not been quite so appetizing.

Nina basely left them to it, saying she must see if Heather was ready for her bath. Upstairs, she could adjust to her surprise at his prompt release. But then, she'd said all along that he could have had nothing to do with the death of that girl. She'd been proved right, for otherwise the police would never have let him go. Would they? She felt rather relieved that Alec was here, however, and that Jenny was not alone with Dan just now.

She went along to Priscilla's bathroom and turned on the water, adding bath oil from a bottle among many on a deep shelf. She had already put out an immense towel with a dense, soft pile. Heather came tottering along the landing just as Nina was going to see how she was faring.

'Are you sure you feel all right?' she asked. Heather looked grey.

'Shaky, but I'll manage,' said Heather. 'Silly, isn't it?'

Nina did not think so at all.

'I'll be nearby,' she said. 'Give a shout if you want anything.' She did not quite like to suggest that Heather should leave the bathroom door unlocked.

While she had her bath, Nina stayed on the landing outside, fearing she might faint, slip, anything. Without warning, overnight, Heather had been transformed into a widow and would, rightly receive much sympathy. She, Nina, would soon be a divorcée, hideous word, and in her case, a woman scorned, though she knew not all divorced women were the same. Some of them had done the scorning and it must feel a great deal better to be, not the rejected, but the one who did the rejecting.

Even so, sympathy and understanding would be pleasant instead of the critical disapproval Nina expected to attract.

I'm being too prickly about it, she thought, and it's only just begun. She leaned her arms on the landing window-sill, brooding, gazing out at the garden as reassuring splashing sounds came from the bathroom.

Below, two heads appeared, one covered in a shabby tweed hat, the other bare, a mass of wiry brown curls like an aureole around the skull. Dan and Alec, walking down the garden, stopped a short way from the house. Alec seemed to be asking Dan a question, and Dan, as he replied, made a large gesture with his arm. The movement lifted his old anorak at the back. Nina saw that his corduroy trousers were slack and made folds over his shrunken buttocks; the boy's jeans, beneath his sweater, were filled tightly with young, firm flesh.

The two men moved across the garden. Had the police really suspected Dan of killing that girl? How many people had noticed his resemblance to the photofit picture? Who had told the police about the likeness? What did he do in London?

Nina brooded on Dan and his secret life for a while, and then her thoughts turned to Alec, who might become her second son-in-law. It wouldn't happen, if it ever did, for a long time; the pair were still so young, and they were a modern couple, less conventional than Sarah and Jeremy.

Nina had not thought of Sarah for at least twenty-four hours. She must telephone her tonight, she thought with guilt, as she heard Heather's bathwater running out. Now she could safely leave her sentinel post. She collected the breakfast tray and went downstairs.

While Heather was dressing, Nina went into the study and dialled the number of Blunt's London offices. She must do this task herself, and before Heather came down and heard her. When the switchboard answered, she asked to speak to Mr Charles Blunt, and explained who she was. Rather to her surprise, she was put straight through – she had thought she might be intercepted by Leonard Blunt's secretary.

Charles Blunt seemed to expect her to have a problem. He sounded pleasant; his voice, to her relief, was not at all like Guy's.

'What can I do for you, Mrs Crowther?' he asked.

'I'm afraid I have some bad news,' Nina said, and plunged in. 'Colonel Jowett had a fall late yesterday afternoon. I'm sorry to tell you he died during the night. Mrs Jowett is here now.'

'Oh, my God,' said Charles, and there was a moment's silence on the line.

It's his father, thought Nina. I've just told him his father is dead. Does he know that it's his father? The words spun round in her head while she waited for him to speak again. When he didn't, she did.

'He can't have known anything about it,' she said. 'He stumbled from the hayloft door and broke his neck. He never regained consciousness.' No need, now, to mention the other injuries; he'd hear about them soon enough.

'I'll come down,' said Charles. 'They'll need some help. Let me see. Let me look at my book.'

'Their daughter is on her way,' Nina said. 'She arrives at Heathrow late this morning.'

'I'll have her met and brought down,' said Charles. 'Can you give me her flight number and time of arrival?'

They were on a piece of paper in front of Nina. She read them out.

'I've got a meeting this morning, and as it's too late to see poor Guy, I suppose I may as well go ahead with that. I'll come on afterwards. How is Heather?'

'Under the circumstances, wonderful,' Nina said. 'But very shocked, of course. She'll be better when her daughter arrives, I expect.'

'Yes,' said Charles, sounding doubtful. 'Can you cope meanwhile, Mrs Crowther?'

'Of course, Mr Blunt,' Nina said, primly. 'I'm very sorry about it. I liked Colonel Jowett.'

'So did I,' said the voice, taut now, on the line. 'It's lucky you're there, Mrs Crowther,' Charles went on. 'Please give Heather my love and say I'll see her soon. Tell her not to worry – I'll deal with everything.'

'I'll tell her,' Nina promised.

As she replaced the receiver, she thought that Heather would be relieved to know that big business was hers to depend upon, and it would be much nicer for Rosemary to be wafted here in a firm's car rather than be met by a young man she didn't know, who would have had to have come in Nina's Metro since the Imp had seen better days. She went into the kitchen making plans in her head. Charles would need a good dinner, and she'd better cater for Heather and Rosemary too. In case they preferred to eat at home, she'd make something in a casserole – but good – that could be divided and taken with them. And Charles might decide to stay overnight. There was a lot to plan.

'Mum, you're swinging into action, aren't you?' said Jenny, grinning at her. 'You like a challenge, don't you?'

'When it's the sort I can handle,' said Nina. 'I can cope with the domestic variety. I'm not good at other kinds.'

'I think you are. I think you've been pretty good these last weeks,' Jenny said. 'It can't have been much fun, especially at first when it was all so strange. And there were those scary telephone calls. Have you had any more?'

'One, and I blew the whistle,' Nina answered. 'There have been none since then.'

'That's something, then,' said Jenny. 'I'll go and tell Alec we don't have to go to the airport. He's helping Dan with something. Poor chap, he spent all night at the police station being grilled about those murders, but he said the police are satisfied that he didn't do them.' For a moment she was tempted to confess her own part in his arrest, but she resisted. She felt ashamed enough as it was. She knew Alec wouldn't give her away.

'I wonder where Charles Blunt sleeps when he stays here,' said Nina. 'There's no way of knowing which was his room.'

The Hall would be full of people this evening. She hummed a little, in the kitchen, planning, and had to remind herself that the gathering was more in the nature of a wake than of a feast.

22

Detective Superintendent Wilshaw and his officers in the Droxton CID, and their colleagues in other forces, were checking Daniel Fenton's accounts of his movements on the days when various girls had died. He had willingly surrendered specimens of his hair and blood, and allowed his fingerprints to be taken, but Wilshaw knew that matching them with evidence from the body of Christine Potter – swabs, hairs – was just a formality. The man was not responsible for that murder, although he had admitted being in London and at Euston station on the day she vanished. They had been able to check his account of his movements and to eliminate him.

'Poor bugger,' said Wilshaw's sergeant, who had returned to Chestnut Crescent and removed from the upstairs room Dan's collection of newspaper cuttings. 'Obsessed with these young girls, eh?'

They'd asked him, in the night, if he had been making mystery telephone calls to the Hall. He'd looked astonished, denying it instantly. Wilshaw had believed him. He'd been upset to learn that Mrs Crowther had been having this trouble and hadn't told him about it. The police did not reveal the source of their tip-off. Oddly enough, no one in the district had pointed out to them the resemblance between Dan and the photofit pictures: those who noticed it thought it just a coincidence, subconsciously reckoning that the killer came either from London or some rough spot, not a peaceful rural area.

In the days after Guy's death, few people in Netherton St Mary, apart from Dan himself, gave much thought to the murder enquiry. A stabbing in Devonshire, where a suspicious husband had returned unexpectedly from a business trip and found his wife in bed with a neighbour whom he had killed with the carving-knife, had pushed it from the headlines. Later, if there was a dearth of stirring news to report and no arrest, the press would whip up rage against the police for failing to find the murderer with headlines such as MAKE OUR DAUGHTERS SAFE.

Wilshaw, when Dan confessed his reasons for going to London so often, had shared his sergeant's pity for the man. He was glad they had been able to release him quickly, before the village had realized where he was, and why. Mud stuck and he would have suffered still more. He'd been through enough.

Police Constable Dawes, the first officer on the scene when a decomposed female body was found near the Droxton by-pass, was one of the officers who examined the Manor hayloft and surrounding area, preparing evidence for the coroner. With him was a detective constable.

'There was some old rubbish stored here,' Heather told them, repeating what she had said at the hospital. 'He must have decided to get rid of it while I was out. He just stepped backwards, when I entered the loft looking for him, and vanished.'

Her firm mouth trembled as she spoke.

'I see,' said the detective constable.

He examined the loft door, which was secured with a wooden bar and some metal bolts, making careful notes. She could have pushed the old man, he knew: one shove would be all that was needed. Such things happened.

'My mother is most distressed, officer,' Rosemary said. 'Does she have to go through all this?'

'Now dear, you know the constable is only doing his duty,' Heather reproved her. 'Is there anything more I can tell you?' she asked.

They'd better examine the bonfire, the two constables decided, and with Heather to lead the way, set off down the garden. They saw just a heap of fine ash: Heather had made quite certain of that, and had put away the garden cart which Guy had used to transport the paintings.

The old man was probably tired, the constables concluded, and had been resting in the loft before fastening the door, though it was odd enough to sit there in the dark. It was their duty to make certain of the truth about the death, but after careful inspection of the scene, they were sure it was an accident.

Charles Blunt was concerned about how Heather would live. The Manor was hers, with no capital transfer tax to be paid on it in her lifetime, but how would she keep it up on the income from her army and state widow's pensions? This was all she would have, Rosemary had said. He had been round the house and was dismayed by its lamentable state. There'd been some odd paintings in an upstairs room; he knew Guy dabbled a bit, but what a shame the old boy had no great talent. They were rather awful daubs. Still, it had given him something to do during the last years.

The house needed repairs. It needed modernization, too; it was habitable as it was only if you were tough; but it was worth a lot of money, enough to keep Heather in comfort for the rest of her life. Wouldn't she be better in some cottage in the village, less isolated? She wouldn't want to move away from her friends.

He'd have to talk to Rosemary about her mother's plans. Irritably, he thought how tiresome Rosemary still was, so arrogant and bossy. She'd been like that as a child, parading her seniority over him and Robin, condescending to them both. He sighed, aware of guilt, even now, that it was he who had survived their shipwreck. He'd swum around and around, looking for his friend in the sea, but Robin had never come to the surface. Only later was his body found. It was ironic that both Robin and his father had met sudden deaths.

Before returning to his new wife in Virginia Water, Charles indicated that all the resources of the Hall were at the disposal of the bereaved ladies. Rosemary had refused his offer to help with the funeral. James, her husband, and she would see to it all, she had said.

Charles hoped the dear old boy would have a good send-off with a rousing hymn or two, something martial.

Guy was buried in the village churchyard. The inquest had been opened and adjourned, enabling the arrangements to go forward and giving the police time to prepare a careful case for the coroner.

The church was filled. Representatives came from every organization he or Heather had been connected with through the years, including the treasurer of the charity from whose presidency Heather had resigned on the day of Guy's death. There were older people from the village, come to show their respect, and among the family mourners, his sister from Scotland and his grand-daughter, the horsey one. Priscilla and Leonard Blunt, nearing the end of their trip, had cut it short to return in time to join the congregation. Priscilla went off to the church looking restrainedly chic in her mink coat over a plain black dress. What must she feel, wondered Nina, watching her go. She would have liked to be there herself, but it wasn't quite her place. She didn't see Heather until afterwards, when everyone came to the Hall for a buffet lunch provided by the Blunts and produced by Nina. The widow wore a navy-blue coat and hat which she must have owned for years. Her grey skirt dipped at the back beneath the hem of the coat. Nina wished she could have got her hands on the coat, let it down or added a false hem, before the service.

Dan, in a dark suit, was at the Hall to help with the lunch. He had volunteered, saying that Nina couldn't manage alone.

Nina knew that she could. This was an area where she had no fears. Nevertheless, she was glad of his support. It was odd to exist behind the green-baize door, now that the Blunts were at home. They'd invited her to eat with them, but somehow or other, she hadn't felt easy about it. Priscilla had suggested she use the television set from the flat in the attic in the evening. She could have it in her bedroom. Nina had done this: she couldn't intrude on their evenings in the study. It seemed that they did not use the drawing-room a great deal in the winter, finding the study snug, with its open fire.

Nina and Dan ate cold salmon in the kitchen while the sounds from the rest of the house grew steadily more cheerful. Charles Blunt had brought them a bottle of hock, and his mother came out, too, to make sure that they were eating. She reported the atmosphere in the kitchen was cosy.

'Maybe they'll get together – make a match,' said Rosemary. 'She seems a pleasant woman. It would solve your problems, wouldn't it, Priscilla? To have them working for you as a couple, I mean. Though I suppose Dan's getting on a bit, now.'

Unaware that they were being bracketed in this manner, Dan and Nina drank their wine and enjoyed their food. Nina felt rather badly about getting so much pleasure from preparing the meal when the occasion was a sad one.

'You should take it up,' said Dan. 'Catering, I mean. There are plenty of folk like the Blunts who'd pay well to have their parties done, and such-like.'

'I'd enjoy it,' said Nina. 'But I wouldn't know how to begin.'

'How much longer are you staying?' asked Dan.

'I'm not sure. I was to have stayed another two weeks, but

they came home early,' said Nina. 'They may want me to leave, now the funeral's over.' She hadn't thought that far ahead herself. She could go to Portugal, she thought: have a little holiday with her mother; but Christmas was coming. She'd never had Christmas without the girls before. Last year, Sarah and Jeremy had come to Silverlea. She'd seen Sebastian unpack his stocking.

'Mrs Crowther – Nina –' said Dan. 'I want to tell you something. It's about that business – you know – when the police took me in the night Colonel Jowett died.'

'But I know already, Dan,' Nina said. 'They made a dreadful mistake.'

'You didn't think I'd killed that girl, then?'

'Of course not. I knew it was quite impossible,' Nina said firmly.

Dan refilled their glasses.

'You trust me, do you?' he said.

'Yes – of course,' Nina said again. 'Why do you ask?'

'I want you to know the truth,' Dan said, twiddling his wine glass, his expression bleak, avoiding her gaze.

'What do you mean?' Nina felt a flutter of fear. What was she going to hear? Was he the killer, after all? The police did make mistakes, let villains walk free, and they hadn't arrested anyone else for that murder.

'When I go to London,' said Dan, 'I talk to young girls at stations. I go up to them, if they're alone and look at all lost, and ask if they've left home and want somewhere to stay.'

'Do you?' Nina's heart began to thump unevenly against the dark grey dress she had selected as appropriate attire today.

'Yes,' he said.

There was a pause. Nina reminded herself that the house was full of people. She was perfectly safe, whatever he might confess.

'If they say they have run away, and haven't anywhere to go,' he went on, still not looking at her, 'I try to persuade them to go back home. I point out that unscrupulous people could come and talk to them, just as I've done, and entice them away, saying they know of a flat or a room, and they might never be heard of again. I tell them what happened to Susie, when she ran away.'

'But she didn't!' Nina exclaimed. 'She was shot in a bank raid.'

'She wasn't,' said Dan. 'We made that up, Ellen and I. We couldn't bear the truth, you see.'

'I don't understand,' Nina said, but her panic was dying down. She'd always known he wasn't a killer.

'A girl was killed in a bank raid. I didn't show you the newspaper cuttings, or you'd have seen it wasn't Susie, whose photographs you'd been looking at. She was someone else's daughter,' said Dan. 'Ellen and I pretended she was ours, because we couldn't accept that Susie had run away and been murdered by a maniac. They caught him, that one,' Dan added. 'He's still in prison, but I suppose they'll let him out one day. I told the police about it and they checked. Of course, as the superintendent said, it didn't mean I hadn't turned into a sex murderer myself,' he added and almost smiled. 'But in the end they were satisfied. I could tell them the names and addresses of some of the girls I'd been able to persuade to go home. There are a few – not many – who listen. Most of them walk away.' They said rude things like 'Get lost, Dad,' and worse.

'Well, you've warned them, anyway,' Nina pointed out.

'Yes,' Dan sighed. 'The day that girl disappeared, I took one home – went with her all the way, on the train. Sometimes I telephone their parents or a friend to meet them.' He always paid their fares back – went with them to buy the tickets and saw them on to the train. 'I'm going on with it,' he said. 'Even if I only succeed with one more girl, it's worthwhile.'

'Of course it is,' said Nina. She was horrified. 'Was the shot girl's name Susie too?' she asked, 'Did that give you the idea?'

'No,' said Dan. 'But the bank raid happened just after the trial. Ellen and I were feeling so dreadful. I mentioned one day that it would be easier to bear if she'd been shot, like that other poor girl. We wouldn't have felt so ashamed.'

'Why did she run away?' she asked.

'We never knew,' said Dan. 'You see, she just disappeared. There was no chance to explain. Perhaps we were too strict, but then one must have rules.'

'Yes,' said Nina.

'When we moved here,' he went on, 'it was easy to tell the

bank story when people asked if we'd a family. Everyone was so sorry. The shooting hadn't happened all that long before – the trial was over, of course, and the men sent to prison. The police caught them, all right. They often do, in the end.'

'Didn't anyone notice about the names being different?' asked Nina.

'Not many people talked to us directly about it. It's the sort of thing that's spread round behind your back, you know, to be tactful,' he answered. 'But one person did. I said she was Ellen's child by an earlier marriage. One lie soon leads to another, you see, and in the end I denied my own daughter.'

What a sad little tale, Nina thought.

'I'm so sorry,' she said.

'I'm glad you know what really happened,' said Dan. 'I wonder if they've finished out there. Shall we clear the dishes?'

That evening, Nina received two propositions. The first was from Priscilla Blunt, who suggested that she should become the resident housekeeper at the Hall, with her own flat – that occupied by the Spanish couple – a wage appropriate to her ability and such a position, and a daily woman to help with the cleaning.

The second offer came from Charles.

'I know my mother's put her idea forward,' he said. 'I promised to let her get in first.'

He had come out to the kitchen after dinner, bringing Nina a glass of Cointreau. They had pressed her to join them for the meal, but she'd refused. Now he sat down at the table, bidding her do the same. Nina, who had been loading the dishwasher, obeyed.

'My idea is that you should cook our lunches at the office – the directors' lunches, I mean. We have a girl who does it now, but she's leaving – wants to go abroad, cook her way round the world, or something. She's looking for someone to take her place, but I'd sooner it was you than a girl – someone mature, I'd prefer – who won't leave us on a whim just as we've all got used to one another.'

'But I'm not qualified,' said Nina. 'I've never done that sort of thing. I haven't got a diploma.'

'You're a bloody good cook, and an excellent hostess,' said Charles. 'And you don't lose your head in a crisis. You'd be a great help with foreign visitors – we get lots of them, now we're exporting and setting up stores overseas. You know we don't only make buns?'

'Yes,' Nina had to smile at this.

'There are seven of us, regularly,' he said, 'and often a guest or two. Sometimes my father's there.'

'I'd have to live in London,' Nina said.

'No, you wouldn't, if you didn't want to. You could commute. I do, after all. You could live in Marlow, say – or Datchet, like my grandfather,' said Charles.

But he wasn't really your grandfather, Nina thought. She knew so much about them, such a big secret. She couldn't stay on in this house, with Priscilla, weighted with such knowledge.

'Think about it, Nina,' Charles urged, and as he looked at her, his eyes were Guy's. She saw the charm – felt it, too – noticed the long, mobile mouth, though the smooth, well-shaven face was fleshy and Guy had been so lean. Hadn't everyone noticed the likeness? She'd come fresh to it, she realized, from outside, and had had the facts that confirmed it thrust at her. People saw what they wanted to see, she supposed: when Sebastian was born, members of both families had declared him the image of this one or that.

Charles was mentioning terms. To Nina, they sounded like the wealth of Arabia.

'Come and see us, before you decide,' he invited. 'Have a look at the kitchen – meet the rest of the board – hear about us from Angela – that's the girl who's leaving. Let's make it Tuesday. Mother plans to keep you here as long as she can, but it's time you had a day off and I'll tell her we've got a date. Come to lunch,' and he smiled at her.

Why not, Nina thought.

'If your mother won't mind,' she agreed, and added, 'I won't be accepting her offer, though I'm very grateful to her.'

'Believe me, the favour would be all on your side,' said Charles.

But he was wrong. Priscilla had held out a helping hand when they met that day in London. She could have ignored Nina's distress, but instead she had offered her an opportunity which had led to this moment. If Nina accepted the position at Blunt's, she would be able to rent a room – even a small flat – until Mr Drew had concluded his wrangling with Martin and extracted some sort of settlement.

In her heart, Nina knew that she was going to lose over that. Eventually, she would get some money, but it would be nothing like half the value of Silverlea, for on paper Martin had managed to make a poor financial showing. Promises, from him, were worthless, she had learned, and she hated him now with a deep bitterness she was sure would never diminish. In destroying their life together, he had demonstrated that it was based on an illusion – her illusion, but she felt a sudden surge of defiant confidence as she contemplated Charles' suggestion – a feeling similar to what she had experienced when, to thwart Sarah's plans to organize her, she had resolved in the beginning to come to the Hall. She would accept the job. She need not commit herself to it for ever; if it didn't work out, she could leave when she had been there long enough to gain a reference. It wasn't, as her idea of marriage had been, a contract for life.

She smiled back at Charles as she worked this out.

'I'm sure I'll be able to persuade you,' he said lightly. 'I'll look forward to that.'

He got his way in most things, Nina decided: like his mother.

There was no need for any action over the promise she had made to Guy, for Rosemary and her husband were going to take over the Manor. Rosemary's husband would soon be retiring from the army, and he planned to start a light-engineering business; suitable premises were available in Droxton and he had a potential partner. They would pay Heather a realistic rent for the Manor.

The day before she left the Hall, Nina went to say goodbye to Heather. She had rented a one-room flat near Watford for three months, with an option to renew, and was starting at Blunt's the following week, to work alongside the departing Angela for a few days.

'You'll be all right, Nina,' Heather said. 'I'm glad things have worked out for you.'

'What about you?' Nina asked. 'Will you find a house in the village?'

'No. I'm going to Cornwall,' said Heather. 'I lived there as a girl, and I want to go back to my roots.'

'Won't you miss your friends?'

'What friends?' asked Heather. 'Without Guy, there's no one.'

'Well – the Blunts,' Nina said. Heather was also putting a distance between herself and family – her daughter and grand-children: but she was used to them, with their army life, being out of close reach.

'I've lived in Priscilla's shadow for a large part of my life,' Heather said. 'Now I can get away. I couldn't before, because of the Manor. Do you know, I almost hate it now – the Manor, I mean. In the end it killed Guy, and it took so much out of us both. I miss him, Nina. It's lonely at night.' She looked at Nina with her large, still beautiful eyes. 'You understand, I know.'

'Perhaps – in a way,' said Nina. She still missed Martin, but he had hurt her so badly that she no longer wanted him. If they were shipwrecked together on a desert island, she told herself fancifully, she would stalk off to the far side of it, immune to his blandishments.

Or would she? She shivered, not sure.

'I want to get away from Priscilla,' Heather said. 'She's always done everything better than I have – she was cleverer at school, and so pretty. But Guy chose me, and nothing can alter that.' Her lined face glowed as she spoke. 'I don't want her to go on patronizing me – giving me expensive presents – that sort of thing.'

'I'm sure she doesn't mean to patronize you,' said Nina. 'She's very kind.'

'When it suits her,' said Heather, and laughed shortly. 'I'm being disloyal to a lifelong friend, Nina.'

But the lifelong friend, decades ago and for who knows how long thereafter, had been disloyal to Heather, Nina reflected.

'It doesn't do to look back too much,' Heather was saying. 'One should remember only the good things, and let the rest go. That's a wise philosophy.'

'Yes,' said Nina. Was it possible that Heather knew the truth and chose to ignore it?

'Come and stay, when I get my cottage,' said Heather.

'I'd like to,' said Nina.

In the morning, she checked her room to make sure she had left nothing behind. Bare of her possessions, the pretty bedroom with its yellow furnishings looked impersonal again, yet here she had wept bitterly; lain terrified, frightened of burglars and anonymous telephone callers; wished malice towards Caroline.

She'd forgotten the pottery cat. It sat on the bathroom window-sill, a silly grin on its painted features. Was it really like Caroline? Nina found that she could not recall the girl's face at all.

How stupid, she thought, picking up the cat. She couldn't leave it here, but it was no longer of any significance. She must have been a bit round the bend to invest it with any, she decided, putting it into her handbag. She'd get rid of it in the dustbin when she went to fetch Dan, who had said he would bring down her cases.

But first she had something to do.

She found Priscilla in her study at her desk. Leonard had gone to the office. Nina was glad she would continue to see him; his genial kindliness must be part of a massive tolerance if he knew the truth of the past. She had enjoyed her lunch at Blunt's, where everyone had treated her like a guest, not a future employee. Charles, saying farewell, had taken her hand and held it for a moment. Nina had remembered, with a sudden stab, Guy on the night when he had surprised her. There might be more surprises ahead, she thought, not certain quite what she meant. The idea was faintly exhilarating.

'Ah, Nina,' said Priscilla. 'Ready to go?' She held out an envelope. 'Your cheque.'

'Thank you,' said Nina, taking it from her.

'I hope it hasn't been dreadfully boring for you here,' Priscilla said. 'I mean – I know there was the accident – that was terrible – but it must have been dull.'

'Oh no – not at all,' said Nina. Her gaze strayed from the elegant figure at the desk to the window. Dan was out there, busy with something. In Priscilla's absence he had been briefly suspected of murder; and in this very room, Nina herself had spent one extraordinary night about which even Heather did not know every detail. Priscilla had no knowledge of these events, had probably not even heard that a murdered girl had been found near the Droxton by-pass, knew nothing of the telephone calls which had been meant for her, not Nina.

'I knew the Hall was in good hands,' Priscilla continued graciously. 'It was lucky for both of us, wasn't it, that we met that day in London?'

'It was for me,' said Nina. 'You'd have found someone.' People like Priscilla always did. 'Here are the keys you gave me,' she added, handing them over. 'And here –' Nina put her hand in her jacket pocket, drawing out the set of keys she had taken from Guy when he fell. 'Here are these,' she went on. 'Colonel Jowett had been unwell before the accident – rather confused. He came up here several times, and once he let himself in. Mrs Jowett knew he had been in the house – she came to collect him – but she thought I'd left the door open. She didn't know about these keys and I've no idea where he found them.'

She held them out to Priscilla.

'Oh,' said Priscilla, accepting them. 'I see.'

There was no more for either to say. The only safety lay in silence, and it was Nina who, after a moment, broke it.

'May I call Dan to fetch my cases?' she asked.

'Certainly,' said Priscilla, laying both sets of keys on her desk. She stared at them, and then, as Nina turned away, opened a small drawer and dropped one set in. Nina left her sitting there, pen in hand, trying to pick up the threads of the letter she had been writing.

Dan stacked Nina's possessions into the Metro. Her green wellingtons went into the boot; she'd need them when she visited Heather. He shook her hand and wished her luck. He'd never see her again, he knew, as he watched the car slowly move forward. She was the only person, apart from the police, who knew the truth about Susie.

But Nina was not thinking of Dan; there was something she'd meant to do, she remembered, some unfinished business which the matter of the keys had driven from her mind. What was it?

Then she remembered the cat.

She stopped the car and opened her handbag, which was resting on the passenger seat beside her. Dan, meanwhile, came up to the car and was beside her as she drew out the small, garish object. She wound down the window.

'Dan, would you drop this into the dustbin?' she said. 'I forgot about it.'

He took it from her, through the car window, looking at it curiously.

'What is it?' he asked.

'Just a silly mascot I had,' Nina said. 'I don't want it any more. It isn't of any importance. I meant to throw it away before leaving.'

'Very well,' he said. 'I'll see to it,' and, holding it in his hand, he watched her drive off.

As she passed the front of the house Priscilla came to the window and waved, and Nina waved back, driving slowly, careful of Dan's gravel.

She'll never be certain of how much I know, Nina thought.

Perhaps one day Charles should be told: when they were all dead – Leonard, Heather and his mother. Or should he? Did it really matter?

Guy and Martin had been alike in their conduct, but Martin had, in the end, acknowledged his action and his responsibility, whereas Guy had drifted on, acting a lie, ending unable to wash his conscience clean.

There wasn't much to choose between them, Nina thought, driving past the Baptist Chapel. Heather, when she moved away, would leave the ghosts of the past and be happy; Nina must do that herself: try not to dwell on what couldn't be changed. It wouldn't be easy: she knew that black days, and more probably nights, lay ahead.

Leaving the village, she put her foot down and drove on fast, towards the by-pass.

Dan waited until the car was out of sight, then turned back to the garden. He put the pottery cat in his pocket. It was odd, ugly, gaudy, everything Nina was not, and a strange thing for her to have owned, but it was all that he had of her.

A policeman walking along a quiet street behind the Bayswater Road noticed a white Cortina parked at a meter, with a man having some small difficulty in opening the door. The man was stout, not young; he wore clerical dress, with a dog-collar. If it had not been for his respectable attire – particularly the collar – the constable would have questioned him about the car and whether in fact it was his. But vicars didn't steal cars.

They didn't, he reflected, as automatically he made a note of the number, very often drive large Cortinas, cars with commodious boots. A Cortina car had been stolen and used to move the body of Christine Potter some weeks ago now, he remembered, and radioed in.

A check was made on the computer, and the white Cortina proved to belong, not to a parson, but to a man whose address was in Kent. It turned out that he was a sales representative.

The police decided not to pick up the thief at once. They trailed him around the streets, and he parked the Cortina near King's Cross station.

The bogus vicar was watched as he followed a young girl who carried a suitcase out of the refreshment room, and arrested as he spoke to her.

CAST FOR DEATH

Margaret Yorke

'The body lay just beneath the surface of the river the hair streaming in the tide, legs splayed with the movement of the water, arms spread, the face downwards.'

That evening, Sam Irwin, noted actor, should have been appearing on stage at the Fantasy Theatre. Instead, his corpse was being hauled from the Thames.

It looked like suicide; but his friend, Patrick Grant, found that difficult to believe. He was determined to find the real reason for Irwin's death; and before long, some apparently unrelated incidents – a series of art robberies, the accidental death of a dog – appeared in a new and sinister light.

'A superior detective story, bang up-to-date.' *Evening Standard*

DEATH ON ACCOUNT

Margaret Yorke

Robbie is a quiet man, passive and unassuming. He is the sort of man who is taken for granted by the people around him, passed by for promotions and bossed around by his wife. Middle-aged, Robbie has never known love, or passion, or power. Oh, in his head he has dreamed his dreams, plotted his plots, planned his revenges – but he knows he would never make any of them reality.

And then one day he does . . .

'Every sentence a well-rounded pleasure' *Manchester Evening News*

'A star in our galaxy of crime writers' *Financial Times*

THE SCENT OF FEAR

Margaret Yorke

Mrs Anderson was afraid that she was losing her mind. She was beginning to forget where she had put things, what she had bought, even what she had eaten. Living all alone in the rambling mansion that had been her home for fifty years, Mrs Anderson was isolated from the town, forgotten by her relatives, and had outlived all her friends.

But Mrs Anderson was not quite alone. She had a visitor. A young man who came every night, through the dining room window. Who helped himself to food and money, who had even made a comfortable room for himself in the attic. A young man who enjoyed power. He could take over the house and make it his kingdom whenever he chose – whenever he needed a place where no one would ever think of looking for him, where no one would find him, no matter what he'd done . . .

'With every novel Mrs Yorke has become more assured' *Daily Telegraph*

'Tense, well written . . . you'll read every word' *Current Crime*

THE COST OF SILENCE

Margaret Yorke

The body lay sprawled, the face contused and battered, the skull crushed . . .

Emma Widnes might have died at any moment, or she could have lived for years. Her husband, Norman, was certainly the kindest nurse his incurable wife could wish for. But then Norman was so pleasant to everyone – a blameless shop-keeper in a quiet town.

The murdered body of Emma Widnes shocked the most experienced of CID detectives, and soon Bidbury reverberated with whispers and conjecture.

And the skeletons could be heard, rattling in the most unlikely cupboards . . .

'Intrigue and deception with a delightfully unexpected twist as a final page bonus' *Financial Times*

'A compelling read' *Irish Times*

A DEMON IN MY VIEW

Ruth Rendell

In a gloomy cellar the figure of a woman leans against the wall. Palely beautiful, she makes no move when the man advances on her from the shadows, puts his hands around her neck and strangles her.

Arthur Johnson is prim, fifty and a bachelor. To the outside world he is the very picture of respectability. No one knows of the dark lusts that bind Arthur to the pale lady in the cellar.

Then, one day, the lady is gone and a new victim must be found . . .

'Absolutely unputdownable . . . it is stamped on every page with the firm mark of a distinguished storyteller at the very height of her powers' *Graham Lord, Sunday Express*

TO FEAR A PAINTED DEVIL

Ruth Rendell

When Edward Carnaby attempts to buy cyanide from his local chemist – supposedly to rid his house of wasps – the news rockets round the town of Linchester.

At a disastrous pary the following weekend, Patrick Selby – the richest man in the community – is unaccountably attacked by a swarm of wasps. He dies during the night. An unfortunate coincidence – or was it?

'The appearance of any novel by Ruth Rendell is a cause for celebration' *The Spectator*

A JUDGEMENT IN STONE

Ruth Rendell

Eunice Parchman applied for the job of housekeeper to the Coverdale family on the same kind of impulse that made her buy a box of chocolates or smother her invalid father. *If* they had been less desperate for help in their country house, they might never have employed her. *If* they had treated her less kindly, she might never have hated them. *If* they had never discovered her terrible secret, she might not have murdered them.

'The best woman crime writer we have had since Sayers, Christie, Allingham and Marsh' *Edmund Crispin, Sunday Times*

'Ruth Rendell is at the very height of her powers. It will be an amazing achievement if she ever writes a better book' *Daily Express*

'This could become a classic among chillers' *H. R. F. Keating, The Times*

Margaret Yorke

'A star in our galaxy of crime writers' *Financial Times*

All the following books are available from your bookshop or newsagent or you can order them direct. Just tick the titles you require and complete the form below.

☐	CAST FOR DEATH	£1.50
☐	COST OF SILENCE	£1.25
☐	DEATH ON ACCOUNT	£1.50
☐	FIND ME A VILLAIN	£1.50
☐	HAND OF DEATH	£1.50
☐	IN THE SMALL HOURS OF THE MORNING	£1.50
☐	NO MEDALS FOR THE MAJOR	£1.50
☐	SCENT OF FEAR	£1.25
	Postage	
	Total	

ARROW BOOKS, BOOKSERVICE BY POST, PO BOX 29, DOUGLAS, ISLE OF MAN, BRITISH ISLES.

Please enclose a cheque or postal order made out to Arrow Books Limited for the amount due including 15p per book for postage and packing for orders both within the UK and overseas.

Please print clearly

NAME ....

ADDRESS ....

....

Whilst every effort is made to keep prices down and to keep popular books in print, Arrow Books cannot guarantee that prices will be the same as those advertised here or that the books will be available.